Demon Bound

ALSO BY NINA K. WESTRA

Demons of Ardani
Demon Bound
Hell Sent

Elves of Ardani
Night Elves of Ardani
Rogue Elves of Ardani
Sun Elves of Ardani
Dark Elves of Ardani

ISBN: 978-1-967722-03-7 (Paperback)

Editing by Noah Sky.

Cover by Nina K. Westra.

ninakwestra.com

DEMON BOUND

DEMONS OF ARDANI

BOOK ONE

NINA K. WESTRA

Contents

ONE

"I have something to show you."

Raiya looked up at her husband, her knife and fork frozen in her hands. He was smiling. It was a smile that said he knew something she didn't.

When Lord Nirlan Han-gal smiled, it was usually because someone else was suffering. In her year of marriage to him, that smile had never preceded anything pleasant.

"What is it?" Raiya asked, carefully keeping her tone neutral. As they finished dinner, she looked down at her plate and realized she hadn't eaten much. She'd been eating less and less, lately.

His smile broadened. "It's a surprise." He went to her, holding out his hand. He would have been angry if she didn't take it, so she stood, letting him lead her by the arm from the dining room into the cold halls of their dark, empty castle.

Long ago, when Uulantaava had been ruled by innumerable warlords scattered across the plains, dozens of men and women had been housed within these halls alongside the nobles they served. These days, it was just Raiya and Nirlan and a few servants. Despite the cold and the emptiness, it probably would have been a nice place to live if she'd been sharing it with someone she loved.

The longer they walked, the more apprehensive she became. When he brought her to the cobweb-laden door that led to the dungeon, she stopped. It had been decades since any prisoners had been kept there, but she very much doubted there was anything there she'd want to see.

"I think I'm feeling a bit sick, actually," she said, a last half-hearted attempt to escape. "I think I should go to bed early."

Nirlan acted as if she hadn't said anything. He opened the door, and she stared into the blackness beyond. He pushed her forward.

She had only ventured into the dungeon beneath the crumbling castle once before. The darkness of the place would have been absolute had it not been for the candle in Nirlan's other hand, and the smell of the ancient stone corridors was one of dank dirt and old mold. She wasn't dressed for the cold, and her thin robe did nothing to insulate her. It was like being inside a grave.

He brought her to a stop in front of another door. Glowing runes were carved in overlapping circles all over it. For a moment, her interest overshadowed her fear, and she began picking out runes she recognized. *Hold. Strength. Imprison.* A locking enchantment. She doubted Nirlan could read a word of it. Eunaios must have crafted it for him. Nevertheless, when Nirlan produced a key and slid it into the lock, it opened smoothly.

Raiya was hit with a dark, powerful wave of something unseen—something that made her shudder. It was not her imagination. Something was there. Nirlan had always had a less-than-savory interest in dark magics, but she'd never felt anything like this strange force that permeated the dungeon.

She didn't have the energy that evening to fake enthusiasm, and there was no point in trying to dissuade him from whatever he was planning. "What is this, Nirlan?"

He looked down at her, and he smiled again. Gods, she hated that smile. She hated how much she'd once found it beautiful.

"Wouldn't you like to find out?" he said.

She didn't reply. He would take her through that doorway, to whatever awful thing lay beyond it, no matter what she said.

"Are you too good to speak to me now?" he asked, his hand squeezing her wrist a little.

He enjoyed causing her discomfort, and he enjoyed trapping her in that discomfort. He loved the sense of control.

She had little pride left, and rarely bothered to defy him. But she was in a defiant mood today. So she said nothing, enjoying and fearing the look of growing displeasure on his face.

He shoved her into the next passage, which was somehow even darker than the previous one. The door banged shut behind them.

"I sometimes wonder if you realize how easy you have it," Nirlan said. His voice was soft, but it seemed loud in the claustrophobic silence of the tunnel. "You've never faced real adversity. You haven't had to work for anything. You don't have any education, talent, or skills, and you don't need any. All you have to do is sit there and be quiet and pretty, and open your legs once in a while. And yet you struggle to do even those simple tasks."

The comment about the lack of skills stung more than the one about opening her legs—because it was true. She kept her expression blank, because she refused to let him see how much the words hurt her.

But adversity? She and her mother had struggled to make ends meet for years. Her father had left her mother when she was young, and her mother had died years ago. She had no other family. She had no trade and no skills other than her knowledge of runes and enchanting.

Her mother had nurtured her love of magic from a young age, using what little money they had to buy her books and finance apprenticeships with mages and magoarchaeologists who were exploring the local Auren-Li ruins. But since Raiya hadn't had the fortune of being born a mage, she would never be able to forge functional enchantments. Runes needed magic to become something more than just markings, and she had none.

There were no academic institutions in remote northern Uulantaava. There was no use for a woman with a passionate love for dead languages and magic she couldn't use. Nirlan had saved her from a life of poverty.

He took his hand off her to quickly brush a stray lock of black hair behind his ear, as if he was annoyed it had strayed. His hair was long, straight, and rarely less than flawless. His skin was light and evenly toned, and his face was perfectly symmetrical. He was a handsome man, in a slender, dandyish way, which was exactly the type she liked. It was one of the many reasons she'd married him. If only looks correlated with quality of character.

"You're spoiled," he said. "I imagine you think you're better than other people because men look at you when you walk down the street."

"I don't."

"You shouldn't. Every time I go into town, I see dozens of younger, prettier girls. They probably have better temperaments than you, as well. Do you realize how lucky you are to be with me?"

"I do."

"Then why do you *insist* on testing me?" he hissed, his temper snapping.

Was it her imagination, or was the corridor getting narrower?

A passing thought came to her, and she swallowed tightly. "I hope you don't mean to bury me down here, Nirlan," she joked, her lips twitching into a nervous, half-hysterical smile. If he did, no one would ever find out. Perhaps her mind truly was broken after so many months of misery with him, because she nearly laughed at the irony of walking into her own grave.

Nirlan ignored her. His lips were pressed in a tight line, and his dark eyes were focused on the tunnel ahead. As Raiya followed his gaze, she could see why. There was a soft glow coming from around the corner at the end of the tunnel. It was a color that seemed almost outside the spectrum visible to mortal eyes, like something that shouldn't exist on this plane. A sense of foreboding squirmed through her belly.

The closer they got to the unnatural light, the worse she felt. She could hardly describe the waves of unpleasant sensation that made her want to run, made her stomach turn. It was as if the light itself emitted fear and hatred. It was physically oppressive, like being in a hot room filled with smoke.

"Nirlan?"

"Be quiet. We've arrived."

They passed beneath a stone arch, beyond which was a vast, high-ceilinged room. A swell of something heavy and intangible washed over her, taking her breath away.

The room was mostly empty, except for the hundreds of glowing runes circling the floor around a large, translucent box, roughly six feet on each side, which was the source of the otherworldly light. The box was a magical barrier of some kind, its sides formed by that strange light. Inside it was a large, dark shape that Raiya couldn't quite make out through the barrier... until it moved.

Vague outlines of long limbs. A head that slowly tilted up to look at her. Eyes that were vibrant, glowing blue, somehow lit from within. The creature was mostly man-shaped, except for the goat-like horns curving from its forehead along the top of its head. It was not human, nor elven, nor anything else she'd ever seen in Heilune, and it was massive.

She took a step backward, running into Nirlan. "What is that?" she breathed.

"Don't you know a demon when you see one, Raiya?"

The demon's eyes met hers. They were flat blue, without iris or pupil, making it hard to judge the direction of its gaze, but somehow she knew it was looking directly at her.

She had found the source of the terrible sensation she'd been feeling. The demon's anger filled the room. But, curiously, the expression on its face was blank.

Was it furious because it had been imprisoned in this dungeon, or was this just its baseline emotional state? It made sense that demons would be perpetually filled with rage. It positively radiated hellish power, even from behind the barrier.

"Why is there a demon beneath the castle?" Raiya asked.

"Because I summoned it. Don't worry. It can't escape its cage."

"Does it... obey you?"

"Not yet. But it will."

Raiya turned to look at Nirlan with disbelief. The only people who summoned demons were fools desperate for power and not too concerned with how they obtained it. In a way, she wasn't surprised. Nirlan had always had an interest in occult lore and magic, though he seemed more interested in the idea of it than in actually learning. She thought it was one of the reasons he'd been attracted to her in the beginning. She had no doubt that Eunaios was the brains behind this, though. Nirlan must have tasked him with obtaining a demon, and Eunaios had figured out how to do it.

Demons inevitably turned on their summoners. They

were immensely powerful beings, halfway between mortals and gods. It was said that they were relentlessly evil, violent and lustful, motivated only by a desire for chaos. They came to Heilune to toy with mortals, to kill and rape and feed. They could cast spells to rival any mage. They were stronger than giants, and even harder to kill. Raiya doubted it could be held captive for long. Nirlan and everyone around him could end up dead by this monster's hands.

"Well?" Nirlan asked. "What do you think of it?"

She tentatively looked up at Nirlan, not knowing what kind of response he wanted. He smiled at her, then pushed her forward. Raiya instinctively dug her heels into the floor, which made her trip and fall to her hands and knees in front of the demon. Suddenly, she was far too close to it. Only the magical barrier kept it from reaching out and touching her.

The box was too small for the demon to stand in, so it was kneeling. It looked down at her, its expression still impassive and somehow judging.

Had Nirlan brought her down here to kill her after all? Did he mean to sacrifice her to the demon? What would a demon do with a sacrifice? Torture her? Eat her? Fuck her and then eat her?

She felt cold, chilled to the bone. She had always feared he might kill her someday, but not like this. "Why did you bring me here?"

Nirlan's hand clasped the back of her neck. She winced as he angled her head up to make her look at the demon. The creature leaned closer to the barrier, cocking its head a little as it stared at her. Its eyes flared brighter in its cold, stony face. Raiya felt faint.

"Do you see the glow in its eyes?" Nirlan said in her ear. "It senses your panic. It's drinking your fear. You're feeding it power."

"Nirlan, please don't do this."

"Don't do what?" he asked innocently.

"Feed me to it."

He played dumb. "What makes you think I'd feed my own wife to a demon? What a horrible death that would be. I wouldn't do something like that unless I had a particularly inadequate wife." He paused. "But perhaps you would prefer him to me, Raiya? I know you're displeased with your life here, despite how hard I've worked to keep you happy. Despite all the wealth I've shared with you, all the gifts I've given you, and the leisurely lifestyle you now enjoy—you still resent me."

"I don't resent you," she said unconvincingly.

"Do you know what he'd do to you?" Nirlan said, still touching her neck in a caress that was verging on an attack. His lips brushed her ear as he murmured to her. "He'd tear you limb from limb. He'd peel your skin away in strips and set fire to your pretty hair. He'd cut off pieces of you until there was nothing left, and he'd lick up all of your blood and pain and terror like honey."

Nirlan had spent a lot of time imagining ways to torture her, it seemed.

"I bet he'd like a taste of this, as well." His hand moved down, cupping between her legs, pressing her skirt down to outline the shape of her body.

The demon's gaze seemed to follow the movement of Nirlan's hand. Raiya held still as his fingers moved slow and hard against her. Twinges of uncomfortable pleasure mixed with humiliation radiated from the places his fingers touched, and she bit her tongue to keep herself from visibly reacting. The demon watched her, its eyes glowing brighter.

Nirlan abruptly let her go, scoffing disapprovingly. Raiya felt heat flooding her face: both shame and hatred. She saw now that he hadn't brought her down here to kill her. He'd just wanted to gloat. He wanted to watch her cower in fear from what he'd done. He was smirking, even now.

Many of Nirlan's motivations in life came down to gloating.

The demon's eyes narrowed slightly—the only sign of intelligence or emotion she'd yet seen from him. Until then, he had looked more like a beast than a man. For some reason, this hint of an intelligent mind behind the horrific visage only made the demon more terrifying.

"What are you going to do with it?" she asked.

Nirlan sighed, as if it was a stupid question. "Make it work for me, obviously. What else are demons good for?"

"You mean you'll make it kill for you."

"Strength is not evil, Raiya. A strong leader benefits everyone. I'll have it patrol the roads. It could protect Frosthaven."

Raiya imagined the demon prowling around the city, unsupervised. She imagined it mercilessly tearing apart anyone who resembled a criminal, anyone who got in its way, or simply anyone Nirlan disliked. Few mortals were equipped to fight a demon.

It could spy for him, fight for him, cast all kinds of spells for who-knew-what kinds of purposes. Nirlan could use it to intimidate or outright remove political rivals. He could loan it out to his friends for their purposes, whatever they may be.

In the Uulantaava of days past, power and wealth had been won in battles fought over months or years in some of the harshest climates in Heilune. Nirlan was not a fighter, and had no army—so he was making one.

A monster. An immortal. A slave.

A demon.

"Once it's bound to me, it will be completely obedient. It will be nice to have some obedience, for a change."

Two

Raiya now knew that "You're not like other girls, are you?" was not really a compliment, but when Nirlan had said it to her when they'd first met, she'd been flattered.

It was almost two years ago, now. She had looked up at him, her attention drawn away from the book in her lap. The man before her was tall and striking, his dark eyes alight with interest. He leaned forward, resting his hands on the table of her booth. His eyes roved over her, taking in her long, dark hair, dark eyes, and tawny skin.

The market buzzed around them, loud and bright while night fell. The Lightbringer festival was well underway. People had strung up lanterns and lit candles, and sparklers and smoke bombs were going off nearby. The air was tinged with the scent of burning wood and grilled food, which somehow made the cold weather feel less harsh.

The man wore fine clothes of silk, white leather, and arctic fox fur—the sort of clothes that few in Frosthaven could afford. Perhaps he was a tourist. Frosthaven was the northernmost city in Uulantaava, the northernmost country in Heilune. Travelers were uncommon enough to be of interest.

Raiya sat up straight, closing her book. No one in town ever wanted to buy from her little booth, but a rich tourist might. "Pardon?" she asked.

"I haven't seen anyone else here reading." He cast an unimpressed glance toward a group of laughing young women on the street. "Most girls would rather be shopping for jewelry or clothes at a time like this. But you're reading a book."

She wasn't sure what he meant, and she felt a little self-conscious. "I see. Are you, ah, enjoying the festival?" she asked, putting on a smile.

"Of course," he said, but he looked a little bored. "I was in Valtos for last year's festival. But this is nice, in its way. More, ah..." He glanced behind him as a group of shouting children ran past, waving sparklers at each other, and he stepped sideways to avoid being struck by one. "...rustic."

Not wanting to give him a chance to move on to another booth, Raiya quickly gestured to the objects propped around her table and hanging from the beam above her. There were stones and bowls and necklaces and other bits and pieces, all inscribed with magic runes. "Are you interested in enchantments?"

"Who wouldn't be?" he said, with a charming smile that dimpled his cheek. Raiya found herself smiling back. "You're the first mage I've met in Frosthaven."

"Oh, I'm not a mage."

"You're not?" He glanced down at the runes with disdain. "What are these, then? Fakes?"

"Oh, no, not at all. They're real runes. I study runic languages. And enchanting, old magic, technology of the Auren-Li period—"

"So you're an academic."

"Well, I wouldn't say that, exactly."

"Why not?"

"I've never been to a university. Nothing formal. It's just things I've picked up here and there, from books, mostly. But I'm not an expert."

"Expert enough to do all this, evidently."

"Yes," she said, allowing herself a little pride. "I made everything here myself."

He raised an eyebrow. "But they don't actually work?"

Her pride vanished as quickly as it had appeared. "No, not exactly. But they would, if you put some magic in them. That's why the runes don't glow. They've got no power." She cleared her throat. "I like to think of them as art pieces, sort of. Like you'd put in a museum, maybe." It sounded stupid, and she tried not to cringe. As if her little crafts were museum worthy. "When I was young, my mother had an enchanted necklace that could turn you completely invisible for a short while. I was always fascinated by it. I've always loved everything about runes and enchanting. The magic, the artistry, the research that goes into them. But I can't use magic, so I just do the part that I'm able to."

The man seemed disappointed. She sensed she was about to lose another sale. But even more than that, she was annoyed at herself for not having been able to hold this interesting stranger's attention. "They make very unique gifts," she said. "Great for collectors of oddities. And they *will* work if you just get a mage to charge them. I guarantee it."

He smiled again, to her relief. "Of course." He glanced down at the table and then picked up the item closest to him —a shaft of white crystal inscribed with a complex mage light enchantment. It could turn all shades of the rainbow and fill a room with swirling clouds of sparkling light and color. Theoretically. Raiya had never seen it in action. "I'll take this."

"Oh! That's a fantastic choice. It's a—"

"Is this enough?" He'd fished out a coin purse and held out several gold marks.

Raiya blinked at them. The man had more money than sense. It was almost endearing. "That's far too much. Here." She took one of the coins from his hand.

Before she could put it away, his hand darted out to catch her wrist. He turned her hand over and put all the coins in her palm, then closed her fingers over them. The warmth of his fingers sent tingles through her. She felt her cheeks heating.

"Can you give me one more thing?" he asked.

"What's that?"

"Dinner with the most interesting girl in Frosthaven?" He canted his head as if to examine her a little more deeply, and there was something sultry in his eyes.

Raiya wondered whether she should be offended by his forwardness. At that moment, though, she could only feel intrigued. He was far more handsome and more polite than the last few men who'd tried to approach her. One of them had been twenty years her senior, and another had been quite drunk. There was a shortage of desirable young men in Frosthaven, to be truthful, let alone ones she had anything in common with. Most of the boys she'd grown up with had moved south when they'd gotten old enough.

The man lowered his voice conspiratorially, giving her a knowing look. "I insist you say yes. I'm so godsdamned bored of chatting about local gossip and whatnot. At least an academic might have something interesting to talk about."

Perhaps he was a bit too candid.

Or perhaps his candidness was refreshing?

What was the harm in spending a few hours with him, anyway?

"I'm not an academic," she said again, with a shy smile. "But I'd be pleased to share a meal with you. If you insist, that is."

"I do."

It was terribly romantic, really, that he'd specifically picked her out of all the other women there.

That was what she'd thought at the time.

She hadn't found out until the next day that she'd been talking to Lord Han-gal's son, who had recently come home after completing his education in Ardani. A whirlwind romance followed, and they'd married soon after. Nirlan's elderly father had died another month after that, and they had inherited the castle and lordship.

"Your wife is looking lovely, as always, Nirlan."

Raiya looked up, drawn out of her memories. The parlor was filled with two dozen or so visitors for one of Nirlan's parties. She smiled like a mage's golem, without real emotion, but she doubted anyone noticed the stiffness. The young man who'd spoken was a noble from a neighboring town, whose name she couldn't be bothered to remember.

Nirlan smiled over at her as if with pride and affection, even though he'd said she was looking old shortly before they'd come out of their dressing room. "As always," he agreed. "I caught the loveliest woman in Heilune." He put an arm around her waist and held her against him, his hand brushing the underside of her breast in a way that definitely verged on inappropriate. Raiya saw the other man's eyes register the touch, a combination of irritation and lust flashing on his face for a fraction of a second.

Nirlan did that whenever another man looked at her. It was a reminder to everyone that he owned her. There were no accidental movements in a room full of people like this. Everything was intentional. Everything was a message. Every seemingly innocent interaction was a subtle battle for dominance.

She had learned that very quickly after she'd first arrived at the castle.

She wandered the room at Nirlan's side while he gossiped and laughed with other important people in extravagant clothing. There were wealthy sun elves from Ysura, a famous artist from distant ra'Hezirat, even a politician from Valtos. Nirlan only befriended important people. Or, in her case, people he found attractive.

"You have quite a book collection," an older man commented. Raiya's eyes reluctantly tracked over the shelves on the wall. The books were covered in dust, unused and forgotten for a long time now. A few of her old rune-inscribed items sat beside them like bookends. She hadn't been able to find the desire to create anything for many months now.

"My wife fancies herself an academic," Nirlan said with a smirk.

"Ah," the man said, looking at Raiya skeptically. "It's good for a lady to have something to keep herself occupied."

Raiya smiled blandly.

Midway through the evening, a hooded figure weaved through the crowd toward them. Nirlan sighed when he saw him.

The hooded man was Eunaios, Nirlan's assistant. He was a mage and a member of the cult of Moratha—the goddess of death—which had been growing in influence in Uulantaava over the last few years. Nirlan had hired him several months ago, and now Raiya understood why. There were not many people who knew how to properly summon and bind a demon, and those who did were usually of questionable repute.

"What is it?" Nirlan said impatiently. "Did I not tell you to stay out of sight?" Eunaios was a rather unattractive, uncharming middle-aged man, deathly pale and shaved bald. He had a dour disposition and a penchant for black robes, which may have been a uniform for Moratha cultists or may have just been his personal taste—Raiya wouldn't have been surprised by either. Nirlan was happy to use him for his magic skills for as long as they could benefit from each other, but obviously he did not want the strange little man putting a damper on his fancy parties. A few of the other guests had given him odd looks as he passed.

"There's a problem with the creature," Eunaios said.

"What kind of problem?"

"It is unwell. You should come and see."

"You're telling me I should leave my own party early to dote on it because it's not feeling well? Does the poor thing have a tummy ache? Ash and blood…"

"If we don't give it what it needs, it could die. And then what will you do? You'll have to find another. It would set us back weeks."

"It can wait a few hours."

Eunaios scowled and retreated, brushing past a group of startled sun elves on his way.

"*Can* they die?" Raiya asked. She knew next to nothing about demons.

Nirlan looked down at her suddenly, as if he'd forgotten she was there. "Of course they can," he said shortly, as if it was a stupid question.

The thought of the demon dying alone in its too-small cage was unexpectedly distressing. Did anything really deserve to die that way, even a demon?

"Perhaps you should see to it soon," she said.

"Just enjoy the party, wife. Drink some more wine."

For a moment, she resented the condescension. Then she decided that she could use some more to drink after all. Wine had become something of a habit of hers recently. There wasn't much else to do in this big, lonely castle, and alcohol smoothed off the sharp edges of life.

Having been given permission, she detached herself from Nirlan's side and went to take a glass of wine from a servant. She took a long drink, then slipped out into the hallway.

She leaned against the wall and closed her eyes, glad to be alone for a moment. Normally, she disliked the silence and solitude of the castle. But Nirlan and his friends were not the kind of company she was looking for.

"Are you all right, lady?"

Her eyes snapped open. One of Nirlan's guests had followed her out into the dark hallway. It was the young noble who'd complimented her earlier.

"Of course," she said. "I'm fine. Thank you. Just getting some air."

He smiled, moving closer. "You're not one for social events, I take it?"

"Oh, I am. I just, ah..." She didn't fit in at these events. She didn't know how to relate to the kinds of things that were important to Nirlan: business deals, rumors about wars brewing in faraway lands, the latest fashions from Ardani or Ysura, gossip about which notables were at odds with whom. The rest of the people here had gone to elite schools all across the continent to learn about these things and connect with other people like themselves. Raiya had spent her childhood running through town unsupervised, swimming in rivers, and reading whatever affordable secondhand books she'd managed to find. When she'd gotten older, most of her time had been spent trying to scrape together enough coin to live on.

"You don't get many visitors so far north, do you? Meeting so many people must be overwhelming."

She wondered if Nirlan would be angry at her for agreeing. She had no doubt that anything she said here would get back to him. "A bit, I suppose."

The man stood in front of her, putting her back to the wall. She saw his eyes flick briefly to her breasts, hidden beneath her dress. "How did a bastard like Nirlan get a woman like you to marry him?"

She smiled half-heartedly. "You think too highly of me, lord."

"Not at all." He leaned in, resting a hand against the wall above her shoulder. She stiffened. She could smell alcohol on his breath.

She tried to sidle out from under him. "I should be getting back."

He put a hand on her waist, holding her still as he leaned even closer. "Stay here a moment."

"My lord, I really should get back to my husband." She tried to push him back, but he dove in, pushing her roughly against the wall as he forced his mouth over hers. His unwelcome lips may as well have been a brand burning her skin. For a moment, she was so shocked that she couldn't move.

"*Raiya,*" came a sharp voice.

The noble unhurriedly dislodged himself from her. Raiya glared at him, then turned to look at Nirlan, who stood in the doorway.

"Your wife is drunk," the man said, smirking.

"Get out," Nirlan said.

"Come on. Don't be that way. You knew what you were doing when you married a commoner. You can hardly complain when you got exactly the sort of woman you bargained for."

Nirlan rapidly approached them, looking close to violence. "*Get out.*"

The noble raised his hands, backing away. "Apologies for the misunderstanding." He bowed, winked at Raiya, and then left.

Nirlan turned to Raiya. He looked furious. Apoplectic.

"I didn't do anything. He forced himself upon me," Raiya said.

There was a tense moment of silence, and he just looked at her with hatred, seething.

Raiya instinctively took a step back. She flinched when Nirlan reached toward her, but he only grabbed her wrist, pulling her back into the room. As soon as they entered, his expression smoothed over, but his grip on her wrist was still painfully tight.

He waited until after the last visitors had left before he punished her, but not a moment longer. He stood in the middle of the parlor with his foot tapping, waiting until the servants had left and they were alone. It didn't take long. The servants in the household were as adept at judging his moods as Raiya was. They all knew to avoid him when he was like this.

"I didn't see you trying to stop him," he said.

"I did try. You're reacting exactly as he wanted you to, Nirlan. He did it just to upset you. This is a petty men's quarrel. Don't—"

He slapped her, his hand swinging so hard and fast that she didn't realize it was coming until after it had happened. She bent over, pressing a hand to her face in shock as her eyes reflexively teared up. It had been a while since he'd hurt her physically, but she remembered this feeling very well. The shock. The betrayal. The humiliation. They all hurt much worse than the slap itself.

"You let him make a fool of me. I suppose I should be grateful that you at least waited until you were out of sight, rather than letting him fondle you in front of the whole room."

She focused on wiping the startled tears from her cheeks. Whatever she said, it would only anger him further.

"Useless," he spat.

She thought he was going to hit her again, but then the door opened. It was Eunaios.

"What?" Nirlan snapped.

Eunaios raised his sparse eyebrows, folding his hands primly into the sleeves of his robe. "The demon."

Nirlan cursed under his breath.

"If you fail to keep it healthy, you'll lose it."

"Yes, I know." He glanced up at Raiya, studied her for a moment, then grabbed her arm to drag her along with them. "I expect you to make this up to me," he said to her. She thought it best not to reply.

THREE

Eunaios didn't look at Raiya as he held open the rune-covered door for them to pass through—not because he was avoiding her gaze, but because she was of no interest to him. He'd more or less ignored her from the moment they'd met. She had no illusions that he might try to protect her from Nirlan.

He probably would have ignored Nirlan too, if Nirlan hadn't been paying for his services. Raiya wondered what he did with his time when he wasn't working with Nirlan. Pray to his strange goddess, maybe? Devise evil plots? Dye his clothes black?

The trek down the dungeon's tunnels was as eerie as Raiya remembered. A palpable malaise had suffused the entire space like a bad odor. She tried holding her breath, which did nothing to keep the uncomfortable feeling off her. Even Eunaios looked like he was feeling ill by the time they reached the demon's cage.

Raiya's eyes went to the box in the center of the room. The creature inside was a lump on the floor. She wondered if it was already dead.

Nirlan went to examine the demon. "What's wrong with it?"

"It's starving," Eunaios replied.

"I thought you said it would only need to be fed once a week."

"Perhaps it was already hungry when we summoned it."

"Wonderful. First the issue with its arm, and now we discover it's a weakling, too."

"The arm will not be a problem. And the issue of feeding it is easily resolved."

"Is it?" Nirlan said, frowning.

"It needs fear, anger, or copulation."

"My dear Eunaios, I hope you're not suggesting I copulate with the thing."

"You don't have to, my lord," Eunaios said dryly. "Having someone engage in sexual activity nearby would suffice. Giving it something to frighten would do, as well. It merely needs a source of emotional energy. It doesn't matter where it comes from. I'm sure there is no shortage of village girls nearby who would not be missed, if you would prefer to just give it something to play with."

A shiver ran up Raiya's spine.

Nirlan seemed to think for a moment, and then he looked up at Raiya. He was still murderously angry, and his ego was bruised. Whenever she saw that look in his eye, she feared for her safety.

She must have visibly paled. It was a mistake to let her fear show on her face, because he enjoyed it. It egged him on. And as she took a step back, he grabbed her arm.

She tore at his fingers, digging her feet into the ground as she struggled against him. "Nirlan, no! Let me go!"

It was with impulsive, joyful cruelty that he flung her through the magical barrier and into the demon's cage. She slipped through the wall of magic as if it were merely fog, then sprawled on the cold floor beside the demon.

It became oddly quiet once she passed through the barrier. She hadn't realized that the dungeon was full of tiny sounds—water dripping, footsteps echoing, wind whispering—until all the noise in the room was muffled. Suddenly, the loudest thing she could hear was the soft breathing of the thing beside her. She froze, afraid of waking it.

It was enormous. Its eyes were closed, as if it was sleeping, but it radiated strength and power. It had pointed ears like an elf's, and an athletic, scarred body with skin stretched taut over ridges of hard muscle, which was fully on display because it wore no clothing from the waist up. From the waist down, it wore only boots and a drape made of folded cloth and metal, not unlike the sarong skirts some men wore in the southern nations of Heilune. Its skin was an unnatural, vibrant blue—an oddly cheerful color for such a terrible creature—and the long, raggedly-cut hair beneath its horns was pure black. There was nothing about it that was not frightening.

She realized, too, that its right arm was entirely missing, cut off at the shoulder and long ago healed over. She'd been so overwhelmed by everything else about the creature that she hadn't noticed it until now.

After a moment, it stirred, as if sensing her presence.

Raiya glanced toward Nirlan. He was watching with increasing wariness. Already he looked like he regretted what he'd just done. Even Eunaios looked stunned. But it was too late to undo his stupidity. She saw their mouths moving as they spoke to each other, but the barrier muffled whatever they said.

A surge of anger tightened her hands into fists. She would die a painful death in a few moments, just because of his foolishness and uncontrolled jealousy.

The demon's eyes opened. Immediately it focused on her,

its cloudy, pupilless eyes sharpening. Raiya tried to scramble back through the barrier, and the demon lunged.

She screamed as its hand wrapped around her ankle and dragged her backward. She tried to dig her nails into the ground, bloodying her fingers. The demon pulled her back easily, flipping her onto her back like she was a doll. She kicked out wildly and hit it with a closed fist. Her hand connected with its chest, which felt more like stone than flesh, and pain burst through her knuckles.

The demon straddled her thighs and loomed over her. It clamped a massive hand over her throat to pin her to the ground. Its eyes glowed as bright as flames.

"Nirlan!" she screamed. She sobbed, waiting for the demon to destroy her.

But instead of killing her, it bent down, burying its face in her neck, and breathed deeply. It pressed against her with a wild desperation, clutching her like she was its lifeline—and if Nirlan and Eunaios were to be believed, that was exactly what she was. It inhaled the scent of her hair and her breath like it was air and the demon was drowning.

Drinking her fear, Nirlan had said.

It paused, looking down at her hand. Blood from her fingers had smeared over its skin as she fought uselessly. Raiya's eyes widened as it released her throat only to grab her wrist and bring her fingers to its mouth.

Astra's mercy, it really was going to eat her. It was going to start by biting off her fingers one by one.

A long, dark tongue came out of its mouth and dragged over her fingers. The texture was surprisingly strong and rough, like a cat's tongue. It seemed to be in no hurry as it licked blood from her hand, lapping at the pads of her fingers and in between them. The demon closed its eyes as if in pleasure.

Raiya stared at it, torn between fascination and disgust.

Her stomach flipped as it took one of her bloodied fingers entirely into its mouth and sucked. There was a spike of stinging pain from the raw wound on the tip of her finger, and a startling arousal that stirred deep in her core as she felt its slick tongue running over the digit. The act was undeniably sensual.

This was not what she'd expected. Did it plan to lick other parts of her, too?

Its pale blue eyes blazed at her as if it could read her mind.

Gods, please, not that.

It wasn't going to kill her quickly. It was going to do it slowly, torturing her first. It was going to draw out every bit of energy it could take from her. Consume her completely.

But she suspected the demon was intelligent. Could it speak Ardanian?

"Tell me what you want," she whispered. The demon watched her closely. Did it understand her?

She was very accustomed to bargaining with unreasonable monsters after living with Nirlan, but she had no idea what she could offer a demon that it couldn't just take from her either way. "Make my death quick and painless, and I'll give you whatever you want," she said quietly. An idea came to her. "I will tell you about Nirlan," she whispered, hoping her husband couldn't hear from outside the barrier. "You want to kill him, don't you? I'll help you escape. I'll help you kill him." She had never seriously wanted to kill him before, but now the thought thrilled her. If Nirlan was going to kill her, then by the gods, she would take him down with her.

The demon's eyes didn't move from hers. Her finger slipped from between its lips, and it rubbed its nose along her wrist as it breathed her in, still gripping her possessively. Its mouth opened slightly, as if it was considering biting her there, and she caught a glimpse of sharp canines.

"Please," she breathed.

There was a flash of blinding light and a loud crack of magical energy. Raiya flinched, and the demon roared in pain. There was another flash, and then it released her abruptly.

A pair of slimmer hands grabbed her and dragged her across the floor, and then she was outside the barrier. She lay still on the floor, trying to regain her composure. Nirlan and Eunaios argued nearby, but the pounding blood in her ears made them sound far away.

"You may have had some trouble explaining your young wife's disappearance if she had been killed," Eunaios said. "I doubt people would believe she had suddenly taken ill."

"I knew it wouldn't kill her," Nirlan snapped. "The creature is not a fool. It wouldn't kill her while she's providing it with energy, and it wouldn't risk angering me when I'm the only one feeding it. It knows it is under my control. It knows it must appease me if it wants to survive."

"If you say so, my lord," Eunaios grunted.

Nirlan was holding a metal baton carved with runes. Raiya recognized the weapon, because she had made it. It was enchanted with a lightning spell, which could discharge on command. Eunaios must have charged it for him. She'd never seen it in working order, and had forgotten it even existed until now.

Her legs felt wobbly and weak, but she managed to stand. She glanced up at the demon as she touched her throat. She was surprised to find that, aside from her fingers, she was unharmed.

The demon was on its knees, panting as it watched them through a curtain of lank black hair.

"When will it be properly bound to me?" Nirlan asked, crossing his arms. "My patience is thinning."

Eunaios frowned. "It takes time to prepare the spell."

"You've been given time, and what do we have to show for it?"

"The demon is already here. Soon you will have complete control over it. Do try to be patient, my lord." He spoke with the tone of someone placating a young child.

Nirlan gave him a sharp look, which didn't appear to ruffle him. Eunaios knew Nirlan needed him. Raiya envied his self-assuredness. Mages with knowledge about demons were more difficult to come by than pretty women. It would be an inconvenience if Raiya happened to disappear, but not a disaster. She had no family or friends left to miss her. He'd find a new wife, and life would go on.

Nirlan turned to the demon. "Do you hear that?" he asked, raising his voice to be heard through the barrier. He stepped closer, swinging the baton casually at his side. "Soon you'll be bound to me. Then we can let you out, and you can wreak havoc on the countryside. You'd like that, wouldn't you?"

Nirlan swung the baton, and arcs of magical lightning burst forth. The demon grimaced and convulsed, defenseless in its cage.

The runes on the baton stopped glowing. It was out of magic. The demon sagged against the back wall of its enclosure as the attacks stopped. Rather than putting the baton back on its hook on the wall, Nirlan handed it to Eunaios. "Recharge this," he said, then turned to leave. "Come, wife."

"Waste of magic," Eunaios commented.

FOUR

As they climbed the stairs to their bedchamber, Raiya realized that her dress had been torn in her struggle with the demon. There was a long rip from the hem to her knee, baring her dark tights beneath. She looked at her hands. The demon had licked all the blood clean, leaving broken nails and pink scrapes on the tips of her fingers.

Raiya's mother had once told her that if a man put his hands on you once, he would undoubtedly do it again, no matter what you did to please him. Nirlan had just thrown her to a demon. Did the same logic apply? Would he punish her that way in the future, risking her life again?

"Do you remember when we used to talk about our dreams, before we were married?" she asked.

Nirlan sighed a little. "What?"

"I said I wanted to recruit a mage to power my enchantments, and you said it was a good idea. I thought I could be a real enchanter and invent things."

"So much for that idea. I've hardly seen you do anything but lounge on the sofa for months."

"And you told me you wanted to make things better in

Frosthaven. You said that after the illness took your father, you were finally going to have the opportunity to make real changes in the town." She gave him a sidelong look, which he didn't bother to notice.

He'd never hired a mage for her, though she'd asked about it many times before he'd implied she was annoying him by bringing it up. Instead, he'd hired Eunaios to help himself with his own goals.

"You probably liked that, didn't you?" Nirlan said.

She looked up at his back as he climbed the stairs ahead of her, her brow puckering. The candle in his hand cast flickering shadows on the walls of the narrow passage.

He glanced over his shoulder to smirk at her. There was no mirth in his smile. "You seem like the type to enjoy having a monster putting his tongue all over you. You were probably thinking about how big his cock might be."

"You were the one who threw me to him like a bone to a dog."

"I didn't expect you to enjoy it so much. You hardly even fought him."

"How do you expect me to fight a creature like that? What else could I have done?"

"You and I both know what you were doing."

After over a year with him, she had thought she was too tired to feel real anger toward him. The anger she'd felt early on had long ago been replaced with emptiness. After a while, she'd given up hope of changing him or her circumstances, and it had been hard to feel anything.

But right now, she was furious. Perhaps some of the demon's anger had rubbed off on her.

Once, one of the servant girls had quietly asked Raiya why she didn't leave him.

"I don't know," Raiya had said, but in truth, there were

many reasons. The primary one was that she was afraid of him, and afraid of what he might do if she tried to leave.

"What if you can't control the demon?" she asked. "What if it kills you?"

"You'd like that, wouldn't you?"

She was mostly unfazed by the accusation. "Why do you think I'd like it if you were killed?"

"Because I know exactly the sort of person you are." As they reached the landing, he stopped, turning around to look down at her. "You think you're so complicated. You think you have such deep thoughts and emotions that no one else could understand. But you're a simple creature. You want to feel special, like every other woman. You want to be doted on. You want to be prized. And you're angry because I won't give you that. Because I refuse to coddle you. Isn't that right?" He put his hand on her waist, nudging his leg suggestively between her thighs. "You're angry now, but we'll make love tonight and I'll make you squeal with pleasure like I always do, and by tomorrow you'll have grown bored of trying to be angry, like you always do."

"I'm not in the mood for lovemaking."

"We'll see." He pulled her through the door to their bedchamber and pushed her toward the bathing room.

She quickly closed the door behind her and tapped the small, rune-covered crystal mage torch on the wall, which lit the room with cold, blue light. She stripped out of her torn, dirty dress. There were bleeding scratches on her knees that she hadn't noticed before then, and a growing bruise on her ankle where the demon had grabbed her. She peeled off all her clothes and hurriedly cleaned the wounds. Nirlan would be annoyed if she lingered there too long, which would make him an impatient lover.

When she came out, he was lounging on the bed. He looked her up and down, frowning a little. He almost looked a touch regretful. She often got the feeling that he felt sorry about things he said and did to her, but that never stopped him from doing them again, over and over.

"Come on, then," he said, jerking his head toward the space beside him on the bed. She sat down next to him.

"What if I had died?" she asked.

He sighed again. "Don't start."

"What would you do if I left you?" she asked, arching an eyebrow. It was either brave or careless, she wasn't sure which. Perhaps she was past caring what he did to her. "What if I decided, 'enough is enough,' and walked out?"

He looked surprised, then he laughed. "And then where would you go? I'm everything you have. I'm your entire life."

"What would you do?" she pressed.

He sighed, slowly pushing her backward onto the mattress. "Raiya, you'll never escape me. We'll be together until the end, whether you like it or not."

IT WAS LESS than a week later when Eunaios announced that he was prepared to cast the final piece of the binding spell.

There was to be another gathering so that Nirlan's friends and peers could witness the event. After all, what was the point of having power if no one knew you had it?

Nirlan supervised Raiya's preparation for the event with a critical eye. She was wearing a deep blue Uulantaavan-style robe secured with a wide belt at her waist. Its sides were split to the hip to the hem, revealing her trousers beneath. Nirlan preferred Ardanian-style dresses, which was exactly why she hadn't worn one.

"Put more makeup on," he said.

Raiya didn't bother to reply, but returned to her dressing table. She looked in her mirror, staring hard into her own dark eyes. Her fingers clenched on the handle of her brush as she dipped it into a pot of pigmented cream. In careful, controlled strokes, she dabbed delicately over the bruise beneath her eye. She was surprised the brush didn't crack in her hand.

She was furious. She had been for days now. Her patience had snapped, and she felt so much hate and bitterness toward her husband that she could hardly stand to look at him, and kept turning away from him instead. She feared that she would do something drastic if she looked too long. Something she'd regret.

When had things gotten so bad? When had her life spun so far out of control?

It had been slow. Like boiling a frog. She hadn't thought she was the sort of person who would end up married to a man she hated, but here she was, standing like a decoration at his side, wondering how long it would be before he killed her, or she killed him.

To match the thick application of cream and powder on her face, she added blush to her cheeks and shadowed her eyes and brows. When she finished, she turned around to face Nirlan, waiting for his stamp of approval.

He frowned. "I prefer you without makeup," he said.

"So do I."

He took her arm to lead her to the great hall anyway. "I'm not in the mood for your nonsense today. This is an important night. Don't embarrass me."

The great hall was already filled with Nirlan's friends by the time they arrived. It was just like Nirlan to be fashionably late to his own event. Eunaios was also waiting there, separate from the others. The man who'd accosted her during the last party had not returned, but she didn't like any of the other visitors much more. She recognized many of them from previous encounters. They were all like Nirlan, more or less, just with different faces—similarly darkly inclined, interested in strange magics and occult practices, and usually unconcerned with things like legal technicalities and traditional definitions of morality.

Nirlan led the group toward the dungeons, flanked by guards. "Prepare yourselves. I promise you, you've never seen anything like this before."

"We've seen your dungeon before, my lord," said one of the men sarcastically, looking around the gloomy tunnels with distaste.

"Your wit is as sharp as ever," said Nirlan flatly.

"He's only joking, of course," said a sun elf woman. "It's not as if you've ever led us astray before, Lord Han-gal. We're all waiting with bated breath to see what you've got this time."

Raiya saw Nirlan's lip curling. "I doubt you'll be so flippant after you see it."

Eunaios opened the rune-covered door to the deeper dungeon, and what could only be described as a wave of physical unease washed over them. Everyone in the group paused, startled.

Nirlan was the only one not fazed. "Come along," he said smugly. He started down the tunnel, his hands clasped behind him, and Raiya reluctantly followed, despite the heavy atmosphere that seemed to be trying to push them back. The group remained uncomfortably silent.

The feeling of ambient power and rage thickened the air, pulsing in Raiya's ears and making her sweat. She almost expected to find the demon waiting to kill them as soon as they stepped across the threshold.

When they entered its chamber, there was a collective intake of breath and a few muttered curses. None of Nirlan's guests were laughing now—a fact which surely pleased him to no end. The room smelled of smoke and heat, though there was no fire burning. It smelled of hatred. It prickled along her skin like clawed fingers.

In the center of the room, encircled with rows of glowing runes on the floor and walls, was the demon. There was no magical barrier around him this time, but his arm was stretched out in front of him, held by a chain going from his wrist to the floor, forcing him to kneel. Another chain ran from a collar on his neck to the ceiling, baring his throat at a painful looking angle.

Reading the runes around him, Raiya saw spells of holding that would keep him in place even if he broke free of the chains. Additional binding runes had been painted in black ink all over his body, across his chest and down his legs, even up his throat and onto the edges of his face. They glowed in dazzling iridescent colors, equal parts frightening and beautiful. They were too small for Raiya to read from a distance, but it must have taken Eunaios weeks of research and planning to find them all, not to mention hours of careful painting.

Something black was dripping down the demon's neck. Not paint—blood. His blood was jet black. Raiya realized that the collar he was wearing had spikes on the inside prodding at his skin. If he moved too much, the spikes would burrow into him.

It was a show of dominance. Nirlan wanted the others to see that he had fully conquered this creature. He wanted it to look dramatic. Raiya was disgusted.

"Ash and blood," someone murmured.

"Is this some kind of joke?" someone else asked.

"It's not real," said another. "Some kind of illusory magic."

That made Nirlan angry. "You doubt me?" He took the lightning baton from where it hung on the wall and approached the demon, who watched him unblinkingly. Raiya had to admit that she was impressed by Nirlan's apparent fearlessness. When he stood next to the demon, he looked small and slight by comparison.

Nirlan raised the baton and dragged it up the demon's exposed chest until it tapped beneath his chin. The tip of the weapon sparked, but didn't shoot. The demon's expression did not change as he glared at Nirlan, but the energetic tension in the air grew.

It was the demon's anger. They could all feel it. It was difficult for Raiya to resist the instinct to turn and run. Two of the others actually took a few steps back.

The sun elf woman was the first to speak. "What do you plan to do with it?"

"Whatever I wish," Nirlan said, putting the baton away.

"Do you mean to say it's bound to you?" someone asked.

Nirlan smiled. "In a few moments, it will be." At his beckoning, Eunaios took a brush and an ink pot from a table against the wall, then began painting runes on Nirlan's palms.

As the others whispered nervously to each other, Raiya's gaze was drawn to the demon. To her surprise, his glowing eyes were already on her.

She stepped closer. There was no barrier between them this time, and it was petrifying being so close to him again. She stopped a few steps short, arm's reach away from a monster from a fairy tale.

The muscles in his shoulders and chest shifted with each breath, straining from the cruel pull of the chains. As she came closer, she could see his thighs flexing with the effort of holding himself up.

He was magnificent. He was pure destructive power. It was in every line, every curve of him. He had been perfectly designed by the gods to seduce and kill.

She did not often see men—or man-shaped creatures—so exposed, physically or metaphorically. There was a secondhand shame in witnessing another person so degraded. Seeing someone helpless, in pain, kneeling and bleeding, filled her with deep unease in the same way that it filled Nirlan with joy. Nirlan would own him soon, and it would only get worse. The demon would be unable to harm him and unable to disobey his orders. He would be a slave.

To tame a creature like this was to spit in the face of creation. Nirlan already owned her, and it was a fate she wouldn't wish on anyone else. As if Nirlan needed more power. As if he needed another person to abuse and demean.

She imagined releasing him from those chains, setting him loose before he was trapped with Nirlan forever. It was a crazy thought. The priests of all Four goodly gods agreed that demons were an abomination. There was no more corrupt or obscene being known to mortalkind.

And yet, he hadn't hurt her when he'd had the chance. He'd spared her.

It was too late to save herself, but maybe it wasn't too late to save him.

Raiya glanced up at Nirlan. He was preoccupied with the spell Eunaios had begun casting as he painted. None of them were watching her. She was inconsequential. She was just the woman on Nirlan's arm. Someone whose name and works would be forgotten by everyone within a month of her death, who would be interchangeable with his next wife, and perhaps the one after that.

She looked down at the runes covering the ground, and a dormant part of her mind awoke—the part that had devoted itself to studying this magic long ago. There were runes for control and submission, commanding and obligation, pain and consequence. Spells for binding were ancient, poorly understood, and rarely cast. They were taboo for good reason.

She inched closer to the demon. Heat and rage radiated from him. His eyes narrowed at her, and she felt his anger intensify. She lifted her shoe to look at the shimmering rune beneath her feet. *Hold,* it read. She scraped the toe of her slipper on the rune, and a tiny piece of the dried black paint flaked away.

Suddenly, the air felt very hot and close, and it was hard to breathe. Glancing at the others to make sure they still weren't watching, she fervently rubbed the toe of her shoe against the rune. Paint flaked away.

"I don't know if you can understand me," she whispered. "And I know you will likely kill me if I release you. But I would rather die now, on my own terms, than by his hand. All I ask is that if you must take my life, take his, as well."

The demon watched her impassively, giving no indication that he could comprehend her words. Raiya's hopes sank, but she didn't stop scratching at the rune.

Eunaios's voice rose behind her as he chanted the words to his spell. The room brightened as the runes glowed. A few more moments, and the spell would be completed.

Raiya ground her shoe against the *hold* rune one last time. Its glow flickered out. She'd erased an entire line in the symbol, rendering it meaningless.

She looked up, meeting eyes with the demon, and dread raced through her.

Finally, Nirlan looked over at her. His eyes flicked down to her feet, then back up to her face. "What are you doing?"

Raiya pressed her back to the wall, as far from the demon as she could get. Everyone in the room was looking at her now.

Apprehension flashed across Nirlan's face. "What have you done?"

The demon pulled at the chain binding his wrist to the floor, carefully, as if testing to see what would happen. The chain pulled up from the metal ring in the stone until the stone shattered.

Nirlan turned and grabbed Eunaios, who appeared frozen. "Finish the binding!"

The demon tore the manacle from his wrist, wrenching the metal into pieces as if it were clay, then reached up to grab his collar. His fingers and throat bled freely as he grasped the spikes and pulled. The metal began to bend.

All of Nirlan's guests shouted and ran for the door, many stumbling over long robes or impractical shoes. Someone near the front of the pack fell, causing a domino effect behind him. Eunaios turned to run with them, and Nirlan grabbed him by the collar, holding him back.

"Finish the damned spell!"

The demon stood straight, his horns nearly touching the high ceiling. He threw the bloodied collar aside and took two long strides forward. That was all it took for him to reach Eunaios.

FIVE

The demon grabbed Eunaios with one hand, picked him up, and buried his teeth in the mage's neck.

There was a spray of red, and a scream that abruptly cut short. Raiya's jaw dropped. Blood cascaded down Eunaios's twitching body, and the demon drank it down like he was starving.

The sun elf woman waved her hand, conjuring a ball of flame that shot toward the demon. It fizzled against his skin harmlessly, leaving no mark. The elf paled as the demon dropped Eunaios's lifeless body and turned his attention toward her. She spun on her heel, only to have him grab her arm and yank her back. She screamed as her arm twisted and dislocated from her shoulder. The demon bent over to tear out her throat with his teeth.

Nirlan looked at Raiya, and outrage tangled with panic on his face before he spun and ran with the others. They'd clustered near the archway, all struggling to get through at once. Nirlan shoved them aside and disappeared into the darkness of the tunnel.

Nirlan's guards put themselves between the demon and

the door, drawing swords, but as the demon stepped toward them, they both looked like they were regretting their courage. The demon grabbed the closest one, picked him up like he weighed nothing, and hurled him against the wall with a horrific crash that left a damp, red smear on the stone.

The second guard slashed at the demon's chest, and there was a dull sound like metal hitting rock. Instead of penetrating the demon's skin, the blade glanced off, like it had hit armor. The demon took hold of the guard's breastplate, driving him to the ground, then pressed his palm against the man's armored chest. The guard's legs flailed as the breath was driven from his lungs. His armor creaked. Bones snapped. His entire chest crumpled inward, and he stopped moving.

The demon watched the remaining people sprint through the door. Shouts of terror echoed down the halls. Bits of mortal flesh and blood coated the floor and had even sprayed on the ceiling. Broken bodies and their parts were strewn across the room.

The demon turned to look over his shoulder at Raiya, his cobalt skin dripping red from his nose to his navel.

All the strength went out of her. Her legs trembled and then buckled, and she slipped to the floor, her back still against the wall. Her heart pounded against her ribs.

She had never known terror like this, so raw and all-consuming. She had thought she didn't fear death. But she feared this. She feared him. It was like he had reached deep inside and grasped some ancient, primitive part of her, the part that instinctively ran from large predators with big teeth. But there was nowhere to run. There was no escape.

The demon's eyes flared bright. Then he turned away from her and went silently out of the room.

Raiya let out a breath, shaking. She was still alive.

She glanced down at Eunaios's broken body. There were

pieces of him scattered across the floor. The demon had done that with his bare hands. Was that Nirlan's fate?

She couldn't stay here now. Everyone knew what she'd done. If the demon didn't kill them all, they would come for her.

She had to run. Now.

Her legs were still trembling as she stepped over the puddles of blood on the floor. She paused to take the lightning baton from its hook on the wall, then followed the sounds of screaming down the tunnels.

She nearly tripped over another body in the stairway up to the castle. Leaning close to the wall at the top of the stairs, she peered into the dim halls. To the left, she heard the sound of metal hitting stone, and another scream. To the right, she heard Nirlan's voice. She recognized it instantly by the harsh, snapping tone he took when he was angry. She strained to make out what he was saying.

"...getting out... find her..."

Her stomach twisted. She went left.

She moved slowly at first, afraid of making noise and drawing attention, but fear made her pick up the pace. Soon she was running.

She had nowhere to go, no time to gather her things. She hadn't planned this far ahead when she'd released the demon. She had thought she'd be dead by now.

Gods, what had she been thinking? What had she just done? She'd upended her entire life in a matter of seconds.

She sprinted down the hall to the parlor. Months ago, she'd packed a tiny satchel and hidden it away there, where Nirlan wouldn't find it—one thing she'd done right, at least. At the time, it had been more of a fantasy than a real plan to leave. She'd never thought she would actually be brave enough to do it.

Looking over her shoulder, she pushed aside the rug

behind the sofa in the corner, then jiggled a loose floorboard. Her bag was right where she'd left it, nestled in a crevice beneath the floor. Digging out the gray, fur-lined cloak and a pair of warm boots that took up the majority of the bag, she hurriedly put them on and shoved her slippers back in the crevice, then slung the bag over her shoulder and slid the floorboard back into place.

It was a start, but she had no clothes other than the robe, trousers, and undershirt she wore. It was not enough to survive outside without shelter for long.

She paused at the doorway, listening. The castle had gone oddly quiet.

"I thought I'd find you here."

She jumped. Nirlan emerged from the shadows in the hall. Raiya took a step back into the parlor, which had only one exit.

"Did you think I didn't know about your little cache?" he sneered. He looked her up and down as if he'd never truly seen her before. "Why did you do it? Why sabotage everything I've worked for?"

Did he really not know?

Raiya clutched her bag on her shoulder, backing up another step. "The demon's coming for you, next," she said. "You should run while you can."

"Oh? Do you know that for certain? Was this your plan all along? To make a deal with the demon and have it kill me and serve you, instead? Clever. I wouldn't have thought you capable of it." He slowly moved toward her, blocking off her exit. "How long do you think that will last? The demon might not have killed you yet, but it will. You're not strong enough to control it. Or do you think you can keep it satisfied with your body? I assure you, that won't take you as far as you think it will."

"Get out of my way."

"You have blood on your hands, you know. Eunaios and the others are dead because of you."

"It's wrong to bind a sentient creature."

"So they deserved to die?"

"Perhaps they did."

He arched an eyebrow, surprised, and perhaps impressed. "I had no idea you were so bloodthirsty, Raiya."

She snarled. "Nirlan, get out of my way. We're done. I'm leaving you."

Fury sparked in his eyes. "We're done when I say we're done, you treacherous, useless—"

He lunged for her. Raiya pulled her baton from the back of her belt and jabbed it toward him. The runes on the metal shaft lit up, and lightning exploded out of its tip with a blinding flash. Nirlan shouted and convulsed.

He collapsed on the floor, twitching, and for a moment, Raiya thought she might have killed him. But then his eyes opened and focused on her. He growled. Unsteadily, he rolled over and started to get up. Raiya leapt over him and ran, her arms and legs pumping wildly.

More blood spotted the hallways here and there, but she saw no one else. Everyone had fled. She was out of breath and clutching her side by the time she reached the front of the castle. There had been a point in her life, back when she'd been spending her time exploring dangerous ruins in search of old enchanting tech, when she could have run a mile without stopping, but it had been a very long time since she'd run anywhere.

She burst through the front doors of the castle, then skidded to a halt. In the middle of the bailey, visible in the bright light of the moons, stood the demon. The bodies of several more guards were scattered around him. He had stopped to stare at the iron portcullis that blocked the exit.

Sensing Raiya's presence, he looked up. She took a step back, drawing a quick breath and turning to run.

He was at her side in a few long strides, grabbing her arm. She struggled, but she may as well have tried to uproot a tree. The demon turned her toward him, meeting her eyes, and she went still, unable to look away. Her heart pounded so loudly that she was certain he could hear it.

There could be no doubt that he was not of this world. He was a good two feet taller than she was, and the horns curving up from the top of his forehead were bestial, but his face could have been carved from marble by the most skilled Auren-Li artists. His cheekbones were sharp, his nose elegantly aquiline. His skin was perfectly smooth, not with youth, but with magic—a kind of agelessness that was inhuman and unnatural. And there was something hypnotic about his eyes. Their swirling, pupilless glow was inexpressive, obscuring his feelings, if he had any. She stared at them, attempting to find a soul within, but she saw nothing.

There was a part of her that felt humbled to witness him, even if he would be her demise. He was like a volcanic eruption, or an eclipse, or a typhoon: a force of nature. Destructive but awe-inspiring.

Instead of ripping into her with his teeth, he merely looked at her, his eyes growing brighter by the second. And then, a spark glowed to life near his shoulder. She realized with alarm that he was casting a spell, channeling her fear into magic.

Traces of bright magenta-violet light ran along his skin, covering the scarred shoulder of his severed arm, and then burst out from his skin in long tendrils, weaving an elongated shape. It coalesced into a new arm, a ghostly apparition of a limb, made of transparent magenta light and nothing else.

Raiya tensed as he shifted his grip on her to his new hand.

It felt just as solid as flesh and blood. He raised his other arm and pointed at the portcullis that blocked the exit.

"What will unlock this cage?" he asked.

She blinked, taken aback. She had not expected him to speak, even though she'd had a suspicion that he could. His voice was calmer and softer than she'd expected. It was as earthy and unyielding as one would expect from a creature of his size, but it held none of the rage and volume she'd anticipated.

A small crease formed between his eyebrows. His grip on her tightened ever so slightly, but the threat was hardly necessary. His hand was large enough that it could have encircled her calf; her forearm felt like a fragile twig beneath it. She was well aware of the danger she was in.

"Speak," he said.

"I—I don't know. I've never seen it down," she stammered. "You could lift it. I'm sure you're strong enough."

"I cannot."

Raiya looked at the portcullis, scanning for a mechanism to open it. "On the wall. There's a lever."

"Raiya!"

She jumped. Nirlan had appeared in the doorway to the castle, but stopped short when he saw the demon. His eyes darted between them both. He wanted her, but not badly enough to fight the demon.

The demon was the first to act. He picked up Raiya, and she cried out in surprise. He carried her against his chest, high off the ground.

"Be still," he growled, his chest rumbling against her as he pulled the lever. She was startled into silence. She didn't have much choice.

She watched Nirlan over the demon's shoulder as the portcullis began to lift. As the iron bars clanked up into place above them and the demon carried her out into the wilderness, Raiya wasn't sure which demon she'd rather be with.

SIX

Bouncing with each of the demon's long strides, Raiya grew dizzy. Her head throbbed. She counted her breaths, trying to keep them even.

She peered up at him surreptitiously, trying to guess his plans, but she quickly looked away when his luminous gaze lowered to meet hers. She hugged herself, having nothing better to do with her body in this awkwardly intimate position.

The demon was scanning as he walked, taking in the miles of waving grass and distant mountains. He studied the land in each direction and then he studied the sky and the stars as if all of it was new to him.

He couldn't have known where he was going. Nirlan and Eunaios had just recently summoned him from the hells. Did he know anything at all about the mortal plane, let alone Heilune? Had he ever even been here before?

She supposed he would do what all demons did: wander the land searching for mortals to sate his hunger for death and destruction. It wasn't hard to guess what part she might play in his plans. He had brought her along as a snack, or a toy to absorb emotional energy from. But how long would that last before he grew bored of her, or before he simply lost control of his rage and killed her like he had the others?

It occurred to her that she was still carrying her enchanted baton in her belt. In all the commotion, she'd forgotten about it. Her hand slowly curled around the handle at her waist, and she felt a prickle of magic as it reacted to her touch, ready to be activated.

The demon glanced down at her sharply. Somehow, he'd sensed the magic. Fear rushed through her, and she quickly let go of the baton. It wasn't powerful enough to keep him down for long, anyway. If she shocked him, he would recover and chase her down again.

The night was deathly quiet. But after a while, Raiya heard the sound of running water. The demon came to a stop beside a creek. He lowered her to the ground, setting her on her feet. Then, ignoring her, he waded into the water and dipped his hands in. He splashed water on his face and over his body, scrubbing away the blood and ink.

Raiya's heart was pounding again, but something about watching him bathe was reassuring. Bathing was a thing that reasonable, sane creatures did, not monsters, right?

When she spoke, her voice was quiet and shaky. "What is your name?"

He looked up, water dripping from his face, and gave her a rather flat, disinterested stare before continuing his washing.

"Do you have one?" she asked.

This time, she thought his expression was one of annoyance. "All sapient beings have names."

Not only could he speak, but he had quite the vocabulary for a monster. Was this how all demons spoke?

"I am Raiya," she said. She had never felt so foolish introducing herself.

The demon brushed the water from his face. Rivulets ran

from the sopping ink-spill of hair that clung to his neck. He stared at her for a long time, and she had the feeling she was being judged... or sentenced.

He waded toward her.

She forced herself to stand still as he approached. He seemed to grow larger with every step, and her fear welled up as if drawn by a pump. He put one hand around her throat—not tightly enough to hurt her, but enough to terrify her further—and took her wrist with the other when she started to resist. He pulled her down to the cold ground and knelt above her. His breath was dry and hot as desert wind as he inhaled her.

"Wait," she gasped, pushing against his chest.

He laid his forearm over her chest to hold her down as his other hand dug into her hair, his fingers coming just short of causing pain as they pulled through the tangled strands. As he moved his face toward hers, she quickly turned hers away. She braced for him to put his mouth on her, to kiss her or bite her or tear her clothes off, but he just breathed her in, over and over, his eyes heavy-lidded. His lips kept coming close to her skin, but they never quite touched. His nose brushed against her occasionally, but it felt like an accident whenever it did. It was as if he longed to taste her, but held back for reasons she couldn't guess.

Raiya's panic ebbed. Fear. He wanted her fear. Nothing else. For the moment.

As her fear dissipated, the demon's movements slowed, and after a moment, he pulled back to look at her. His eyes were blazing like otherworldly suns, but now that she was not brimming with terror, his hunger seemed to wane.

"Are you quite finished?" Raiya asked quietly.

The demon tilted his head a little.

It was foolish to be snide. Nirlan always said her tongue was too sharp for her own good. But if the demon cared about her attitude, he didn't show it. He studied her for a long moment, as if she was as strange to him as he was to her.

And then he released her. He trudged to a nearby rock, where he sat down, looking oddly tired. Raiya sat up and straightened her hair. The ground had made her back damp, and now that the demon's unnaturally hot skin wasn't smothering her, she shivered with cold.

He was still watching her. But he did not seem about to devour her, nor pick her up again. Still trembling slightly with the adrenaline of the encounter, she opened her small pack. The demon's eyes narrowed with suspicion, but he didn't move to stop her.

She pulled out a threadbare blanket the color of slate and threw it around her shoulders. It was insufficient for Uulantaava nights, but it was all she'd been able to fit in the small bag. Also inside the satchel was a little money and, most importantly, her enchanting stylus and her old journal filled with rune translations and spells. Touching the soft leather cover of the book and the smooth steel of the stylus made her feel a strange combination of nostalgia and guilt. She closed the satchel without opening the book.

The demon had stopped looking at her. He seemed to be thinking.

"How often do you have to do that—feed?" She didn't know what else to call it.

The demon's eyes slowly shifted to her again. "I am always hungry," he said. "And your smell is enticing."

A chill went up her spine.

"Do you plan to return to the hells now?" she asked.

"No."

It was what she'd expected. If she'd been summoned and trapped on another plane, she would want to find a way home, but demons were different. Their desires and motives were inscrutable to mortals.

She took a breath. "Are you... going to kill me?"

"No."

The answer came surprisingly quick. It stunned her into silence. He could be lying, of course. He probably was. On the other hand, he'd given her no reason to doubt him so far.

"Why?" she asked.

He didn't answer.

"Should I consider myself your prisoner?" she asked.

He thought before answering. "Yes," he decided.

Her heart sank. "What will you do now?" She took a slow step toward him. To her surprise, he stood up abruptly. She flinched.

"I know you have a weapon," he said. "You should not attempt to use it." Every time he spoke, it was in the same calm, matter-of-fact tone. His words sounded like a threat, but there was little about his voice that was frightening, even if the rest of him evoked terror.

He came toward her again, and she couldn't help but feel another flash of dread. Darkness and anger still emanated from him, though it was nowhere near as strong now as it had been in the dungeon.

She watched his huge hand close around her wrist, and she forced herself not to cower as he raised her palm to his nose and inhaled deeply. Images of torn corpses and blood-spattered stone flashed through her mind.

He tilted her hand to run his thumb thoughtfully over her palm and then up her index finger, which flexed slightly under his touch. He watched her small, pale fingers curiously. Was it possible she was the first mortal he'd met? Had he ever seen anyone like her before?

As if he couldn't stop himself any longer, he pressed his mouth to her skin. His lips parted, and she saw the tips of sharp fangs inside his mouth. She imagined those teeth biting through her flesh, severing fingers, draining her of blood.

"What if I stayed with you willingly?" she said in a rush, before she could feel the prick of his teeth.

The demon looked at her, frowning.

Raiya swallowed. He wanted to keep her around so that he could feed whenever he liked, which meant he wouldn't kill her right away. But the problem with relying on fear for feeding was obvious. Eventually, her fear would fade. And then what tortures would he have to invent in order to inspire new fear in her?

"I'll let you use my body," she said, her stomach flipping. "To feed from. I won't fight you, and I won't try to escape."

The demon studied her skeptically. He glanced pointedly at her trembling hand. "You will give yourself willingly?"

"Yes. With some caveats."

He dropped her hand. "What caveats?"

"I don't want to be physically hurt. I don't want to be bruised or bloodied. I don't want to be forced." She didn't know how demon feedings worked, exactly. She hoped he didn't require any of those things. "But I'll do my best to… satisfy you, otherwise."

He narrowed his eyes. "Why would you agree to this?"

"Because you can offer me something in exchange. I want you to protect me from my husband."

"Your husband?"

"Nirlan. The one who summoned you."

"He is your…" He seemed to struggle for a word. "…Your mate?"

She wished she could deny it. "Yes."

That seemed to throw him off. He thought about it for a long time.

"No one willingly submits to a demon," he said eventually. "The only mortals willing to deal with my kind are the ones like your master. Those mortals only summon us when they know they can make us submit."

Her *master*. That was what he thought her relationship with Nirlan was. She almost laughed, because he wasn't wrong.

"I don't want to control you," she said carefully. "I don't want to be controlled, either. Neither of us has to submit to the other as long as we stick to our agreement. We could be equals."

"Equals?" He said the word like it was foreign. He wasn't saying no, but he wasn't saying yes, either. She needed him to say yes. She needed protection from Nirlan, and from the world. She had nowhere else to turn.

Steeling herself, she tentatively reached toward him. Her fingers slid beneath the wrapping at his waist.

A wave of anger pulsed in the air. The demon grabbed her wrist. "You will touch me only when I grant you permission," he said through bared fangs.

She shrank. "Of course. I'm sorry."

"Do not touch," he growled again.

"I'm sorry. I didn't know. I won't do it again."

He released her, and she took a few steps back. The night seemed to be growing colder by the minute. She shivered.

The demon's anger seemed to cool. "You want an alliance," he said.

"Yes."

"You are wise to make this offer."

"Um... Thank you."

"I agree to your terms."

She was flooded with relief, and then dread. What kinds of things would she need to do to please him?

Perhaps she should start with the basics. "Will you tell me your name, then, since we're allies?"

He gave her a disapproving look. "My name is Azreth." He eyed her satchel. "Mortals must sleep every night and eat every day."

She wasn't sure whether that was a question. "Yes."

"Then we must allow you time to rest, and then we must find you food to eat. Sleep now."

"Now?"

"Yes. It is night." He waved toward the dark sky.

Bewildered, she glanced around at the damp, frosty ground, and wrapped her arms around herself. "I need to find a safe, warm place before I can sleep. It's too cold out here."

Azreth took a breath, then let it out. Raiya interpreted it as thoughtful, rather than annoyed.

When he reached for her again, she was stiff but unresisting as he turned her around and pulled her against him. He sat down on the ground, putting his back against a rock and setting her in his lap. His long, dark limbs folded around her, enveloping her in warm skin and a smell like heated wood. Despite his near-nudity, the cold did not seem to affect him.

"You must stay with me. You will be warm enough," he said.

"Oh."

He gave her a long, inscrutable look. "Turn on me, and I will destroy you," he reminded her matter-of-factly.

Raiya just nodded wearily.

"Now go to sleep."

Easier said than done.

She tried to force herself to relax, reluctantly laying her head against his hot chest. His heart thumped loud and heavy beneath her ear, beating far slower than any human's.

SEVEN

S he awoke to the light of dawn creeping over the horizon, and a large, warm mass against her side. The previous day came rushing back to her, and she stiffened.

There was a demon beneath her. She could feel his chest expanding, lifting her slightly with each slow, deep breath. She peered up at his face. He was looking back at her with his strange, hollow eyes.

"Have you slept enough?" he asked.

"Yes," she said, her voice small.

He unwrapped his heavy arms from her, freeing her.

"How long have you been awake?" she asked.

"I did not sleep."

"Don't you need to?"

"No."

Demons didn't sleep. Of course. That would be too simple.

Azreth stood up and stretched, lifting his arms high over his head—and like when he'd bathed, Raiya was struck by what a strangely human gesture it was. In the morning light,

59

she could see him much better than before. She realized his skin had a faintly iridescent quality to it, subtly changing tone depending on where the light hit it. The color gradually darkened near his hands and feet.

The demon looked down at her, and she realized she'd been staring.

"I must feed now," he said.

Raiya tensed. "Oh. Give me a minute." She went to the creek to complete her morning ablutions. She rebraided her hair and scrubbed her face until all the makeup from last night came off, which took some time, but Azreth didn't interrupt her.

When she returned to him, he frowned at her. "You're injured."

She remembered the bruise around her eye. It was old enough that she couldn't feel it anymore. "It's nothing. I can perform just fine, I promise."

He hesitated. "Did I do that to you when they put you in my cage?"

"You don't remember?"

He frowned at her and said nothing.

Had he been so unwell, so out of his mind with hunger, that he couldn't remember what had happened that night?

"No. This was my husband."

His hand went to her throat, lightly touching the old scrapes there. He pulled her collar down to follow the marks to her collarbone. Those ones were indeed from Azreth, as were the scratches on her ankle, which were hidden by her robe and trousers. Raiya just watched him defiantly.

He put her collar back into place. "I have heard that humans only take willing mates."

"Usually."

"Did your husband force you into marriage?"

She felt an ashamed flush climbing up her neck. "No, he didn't force me."

One of his eyebrows arched slightly. "So you formed an alliance with him, agreed to be equals, and now you have betrayed him."

She frowned at him, fully understanding his implication that she was untrustworthy. "Yes, I suppose I have."

Azreth waited for further argument, and she gave none. "I must feed," he repeated.

"What do I need to do?"

"Arouse yourself."

Raiya scoffed a little. Did he really expect that she would be excited about this? Or that she could excite herself on command? "I can't," she said shortly, partly because she was frustrated by the path of the previous conversation. "Just... just do what you want with me."

Azreth hesitated, then reached for her, putting an enormous hand on her jaw. She saw interest flare in his eyes.

Her heart beat faster. "Remember our agreement," she said, knowing perfectly well that she had no way of enforcing it.

"You do not want to be bruised, or bloodied, or forced," he repeated verbatim, surprising her.

His fingers drifted down her throat. She would have expected claws, but his hands were just like any other man's: strong and dexterous with appropriately sized, flat fingernails. And they were blue. She supposed that part was a little different from the average man.

He moved slowly, watching her face all the while, as if he was testing to see how far she would let him go. He thought she was lying. This was a challenge.

She stiffened further when his hand slid down her chest, between her breasts. A twinge of anticipation pulsed between her legs. But more than arousal, she felt shame, anger, and fear.

Azreth's hand slowed, then dropped. He glared at her.

"What?" she asked.

"You said you would be willing."

"I'm trying," she said quickly. She feared what would happen when he lost patience with her. "Keep going."

He began to reach toward her, then stopped again, making an irritated sound in the back of his throat. "If you cannot do this, then you must find someone else who will."

She hadn't guessed he would suggest an alternative, rather than simply taking what he wanted from her.

"I can do it," she assured him, but she had her doubts. Would he even fit inside her? What if he couldn't? "I could... use my mouth," she offered. Her cheeks burned.

His lips curled with irritation. "That is not how it works."

"Then how does it work?"

"The energy I feed on comes from others. From you. My body is not relevant. Only yours matters."

She blinked. She was a fool. *Arouse yourself,* he'd said. That was what he needed. She had to come for him. Oh, gods.

"Do you know how to pleasure yourself?" he asked.

"Of course I do."

"Then do it."

He didn't need to be involved at all. Fascinating. "Do you need to... watch me?" This entire situation was beyond the pale.

There was a faint flare of light in his eyes. "No. But I must be nearby."

Raiya looked around. They were in a wide, empty plain dotted with stones. There were no other living things nearby, and the castle and nearby roads were all far out of sight.

She slid to the other side of the boulder they'd slept against and sat down in the grass. After a moment, she heard Azreth sit on the other side of it, giving her some privacy—but not much.

"I'm going to begin now," she said uncertainly.

Azreth said nothing.

She closed her eyes and sighed softly. This was among the most outrageous things she'd ever been tasked with. But she was going to find a way to make it work. There was no point in delaying.

Eyes still closed, she lifted a hand to her breast and gently pinched its peak. A soft flutter went through her as her nerves awakened.

"Good," came Azreth's deep, toneless voice, and Raiya's eyes flew open. She glanced up to see if he was watching, but he was still on the other side of the rock.

She shifted her other hand to the apex of her thighs. Knowing he was so close put her on edge. It made her body respond quickly. She pressed her hand between her legs, over the fabric of her trousers.

She imagined her fingers were someone else's. She imagined a man. A tall man with strong hands. He was stern and powerful, but gentle and handsome. His fingers were big and bold as they touched her, as they penetrated her.

Her hand slid quietly beneath her clothes. She felt like she was a girl again, surreptitiously touching herself in bed after everyone else had fallen asleep. She supposed there was no point in trying to be quiet when he already knew exactly what she was doing, but she tried anyway.

The handsome man in her fantasy struggled to hold her focus while the demon was right behind her, observing her every move through this strange sixth sense he had. He would know when she'd touched a sensitive nerve. If she made herself come, he would feel it. Gods. She may as well have just allowed him to watch—it would have been the same.

"How long should I continue?" she asked.

"As long as you can," he replied, sounding very near. Raiya couldn't help but look up again, just to make sure. He had remained on the other side of the boulder where he couldn't see her, just as he'd promised. Her nerves settled. She closed her eyes again, trying to relax. Azreth's voice was strangely reassuring. Calm and steady. Patient and confident. "You are doing well."

The low vibration of the words combed over her, and a shiver went through her. She hadn't expected his approval.

She dipped her fingers deep into herself, tipping her head back against the rock. Her flesh had grown thick and slick.

For a long time, Azreth didn't speak.

"Is this working?" she asked breathlessly.

"Yes," he said. Then, again, "Yes..." His voice sounded heavy with arousal. Or was it hunger? Did he want her body, or did he just want to feed from her?

Fleetingly, she imagined it was his fingers touching her, stroking her and dipping inside her, making her back arch.

Is this so bad? he might say, smirking.

No. It wasn't.

What would it have been like if he had insisted on making her come, instead of letting her do it alone? What would it be like to be fucked by him? Big-and-brutish was not her usual type, but he was undeniably beautiful.

She wondered how he would do it. She imagined him palming her breasts and pinching her nipples until she cried out. She imagined him towering over her, his hands locked around her ankles and spreading her thighs wide as he thrust into her. His cock would be too big for her, and she would struggle to take him, but he wouldn't be deterred.

He'd be in absolute control, stretching her to her limit until her body yielded completely. He would take her until she was a gasping, whimpering heap.

You are so wet for me, he'd say. *Come for me, mortal.*

Climax exploded through her. She pressed her lips together to keep from moaning aloud, but a whimper managed to escape as pleasure ravaged her body.

She stifled her ragged breathing and quickly withdrew her hand from beneath her clothes. It had been a long time since she'd been so aroused.

Gods. If he could sense what she felt, he would know exactly when she'd thought of something that excited her. Maybe he would wonder what she'd been thinking of. Maybe he would even guess correctly.

When she heard him moving, she hurriedly got to her feet and pushed a loose lock of hair behind her ear, conscious of her crooked robe, damp fingers, and bruised, flushed face. She was a mess. She went to the other side of the boulder, folding her hands in front of her to keep them from fidgeting. Her demon voyeur surveyed her coolly.

The real Azreth was less flirtatious than her imaginary version of him. His lovely, pouting lips were unsmiling, completely without humor or sultry cockiness, but his eyes did linger on her longer than she expected them to.

"Good," he said simply. That was it.

"Do you know where you're going?" Raiya asked, trailing beyond Azreth as they waded through the dry grass.

"Away from your master."

"My husband."

"Yes."

She'd almost expected him to go back to the castle to kill him, now that he'd fed and restored his strength. "You're afraid of him?"

"He is a powerful man. He has many fighters and magics at his disposal."

Raiya was impressed by the accuracy of his assessment. "He does not give up easily, and he doesn't like losing. If we aren't careful, he'll find us, and he'll put us under his heel again."

Azreth had been walking a few steps ahead of her due to his long strides, but now he slowed his pace to walk beside her. He looked down at her thoughtfully. "Since you're his mate, you know him well," he said, as if it had just occurred to him.

"We don't say 'mate' here. I'm his wife. And yes, I do."

"Tell me what he will do next. What methods will he employ to find me?"

She shifted uncomfortably under his gaze, running a hand down her braid. "I'm not sure. But I know he won't limit himself to methods that are legal and moral, and he'll be relentless. It's a matter of pride. But you got rid of his mage, at least. That will give you a good head start."

A farmhouse appeared in the distance. Raiya grew alarmed when Azreth altered his path to guide them toward it.

"Where are you going?"

"There is a house. We will find food there."

Raiya thought of the bloody mess left behind at the castle. Azreth looked down at her, as if sensing her sudden spike of fear.

"Wait," she said. "I don't think that's wise."

"Why not?"

"What if there's someone inside?"

"I will kill them."

"No!" She ran in front of him to block his path. "Stay here and let me go alone. Please."

He kept walking. "You will stay with me."

"But—"

"No," he said sharply, frightening her into silence.

She prayed there was no one in the house.

As they got closer, she saw her hopes were in vain. There

was a young man working in the field by the house. He stopped and stared, mouth agape, shovel motionless in his hand. Then he ran to the house, stumbling over his own feet in his hurry, and slammed the door behind him.

Raiya's stomach turned. "Azreth, please, wait."

He stopped in front of the entrance. The house was quiet. He attempted to push the door open, and he met resistance. It had been barred.

Raiya flinched at the thunderous crash of Azreth's fist against the door. The wood splintered, and there was a shriek inside the house. Azreth hit the door again, which shattered it into pieces. It was bizarre to watch someone wreck such havoc so casually. Usually, violence followed anger, but he was completely calm. He nudged the remnants of the door aside and stepped over the threshold. Raiya hurried after him.

The house was a single large room with a kitchen on one side, two beds on the other, and a low table in the middle. From the corners of the room, a small family watched them. A woman, a young boy, an older girl, and an older man. Raiya couldn't see the young man they'd seen outside.

Azreth didn't do anything at first. He stepped into the room, giving the terrified humans only a passing glance. It was clear he didn't consider them threats, which she hoped meant he would leave them alone. He looked around the room, and his eyes focused on the kitchen.

Something moved behind him. The young man appeared, leaping out from behind the splintered door and wielding his shovel above his head in both hands like a sword. He brought it down on Azreth's back. The shovel bounced off Azreth's body, making the man stumble backward.

Azreth turned. He grabbed the shovel from the young man's hand and threw it across the room so hard that it stuck in the wall. There was a jumble of movement, and then Azreth cried out in pain and hunched over. It took Raiya a moment to make out what had happened.

The older man had pulled an iron poker from beside the hearth and attacked Azreth, embedding it in his side. The pointed end had easily penetrated where swords had failed, and he was bleeding.

The air pulsated with his pain and fury. Face screwed up with agony, Azreth grasped the end of the poker and wrenched it from his body. A gush of black blood flowed out, sizzling on the cold iron as if the metal were fresh from the forge. Azreth threw the poker away from him like it was poisonous. With one hand, he struck the younger man, which sent him flying, then he strode forward to grab the older man by the front of his shirt. He raised him off the ground, letting his feet kick helplessly in the air.

"Azreth!" Raiya rushed to stand in front of him, pulling at his arm until turned toward her, his expression furious, and for a moment, she thought he would simply kill her with one strike of his deadly fist. "They're just afraid! They're only farmers. Please let them go!"

Azreth bared his fangs at her. The younger man was on the floor, cowering. The girl on the other side of the room was on her knees, sobbing as she prayed aloud to Astra. The young boy was screaming as he hugged the older woman's legs. A piercing wail met Raiya's ears, and she realized that the woman was holding a baby—a shrouded bundle in her arms. The wide-eyed woman clutched the infant tighter against her chest, as if afraid the sound would draw the demon's attention. Azreth looked toward the baby, his brows pinching together.

"They were afraid you would hurt them," Raiya said. "They can do you no harm. You don't have to do this. Please. Please, don't kill them."

Azreth glared down at her, still holding the older man

aloft. His eyes shifted to the man, then to the weeping children and the woman.

Slowly, Azreth lowered the man. As soon as his feet touched the floor, the man backed away to huddle beside the woman and children. Raiya sagged with relief, astounded.

Azreth glanced back to check on the younger man, whose eyes widened upon catching the demon's gaze. At the same time, something on the stove bubbled over and hissed. They'd been in the middle of cooking.

When no one moved, Azreth went to the kitchen, holding the wound at his side with one hand. He ignored the overflowing pot and took the raw deer leg that was sitting on a chopping board beside the stove. He gathered a skin of water and a few other scraps, too, before heading for the door.

Raiya glanced over at the young man kneeling on the floor. His eyes sharpened with curiosity when they met hers. He looked torn, like he didn't know whether to hate her or pity her. His eyes asked a silent question: Was she the demon's prisoner, or his accomplice?

"Human," Azreth said expectantly as he stepped over the shattered wood.

Giving the family one last ashamed glance, she hurried after him.

EIGHT

When they were a safe distance away from the scene of their crime, Azreth turned his attention to his wound, which he'd been doing an admirable job of ignoring. There was discolored flesh around the hole where the poker had stabbed him, almost like a burn.

"Iron is poisonous to you, isn't it?" Raiya said. "That's why you couldn't lift the portcullis with your hands."

He gave her a steady, warning look. *Don't get any ideas,* the look said.

The wound looked painful, even if he was good at hiding it. "Are you all right?" she asked.

He gave her another look, thinking before he spoke. She was coming to realize that he was very cautious, always suspicious, rarely acting or speaking without careful consideration.

"It is a flesh wound," he said. She couldn't tell whether he was telling the truth.

"Those swords the guards used in the castle were steel, and they did nothing to you. Steel is made with iron."

"Steel is mortal-made. It is not pure enough. It is not of the earth." He placed his hand over the wound, and a pale

71

glow bloomed around his fingers. A healing spell. When he moved his hand away, the wound was a little smaller, but not much. Maybe he needed more magic. More energy.

Nervous, she waited for the command—*arouse yourself.*

Instead, he offered her the deer leg. When she informed him that she wouldn't eat raw meat, he made a fire, setting a pile of twigs aflame with a wave of his hand before tearing the meat into pieces. Raiya set the small chunks onto a stone beside the flames to cook, and Azreth lifted the rest of the leg to his mouth and bit into it, raw. She watched him with morbid fascination.

"Do you need to eat?" she asked, since he had not seemed averse to answering her questions so far. "Or do you just enjoy it?"

"My body does not require as much care as yours," he said. "But I must eat on occasion, or I will grow weak and die." He took another slow bite, ripping the wet, bloody flesh.

Raiya looked down, feeling bile creeping up her throat. She kept thinking about what might have happened to the farmers if she hadn't been able to calm him.

And yet, she had.

"Human," he said.

"Yes?"

He scanned the empty plain around them, his knees bending slightly as if preparing for a fight. "What is that sound?" he asked quietly.

The hairs on the back of her neck stood on end. She couldn't hear anything. "What sound?" she whispered.

He crouched beside her, watching the tall grass gently wave in the breeze. He was silent, not even breathing, and the muscles in his shoulders and thighs were taut, ready to spring. A natural predator. From this close, she could smell him again, hot and dry and somehow intoxicating.

"There," he murmured. And Raiya realized there was indeed a sound nearby—something she'd ignored.

"You mean... the bird?" she asked, raising an eyebrow.

The chirping song came again. "That," Azreth said. "What is it?"

Raiya laughed, releasing nervous tension. "It's just a little bird." She searched their surroundings until she spotted it—a tiny warbler perched on a long blade of grass. She pointed to it as it flew off. Azreth stared after it, perplexed.

"Do you not have birds where you're from?" she asked.

"In the hells, small animals stay silent and hidden. They would be killed by larger animals, otherwise."

He was less prepared for the mortal plane than she'd guessed. There was so much he didn't know about Heilune. Even the simple things. She wondered how long he could survive here on his own.

There were people here who hunted demons. Paladins, bounty hunters, soldiers and even city guards. This world was against him. Even with all his power, he could not stand up to it forever.

"Will you explain something to me?" she asked tentatively. "I always thought demons came to our plane because they were mindless creatures hellbent on tormenting mortals. But you are far from mindless, and you haven't tormented me, at least. So why do you not return to the hells? Heilune is dangerous for your kind."

He stood up, brushing dirt from his knees. "Whatever awaits me in Heilune, it is better than what I left behind."

Raiya raised her eyebrows. Did even demons consider the hells to be, well, hellish? Or was Azreth's situation unique? "What is it like there? I have studied much of this world, but not much is known about yours."

"We have talked enough about the hells," he said abruptly. "That book you have. There are runes in it."

Her lips parted in surprise. "You searched my bag?" She realized he must have done it while she was sleeping in his arms. Not that she'd ever trusted him, but it felt like a violation of trust anyway.

"Yes," he said, unapologetic. "To help me decide whether you pose a threat to me."

"Oh?" She crossed her arms, amused by the idea that she could be a threat to him. "And *am* I a threat, in your estimation?"

He didn't answer the question. "You know runes. You read the runes in the dungeon when they tried to bind me. That's how you knew how to break the mage's spell so thoroughly."

"Yes," she admitted.

"Are you a mage?"

That was a bit of a knife to the heart. "No. Nothing so glamorous."

She wasn't sure whether he was pleased or disappointed, but hearing this information made him stop to contemplate something. She waited.

"I would like to amend our agreement," he said.

She furrowed her brow. Their agreement was precarious enough as it was. "How so?"

"I require assistance with this." He held out his hand. On his palm was a silvery, glinting square of runes. The ink had washed away, but the runes remained branded faintly into his skin. She had thought they'd broken the enchantment before the runes had a chance to become permanent. It appeared she was wrong.

"I was too late," she murmured.

Azreth's lips twitched downward. "What do they say?"

Raiya hesitated. She could lie if she wanted to. He would have no way of knowing. She could tell him that they would kill him if he didn't return to his own plane, perhaps.

She glanced up at him. For a moment, she caught a flicker of something vulnerable in his expression.

He was alone here. Except for her.

Giving him a wary look, she put her finger to his palm. His skin was hot beneath the pad of her fingertip. Touching him felt like a sin.

"This one says 'death,' or 'final,'" she said. "This part stipulates a promise. And this one means 'lifelong,' or 'forever.'"

"What do they do?"

"I think it's a piece of a kind of soulbinding. A spell that will keep you partially bound to Nirlan."

"Bound in what way?"

"I'm not sure. It's half a spell. Since it was interrupted, I can't know for certain what the effects are. It could mean nothing... or it could mean that something bad will happen to you if you're away from Nirlan for too long."

There was a sudden heaviness to the air between them—Azreth's quiet anger. "Can they be removed?"

"I'm not sure. There may be a way."

"Help me find one, and I will protect you from the mate you betrayed."

She bristled, but didn't bother to defend herself. She had a hard time explaining why she had married a man she had come to hate. People always took Nirlan's side. "You're already doing that, remember?"

He straightened, his eyes intense. "I will protect you from any other dangers we cross. I will ensure that you are fed and sheltered and healthy. I am strong and capable, even in this unfamiliar land. If you do this for me, I will destroy anyone who crosses you. You have my word."

Raiya stared at him, eyebrows rising.

"Do you doubt my abilities?" he asked.

"No."

He narrowed his eyes at her. "You must uphold your end of the agreement. Betray me, and I—"

"You will destroy me. Yes. I know."

"You cannot outwit me. Plot against me, attempt to deceive me, and I will know."

She dug in her bag and, for the first time in months, opened her old journal. There was a certain excitement to it all, she had to admit. Despite the dire circumstances, it was a thrill to have a mystery to unravel. She began copying down the runes on Azreth's hand onto the paper. "I would have helped you regardless of our agreement. I don't need anything extra in exchange. No one deserves to be enslaved."

He frowned. He looked like he didn't understand and was trying to decide whether she was lying. She supposed she should have expected that.

"But if you want my help, there are a few other conditions you must agree to," she said.

"You said you didn't need anything."

"These things are not for me," she said, closing her book and placing it back in the bag. "You can't barge into places where you're not welcome. If you don't want to end up on the end of a Paladin's sword, you must listen to me."

"I will not lie down for those who bear weapons against me."

"Then don't break into their houses and steal from them," she said sharply. "I won't help you if it means bullying people weaker than you. I've spent too much time around bullies of late."

She realized her temper had gotten the best of her. She'd raised her voice.

Azreth didn't react. He thought for a moment. "I have no desire to hurt the weak."

She raised her eyebrows. He seemed earnest. "Well... Good."

He gave her a long, interested look, his expression difficult to read. She felt like she was being studied. Which was fair enough, because she was studying him back.

Finally, he looked down, raising his flesh-and-blood palm and pointing at the runes with his magically conjured fingers. She'd never seen a spell like that, a replacement for an entire body part. She wondered if he'd invented it himself after he'd lost his arm.

"What must I do to get rid of these marks?" he asked.

He was asking her to decide what they should do next. It was jarring, being asked for advice. No one had ever looked to her for her expertise before. And certainly no one had ever looked to her for leadership.

She had been living passively for so long now that she wasn't sure whether she remembered how to do anything else.

She ran her hand over her braid. "It will not be easy," she said slowly. "I have no experience with enchanting or disenchanting living things. We will need help. I think we should start by making sure we live long enough to look for a cure." She pulled a silver bracelet out of her bag. It was a simple, solid ring of metal, tarnished from lack of maintenance, with an opening on one side so it could be slipped onto the wrist. Tiny, dull runes lined the band. "I was going to use this when I left Nirlan, but you should probably take it. It's a simple glamour. It will help you blend in with mortals. It won't make you invisible, but it should be able to alter your appearance enough to keep people from attacking you on sight."

He took the bracelet from her, eyeing it as though he expected it to bite him. It looked tiny and delicate in his hand.

"It needs to be charged with magic first," she said. "I've never actually used it before."

"I can charge it."

She hesitated, glancing down. "Enchantments require quite a lot of magic."

"Then I will need to feed."

"Is there something that will give you more power than what I did before?" she asked, blushing faintly at the memory. "Something that I'd actually be willing to do, I mean?"

"Stronger emotions are better," he said. "The easiest avenues to power are pain and sex. In the hells, demons often torture each other for it."

"That wouldn't be my first choice."

"It is not anyone's first choice."

She was beginning to understand why he wasn't keen on going back there, if losing a fight meant being subjected to that. "Then sex is easiest?"

"Yes. The effect would be greater if I touched you this time."

Raiya's heart rate jumped. She saw his eyes flare in response. He already sensed it. "Touch me how?"

"It doesn't matter. But being in close proximity to you will make the magic stronger. Even better if I am touching your skin." It was hard to tell if he was excited by the prospect. As usual, his expression was wooden. She wasn't sure if that made her feel more comfortable, or less.

"Then... let's do that," she decided.

He needed no further encouragement.

NINE

Azreth wrapped an arm around her to pull her closer.

The movement startled her. A rush of something—fear or lust—turned her insides to liquid as she braced her hands against his chest. She wasn't ready for whatever this was. "Wait."

Azreth canted his head slightly. His hands rested on her back and her waist, waiting. She had not expected him to stop.

She took a breath, calming herself. This was just a transaction. She didn't belong to him. She was doing this for power. For herself. For her enchantments.

Thinking of her enchantments firmed her resolve. Finally, she had a magic user to power her creations.

When she didn't say anything more, he turned her around so that her back was against him. Holding her, he sank to the ground, seating her in his lap. He was a massive pillar of warmth against her back, his arms enfolding her and steadying her like when they'd slept together.

"You would like my assistance?" he asked. The velvety softness of his voice penetrated through her body and sent shivers up her spine.

"Yes," she said. "Please."

He paused, as if surprised.

"We may as well get it done with quickly," she added, not wanting him to think she was too eager.

"...Yes." His arms draped languidly over her as he bent his knee, raising his thigh between her legs. She drew in a breath as thick muscle pressed against her. She got the feeling he wasn't particularly in a hurry.

"Have you done this before?" she asked.

"Not with a mortal." His hand moved to her thigh, a firm touch that edged dangerously close to her sex.

"Do you know what you're doing?"

"You will have to let me know."

He cupped her through her trousers. Raiya froze, her heart racing. It was the same way Nirlan had touched her in front of him. She knew they were both thinking of it.

Unhurriedly, he pulled her robe up over her waist. She braced herself against him, feeling trapped with him on every side of her. And yet, she liked the feeling.

She closed her eyes as he caressed her sex. They lapsed into a silence that felt very awkward, but she felt that interrupting the moment by talking would be even worse.

He pulled her thigh with one hand, gently spreading her legs further.

She told herself there was nothing dehumanizing or embarrassing about this. This was for her. This was for power. This was for a new life away from Nirlan.

Her hips wriggled involuntarily as his fingers rolled over a sensitive point. And as she shifted, she felt a hard column beneath her, its length pressing against the cleft of her backside. Her eyes snapped open.

Azreth tilted his head, breathing deeply against the top of her head. "You smell like lust," he murmured, breaking their silence.

She opened her mouth, but no sound came out.

She tried to push against him to readjust herself, and he responded by pulling her tighter against him. He grabbed her wrist, pinning it to her side, and his palm clenched hard against her mound. She gasped, unable to escape the grinding of his hand. His body was as solid as stone. He was so much heavier and stronger than Nirlan.

It was too easy to enjoy him. Far too easy.

His hand moved up to the waist of her trousers and began to slide beneath. When she felt his fingers seeking the edges of her undergarments, she was stricken with sudden panic. It was all too much.

"No. Wait." She tried to shift her hands to stop him, but he was immovable. He paused anyway. She felt his head lift.

"Why not?"

"I just—just please don't."

He paused another beat, then withdrew his hand from beneath her clothes. His nose and mouth touched the side of her head—almost, but not quite, a kiss. Almost... like an apology.

"Be at ease," he murmured.

A wave of emotion crashed over her, and tears stung her eyes. She hadn't really thought he would stop when she asked. She wasn't used to people stopping. And it had been a long time since anyone had touched her sweetly—even if this was all for function, not fun.

She realized that because he could sense her arousal and her fear, and probably other things, he could somewhat sense what she wanted without her even saying anything. And so, without her having to clarify, he seemed to sense her desire to continue. His fingers explored her greedily, but not roughly.

He found a spot that made her gasp. She turned to jelly, her head tipping back onto his shoulder.

"There," she whispered.

"I know."

His cock pulsed beneath her, pushing upward as it sought her channel. At that moment, she longed for it. Her body felt empty, unfilled, unsatisfied. It yearned for him.

Gods, how did he do this to her? Was it magic? Was she being bewitched?

As his strong fingers flexed against her—skillful for someone who'd never met a mortal woman before—she gave a moan that she struggled to suppress. She grabbed his arms, holding on for dear life as she climaxed. Her entire body tried to arch, but he held her fast. Her hips bucked against him, and he moved along with her, his body taunting her. There was far too much cloth between them.

And then she heard a satisfied moan behind her, as if Azreth was experiencing his own climax of sorts. His arms crushed her against him. His fingers clenched on her arm, hard enough to border on pain. His hips rolled against her in a way that made her lightheaded.

"You taste fantastic." The words grating out of his throat sounded like metal and magic as his voice took on an impossible two-toned aspect. Raiya's hair stood on end. It was exactly what she would expect a demon to sound like. It was inhuman. Terrifying. Demonic.

"Taste?" she asked. Suddenly she was thinking about him licking the blood from her fingers. She was remembering him wild with hunger, losing control, tearing bodies limb from limb.

His arms were still locked around her, and his cock was thick between her legs.

"Yes," he sighed, and his voice had returned to normal again. "Like nothing else I've ever experienced."

She didn't know what to say. Should she be flattered, or worried?

He released her, and she slowly shuffled her clothes back into place before climbing from his lap. She fussed longer than necessary, afraid to turn back around and look at him. When she finally did, he looked lazy and satisfied, his eyes half-lidded, like he'd just had a feast and possibly eaten too much.

She was pretty sure that some sort of coda was appropriate for this interaction, but what? Should she thank him for a good time? Remind him that she'd only done this out of necessity? Should she address her teariness earlier?

Instead, she thought about what he'd said a moment ago. *Like nothing else I've ever experienced.*

"If you'd never met a mortal before now, how did you feed in the hells?" she asked.

He tilted his head back to look up at her. His eyes were blazing cerulean. "We feed on emotional energy. Demons have emotions."

"You fed on other demons?"

"Yes."

"Like this?"

A tiny crease formed between his brows as he got to his feet. The lazy, satisfied look was gone. "No."

Curiosity ate at her. She had to force herself not to ask again. Instead, she pulled the bracelet from her pocket and held it out in her palm. Azreth looked down at it blankly.

"Our agreement?" she reminded him.

He gave her a look that seemed faintly disapproving. But he picked up the bracelet and held it lightly between his hands. A light grew between his palms as magic pulsed through the air, flowing into the bracelet. Raiya watched, rapt. It was a rare joy to have one of her creations actually imbued with magic.

How amazing it must be to be able to have magic at your fingertips. He used it like it was completely natural, like an extension of his body. Like he thought nothing of it.

She glanced up at his face, expecting him to be focused on his magic, but he was watching her. Watching her watching him.

"Are mortals preferable to demons for feeding?" she asked. "Is that why your people come to Heilune? Because we... taste better?"

"They are preferable," he said, "because they are soft and weak and easily frightened. Your plane is a feast for us."

She bristled. "We are not weak."

He gave her a look. He wore no particular expression, but somehow it seemed like an argument anyway.

"We're not weak," she repeated.

"You are not strong," he said slowly. He spoke matter-of-factly, as if trying to convey that he didn't intend it as an insult. "Mortals are small and easy to break. They cannot put up much of a fight. It is different in the hells. We must fight every day in order to survive. That's why many try to make their way here, even when it comes with great risk." He glanced up at her, shrugging one shoulder. "That, and you taste better."

"Perhaps other demons would have an easier time if they all behaved like you." She hesitated, weighing whether she should say what she was thinking. She crossed her arms tightly over her chest. "It isn't so bad being fed from when you do it like that."

His eyebrows went up a touch. She felt herself blushing.

He lowered his gaze to the bracelet again. "Perhaps. Not everyone has such a willing donor on hand."

Donor. She preferred that to "victim."

The light between his palms faded as he finished charging the bracelet. When he held it out to her, light shimmered from the runes. Raiya smiled, excited to see it work.

"Put it on," she said.

His eyes narrowed. "You first."

Raiya's smile faded. Just like that, the speck of goodwill between them seemed to evaporate.

"I can tell you are a man who does not trust easily, Azreth." she said dryly. She took the bracelet and slipped it onto her arm. She sensed the enchantment latch onto her mind, waiting for instruction. She willed it into action.

Magic darted over her skin, and her complexion darkened to a cobalt blue to match Azreth's. She rapidly switched through all the colors of the rainbow.

"It changes your coloring," he observed.

"Yes. And it didn't even strike me dead in the process." She took it off and held it out to him. "Now will you use it?"

Hesitantly, he took it from her and slipped it over his wrist. He had to bend the metal open wide, but eventually it fit.

He changed his skin to the same sandy color as hers, and his hair remained black. She was relieved when his horns disappeared. She'd been afraid the illusion wouldn't cover them. It wasn't the strongest glamour she'd ever seen, but for the work of a mediocre non-mage enchanter, she thought it wasn't bad.

"Your eyes," she reminded him.

Pupils and irises and whites appeared. Brown eyes, like hers. He looked down at her. It was unnerving to suddenly be able to track his gaze so precisely, for some reason. His eyes felt more intense when she could see them looking directly into hers.

She looked him over. Disguised as a human, she found that he was very conventionally attractive, which almost made her laugh. It wasn't enough that he was a seven foot tall, bare-chested man with a body that looked to have been sculpted by the gods—no, he had to have a pretty face, too. It was almost too ridiculous to be believable.

He was going to attract attention no matter how much they changed him, but at least he wasn't blue. "It's a shame it can't make you look any smaller," she said. "If people ask, tell them you're half giant. We need clothes for you, too."

"I do not need protection from the elements."

She arched an eyebrow. "Have you seen anyone else here walking around topless?"

"Topless?"

"Without a top. A shirt."

He thought about it. "No," he realized. "It looks suspicious?"

"You could say that." She pulled her blanket from her bag and held it out to him. He fastened it around his shoulders, then bent down so she could pin it into place. The fabric wasn't thick, but there was a lot of it, and it covered most of his upper body, draping over him like a shawl.

She stood back to check their work. "You could almost pass for a native Uulantaavan," she said. "As long as you don't bite anyone."

He lifted his makeshift cloak so that both his arms were free. The strange glow of his phantom limb was gone, and it had the appearance of real flesh. He gave it a lingering look, turning his hand over and back.

"What now?" he asked.

She paused, surprised again to be the one making decisions. "There are no other scholars in Frosthaven who could help with your binding, let alone enchanters. We'll need to go farther afield to find the information we're looking for." And she was eager to put more distance between her and Nirlan.

"How much farther?"

She grimaced. It was probably best to be honest. "I'm not sure. We should head for Ontag-ul for now. It's the next town down the road." And it was still many miles away, especially since Azreth had brought them west instead of south along the north-south road when he'd wandered away from the castle. It would take days to get there.

"And if we don't find answers there?"

"Then we will have to keep searching."

He nodded. "I will follow." The statement was oddly comforting.

TEN

"We are being followed," Azreth said.

Raiya looked up at him. They'd been walking for several hours and had made it to the road south of Frosthaven. The sun had risen high and started to fall again, its light gray and cold.

She glanced over her shoulder, and sure enough, there was a figure in the distance, jutting up from the horizon between grassy hills. A rider.

"It could be just another traveler," Raiya said.

Azreth jerked his chin to point at something on their right.

In the fields off the side of the road, there were two more figures. When Raiya looked around, she found yet another flanking them on the other side. They were very far away, trying not to be seen before they'd had time to surround her and Azreth. They'd succeeded.

"Ash," Raiya cursed. They couldn't outrun mounted pursuers.

The riders came closer, slowly but surely. They were being

cautious. They rode behelgi—Uulantaavan giant elk. Raiya spotted silver armor and red cloaks.

"Paladins," she said. "Followers of the god of justice, Paladius. They hunt demons, among other things."

"I know what they are," Azreth said coldly. He stopped walking, then put a hand on her shoulder and pulled her in front of him.

"What are you going to do?"

He gave her a look.

"Azreth, don't do anything rash. Paladins fight for good. They help people. Supposedly." Her own father had been partial to the god Paladius. She didn't remember her father well, but what she did remember was not altogether pleasant. Paladius was not the most forgiving deity. "They are capable of seeing reason. If we can convince them you don't mean anyone harm, they won't hurt you. Maybe they could even help us. Don't do anything until I say so."

"You do not command me."

"I'm asking you as a favor. Please don't hurt anyone."

He quietly watched the riders. His glamoured eyes were unnaturally steady. He never blinked.

The Paladins were careful as they approached, even though there were five of them that Raiya could see, and only one of Azreth. But the closest one smiled at her when he pulled his mount to a stop a few strides away. He had sandy hair and a pale complexion, and appeared to be the youngest among them. An Ardanian by blood, by the look of him. The symbol of Paladius, seven swords forming a septagon, was emblazoned on his cuirass and his cloak. He glanced uncertainly back at one of the older men, who gave him a swift nod.

"Well met, lady," the young man said. The antlers on the behelgi he rode were enormous, and it made Raiya wonder whether the beasts were trained to fight for the Paladins. The man glanced up at Azreth. Azreth just stared coldly at him.

"Well met," Raiya said quickly. "My companion is mute, but he wishes you a good afternoon as well."

The man nodded politely. "I'm Paladin Adamus of the Temple of Paladius."

She didn't want to tell them her name until she knew she could trust them. Azreth looked down at her. She could feel his cool judgment as she hesitated. "Good to meet you," she said.

Azreth shifted a fraction, merely moving his weight from one foot to the other, but the Paladins reacted instantly. Several hands darted to sword hilts. Two of them jerked their behelgi's reins, making the animals twitch.

"Is there a problem?" Raiya asked.

Adamus was one of the ones who'd reached for his sword. He tore his gaze from Azreth to look down at her, and a crease appeared between his brows. He looked a bit younger than Raiya. She didn't get the impression he was their leader. She wondered if the others had chosen him to speak to her because they thought she might be more agreeable toward someone close to her own age—someone more approachable than the stern-looking men who accompanied him.

"Forgive us, lady. We've come searching for a young woman matching your description. We think she may be in trouble. We want to help her if we can. She is said to possibly be traveling with a... strange man."

Azreth's hand tensed on her shoulder. He was impatient. Or, he was worried that she would take them up on their offer.

She considered it.

"I see," she said. "I don't know anything about that."

The Paladins exchanged glances. "If you do see her, please let her know that we're at her disposal," Adamus said. "I expect she's under duress and afraid for her safety, but we're here to help, no matter her circumstances. Do you, uh, take my meaning, lady?"

Raiya was stunned that he was saying all this right under Azreth's nose, as if he wouldn't understand. But then she remembered that she'd also thought demons were dumb beasts before she'd met Azreth.

Still, the man seemed earnest. She found herself wanting to trust him.

She thought about the journey that awaited them—sneaking around in their search for a way to remove the binding, begging or stealing to obtain food and shelter, running from Paladins and city guards. They faced a lonely road.

"I do need help. I'm Lady Raiya Han-gal of Frosthaven. My husband threatened my life, so I ran from him." Azreth made a soft sound of annoyance as she said all this, which she ignored. "My companion needs help, too. We need protection."

Adamus raised his eyebrows, turning to his companions. He said something under his breath. Raiya could barely make it out from where she stood. *"That's not the story the lord told us..."*

She felt the blood drain from her face. Nirlan had sent them? She glanced up at Azreth. He gave her a look that was mostly blank but somehow still conveyed *I told you so* perfectly clearly.

She hurried to go on. "If you listen to our story, I'm sure you'll—"

Azreth spun suddenly, throwing her off balance. When she looked up, there was an arrow caught in his fist and an archer in the distance whom she hadn't seen before. He glanced down at the arrowhead before he threw it aside. It was an unusual, rough-looking metal. Iron.

Before she could react, someone grabbed her around the waist and half shoved, half threw her across the road. She landed flat on her stomach in the dirt with the wind knocked out of her.

Across the road, Paladin Adamus leapt down from his behelgi. "Lady Han-gal, stay back! We'll take care of this!" She tried to shout at him, but she had no air. She clenched her fists in the grass, struggling to regain her breath.

Azreth dropped the glamour. Raiya doubted it came as a surprise to any of them, but there was still a beat of hesitation when they saw him—blue skin, glowing eyes, horns and all.

A Paladin attacked Azreth from behind, attempting a jab at his back. Azreth twisted sideways, and the blade narrowly missed him just as another Paladin came at him from the other side with an iron-tipped lance. Azreth saw it in time to step aside again, grabbing the shaft of the lance and jerking it away from its wielder. Reversing its momentum, he jabbed the butt of the lance back at the Paladin's chest, shoving him to the ground and leaving a deep dent in his armor. He spun and swung the lance into the next Paladin's side so hard that the shaft broke in half, then he threw the pieces aside. Adamus was more cautious than the others. He stayed back, wisely keeping out of Azreth's reach.

They were going to kill him. Or he was going to kill them. Raiya was terrified of both possible outcomes. She struggled to her feet and started toward them, but the Paladin closest to her grabbed her arm.

"Stay back," he said to her.

She tried and failed to jerk her arm away. "Get off me!"

"Keep out of the way and don't make trouble, girl." His gauntleted hand was digging painfully into her.

"What is the matter with you? Let me go!" She jerked and kicked until she managed to slip out of his grasp. But before she could take two steps, he tackled her. His heavy, armored body pinned her to the dirt, scarcely allowing her to breathe. She struggled, and his arm locked around her neck, further cutting off her air. She tried to call out, but only a soft, stran-gled noise came out. Panic gripped her as her vision spotted.

And then, the atmosphere around them condensed. It was an invisible dark cloud. An oncoming storm. A heaviness that was more than physical. It was fury, deep and vibrant red like heated metal.

The Paladin suddenly lifted off her. She gasped for breath as she looked up. Azreth was above her, holding the Paladin by the collar of his cuirass. The air trembled with his anger.

He crushed the Paladin between his hands. Raiya heard bones shatter, and she flinched away as blood spilled from the Paladin's armor. Azreth threw the body aside with intense contempt.

It was quiet again. All but one of the Paladins were down.

Adamus stood a dozen strides away—less, for Azreth—staring at them both, his sword drooping in his hand. Azreth moved toward him, and to the Paladin's credit, he didn't run, but he didn't raise his weapon, either. He let his sword drop to the ground and held up his hands in surrender.

Azreth grabbed him by his collar, lifting him off the ground. Raiya was about to ask him to spare the man, but Azreth spoke first.

"Your archer tried to kill me. He hid like a coward and tried to shoot me while my back was turned."

The Paladin looked surprised. Perhaps, like Raiya, he hadn't known Azreth could speak. He kicked the air, shifting in Azreth's grip. "Yes. It wasn't right. And it wasn't right for them to be so rough with a lady. I apologize on their behalf."

Azreth glared at the man. He seemed vaguely taken aback by the apology, and it took him several seconds to decide how to react. "An apology means nothing when not accompanied by action. What will you do as a service to her?"

Raiya glanced up at him in surprise.

Adamus's gaze snapped to Raiya. "Well... truthfully, I have

little to offer. I'm not of a high rank in our organization, and I don't have the power to stop anyone from coming for you. But I meant what I said about wanting to help. My offer stands. I'm at your service."

Azreth looked down at Raiya. When she nodded, he slowly lowered the Paladin to the ground. Adamus straightened his armor, watching them warily.

"Are you all right, lady?" he asked.

"Fine."

He gave a short bow. "I'm sorry you were mishandled."

"I'm fine," she assured him, crossing her arms. "Nirlan sent you?"

He nodded. "The lord said that..." He glanced up at Azreth and lowered his voice. "He told us he interrupted you while you were attempting a ritual to bind the demon."

Raiya scoffed. This was an audacious lie, even for Nirlan.

"Lady, many people have done desperate things to escape a cruel lover. Nothing you've done is unforgivable. You are not beyond saving. We can still help free you from your husband and your demon both."

The interaction she'd just had with the Paladins had quickly soured her toward them. She didn't want to escape one overbearing man just to run to another. "Thank you, but no."

"Whatever the demon has told you is a lie, lady. He will turn on you. Demons always do."

Truthfully, she feared he was correct. She was most likely a fool for allying with a demon. She looked up at Azreth. A muscle in his brow twitched.

"There are other Paladins," Adamus said. "Many more than just us. Truly, I do not mean this as a threat, but you won't be able to evade them forever. You should send the demon back to the hells and turn yourself in."

"This man has nothing of value to offer us," Azreth said.

"We should kill him now. He will shoot us as soon as we turn our backs on him."

Adamus blanched. "I won't."

Even Raiya doubted him.

"Paladius commands his Paladins never to fight dishonorably," Adamus said, putting his hand over his heart. "I will not betray an opponent who has shown me mercy. You have my word."

"Then he will return later with more Paladins," Azreth said. "And we will have to fight him again. If we kill him now, there will be one less for us to fight later."

Adamus looked regretful, but gave another little bow. "That, I cannot deny. I have a responsibility to protect the people of Frosthaven and beyond. But I hope this can be resolved without bloodshed."

Azreth looked down at Raiya. He was deferring to her.

So she addressed Adamus. "I suggest you start walking the other way and don't turn back until you reach Frosthaven. Go quickly, before anyone changes their minds."

Adamus's eyes widened. Then he quickly dipped into another, lower, bow. "Wise advice. I remain at your service, should you need me."

She and Azreth watched him hurry down the road. Azreth watched him closely until they could no longer see him.

"Is this normal on your plane, to simply release enemies just because they ask for it?" he asked.

"Sometimes, if they've surrendered. It's considered dishonorable to execute someone after they throw down their weapons. There are certain rules for conflict."

He frowned. "Rules? Who makes the rules?"

"No one, I suppose. It's about honor, like I said."

Azreth was silent. After a few beats, one of the behelgi caught his attention. Stepping over a dead Paladin, he approached it. The behelgi raised its head, eyeing him suspiciously.

"I suppose it's different in the hells," Raiya said.

"In the hells, no one would bother to ask for mercy," Azreth said, "because no one would ever grant it." He slowly reached toward the behelgi, as if to pet it. But as soon as he came near, it sprinted away. It seemed that animals were not immune to the frightening aura he exuded.

Azreth lowered his hand and resigned himself to watching the animals from a distance—a scene which struck Raiya as quite sad. She came to stand beside him.

"Do you... like animals?" she asked, wondering whether they had any domesticated animals in the hells. Somehow, she doubted it.

He glanced down at her, then up at the behelgi again. She got the impression he was confused by the question.

"Are they in danger here without their riders?" he asked. "Will something kill them if they're left alone?"

"Possibly."

He watched them, frowning. All except the one he'd startled were grazing placidly, unaware of any dangers.

"You want to protect them," Raiya guessed, surprised.

He hesitated to answer, as if he was reluctant to admit it. "Yes."

"Why?"

"They're peaceful."

She gave a decisive nod. "We'll take care of them."

It took her some time to round up all the behelgi. While Azreth stood back, she tied them end to end and made a little train, held the reins of the one in front to guide it, and then they were on their way.

"Thank you," she said. "For defending me."

Azreth glanced down at her appraisingly. "We have an alliance."

Eleven

As the sun began to set, Azreth veered closer to Raiya. The behelgi shied away as he approached. "There's a settlement ahead," he said.

"Really? I didn't think we would reach the city this soon."

"It does not look like a city."

Raiya squinted toward the horizon. In the waning light, she could see a cluster of colorful tents in the distance. In the field beside them, there was a large herd of behelgi.

"Roamers," she said, frowning. "They're nomads. They take their herds with them where they travel." She hadn't expected to find them here, but she realized she should have—winter was coming, and they would be moving south toward a warmer climate. "My mother was a Roamer, though I'm not sure which clan. She was born among them and traveled with them all her life until she moved to the city and met my father." That was all far in the past. Raiya knew little of their ways, but her mother had spoken fondly about that time in her life.

Azreth's steps slowed. He waited for further explanation, or advice on what they should do now.

"We could trade the behelgi to them for some supplies and a place to rest for the night." She gave him an apologetic look, knowing that rest was only necessary for herself. "Perhaps I should go ahead alone while you go around them. It would be easier to avoid—"

He shot down the suggestion with a simple, hard, "No."

Apparently, he still didn't trust her not to run off without him. Raiya crossed her arms. "Then what do you suggest?"

"Are these people dangerous?"

Her inclination was to say no. It was widely known that Roamers didn't always follow Uulantaavan law to the letter, but perhaps that would be to their advantage. They didn't tend to welcome lawmen or soldiers among them. It was said that their camps were safe havens for those skirting the line between lawful and unlawful. *A bunch of freaks and criminals,* her father had once said. That sounded like Azreth and herself.

But demons weren't welcome anywhere. Not even in a Roamer camp.

"I don't think they're dangerous. But you should keep your glamour on," she said.

"Perhaps I shouldn't. I am growing hungry."

She looked up at him in alarm, and she realized he was being facetious. "Are you suggesting you'd like to remove the glamour and run through their camp just to frighten them and feast on their panic?"

He gave her a look that was almost wry. "That is what every demon would like to do."

Surprised by his sense of humor, dark though it was, she actually smirked. "Please do restrain yourself, if you can manage. You can feed from me later."

She'd spoken without thinking, but as soon as the words were out of her mouth, she felt awkward. There was a stiff silence.

As they walked closer, a sentry approached them. She was a dark-haired, tawny-skinned Uulantaavan woman, like Raiya, with a bow slung over her shoulder and a sword at her side. To Raiya's surprise, she seemed unfazed by Azreth's size.

"*Chianyehseg,*" she said, giving the traditional Uulantaavan language greeting, then switched to Ardanian. Hardly anyone outside of the most isolated pockets of the country still spoke Uulantaavan as their primary language. "All are welcome here, provided they cause no trouble and they have something to contribute to the betterment of the clan."

Raiya gave her a polite nod. "*Chianyehseg.* We have something to contribute." She motioned to the behelgi behind her.

"All of them?"

"That's right."

"Hm." She studied them briefly, skeptical. "Follow me. I'll bring you to one of the shepherds."

The camp consisted of several concentric circles of large, elaborate tents beside the road. There was a large cooking fire in the center of the camp, and several smaller fires dotted around the tents. A group of sun elves was preparing food, using their fire magic to tame the flames beneath pots and grills. Nearby, there was a trio of musicians playing a khuur, dombra, and drums for an enthusiastic audience. Children shouted and laughed as they played in the fields.

Azreth stared at everything warily, his eyes tracking every movement. He watched the children especially closely. Raiya thought he looked a bit like a nervous cat, ready to slink away in a hurry if someone made too loud a sound.

Originally, the Roamers had been a collection of northern Uulantaavan tribes, but over time, the clans had expanded to include people from various origins. They had a reputation for picking up outsiders and loners from wherever they stopped. Some even said that they kidnapped children to add to their numbers, though Raiya was almost certain that was a myth.

She could see some foreigners among them: a number of olive-skinned Ardanians, two ra'Hezirati from the deserts far to the southeast, a woman with oakmoss-colored skin and pointed ears who must have had some orcish blood in her, and the tall sun elves by the cooking fire. The latter were especially of interest to Raiya. Foreigners were rarely seen this far north, and non-humans were particularly uncommon.

The sentry brought them to the shepherd—a rotund, stern-looking old woman with a cane of gnarled wood. She looked over the behelgi with a discerning, critical eye as the sentry returned to her post.

"Are they stolen?" she asked, getting right to the point.

Raiya gave a nervous smile. "Would you buy them if they were?"

The woman was already circling the behelgi. Either the animals were well trained or she was just good with behelgi, because they allowed her to poke and prod them freely. "Doesn't matter unless they've got a brand on them, and it seems that they don't."

"You're not worried about being accused of stealing?"

She shrugged. "We'll be accused of stealing either way. Doesn't make much difference."

"I see."

"The animals seem to be in fair condition. What's your price?"

"I'd be happy just to see them go to a good home. How about thirty marks, a place to sleep for the night, and enough food for two people for the next few days?"

The shepherd snorted. "Enough food for *him?*" she asked, jerking her chin at Azreth, who squinted back at her. "He looks like he eats for three."

"Enough for two is fine."

The woman made an indecisive sound, as if Raiya was

asking too much. Raiya, who knew the animals were worth significantly more than what she was asking, just smiled.

Eventually the shepherd relented, handing over a small pile of coins and then pointing her to one of the smaller fire pits. Raiya relinquished the train of behelgi and went where she was told. Even without looking, she felt Azreth's weighty, dark presence following silently.

She sat down on one of the hides that had been laid beside the fire. No one else was around it yet—most were gathered near the musicians. Azreth reluctantly knelt beside her, resting his hands on his knees.

They were left alone there for some time, and as Raiya listened to the distant music and laughter and the fire crackling, her breathing began to slow. Her muscles loosened. She let out a long breath and closed her eyes and tilted her head side to side, stretching her neck. She hadn't realized how tense she'd been for the past few days.

No. It had been more than days. Weeks. Months, even, since she'd felt like this. *Safe.* That was what this feeling was. She felt safe. For the moment. She wanted to grab on to that feeling and hold it for dear life, because she knew it was going to slip away before long. She wanted it to last. She wanted to keep it for as long as she could.

Azreth was still scanning the camp restlessly, like he was deep in enemy territory. Maybe to him, it felt like he was. She didn't know how anyone could feel that way in a place so cheerful, though.

She suddenly felt guilty for bringing him here. She didn't think he would attack anyone, but if he did, she would be responsible for it. She'd brought a terrible danger into these people's home—a danger they'd never truly agreed to host.

"What's wrong?" she asked him.

"There are many people here."

"Does that worry you?"

"I did not think there would be so many."

She raised her eyebrows. "We haven't even reached a town yet. There are only, what, two hundred people here?"

"There are more in the cities?"

"Of course."

His fingers balled into fists on his knees as he continued eyeing their surroundings.

Raiya wondered if the Roamers would even be able to harm him if they wanted to, which of course they didn't. Their tent stakes looked like they might have been iron, she noted. She wondered if being stabbed through with iron could actually kill him, or if it would only hurt. Somehow, she suspected he wouldn't appreciate her asking.

"My strength is waning," he said pointedly.

She tried not to show how nervous that statement made her, with all these vulnerable people nearby who would be subject to his hunger if it grew too great. "I'll help you. Tonight, once we find someplace private."

Some of the tension in his face disappeared, but it gave way to something vaguely tired. He looked away.

"Can you wait that long?" she asked.

"Yes."

"Are you sure? Is it... If you feel any strong urges to... do anything, will you tell me?"

"I am not a wild beast."

She gave him a sidelong glance and said quietly, "I've seen you lose control before."

He didn't say anything, and didn't look at her. Upon reflection, Raiya supposed she wasn't being entirely fair. Even when he'd been starving and Nirlan had thrown her to him, he hadn't hurt her.

"Don't panic," came a girl's voice.

Raiya and Azreth both turned, and Raiya's eyebrows shot up.

Standing tensely behind them was an adolescent elven girl. Her skin was somewhere between blue and dark gray, and it made her look almost as alien as Azreth. Based on the way her bright green eyes were glancing between them, it was clear that she was, in fact, accustomed to people panicking when they saw her. Her black hair was artfully arranged into a collection of narrow braids. Her clothes were strange and elaborate, presumably of night elf make, and she wore unusual armor of black leather, along with a sword at her side. She was also holding a large basket in her arms.

"I won't," Raiya said. She smiled, trying to convey calm.

The girl looked relieved. She moved toward the fire and set down the basket she carried. "Fu-lon told me to take care of you. I'm Jai."

"I'm Raiya. This is Azreth."

The girl shot Raiya a shy smile as she started taking small, wrapped packages of food out of her basket.

Raiya had never seen a night elf in her life. Anyone who did was unlikely to live to tell about it. Like the Roamers, the night elves had a fearsome reputation that stretched far beyond their borders. Jai seemed harmless, but where there was one night elf, there were probably more lurking in the shadows nearby.

"How unusual, seeing a night elf this far outside of the Varai forest. Are there any others here?" Raiya asked, trying to sound nonchalant.

Jai sighed. "It's only my brother and me. We aren't going to sacrifice you to our goddess. I promise. Yes, we're really members of the clan. Yes, it's unusual. No, we don't go on raids, and we're not highwaymen."

"Of course not," Raiya agreed, as if she hadn't been thinking exactly all of those things.

Jai seemed mollified. She put a tea kettle over the fire.

"Is your brother older or younger?" Raiya asked.

"Older. He's a dick. But usually he goes out hunting at night, so you won't have to talk to him."

"Ah." If the Roamers had accepted them, they probably weren't murderers. She inched a little closer to Azreth nonetheless. He peered over at her questioningly.

Jai proudly handed them both plates of food she'd put together from the things in her basket, then glanced up at them as if checking their reactions. "I hope you like it. These are potato dumplings, and this is mutton. The tea leaf salad is my favorite. Oh! I forgot tea. I'll be right back." She hurried off into the sea of tents. Azreth stared after her.

"She is a juvenile?" he asked quietly.

It struck Raiya as an odd question. "Yes. She looks about fourteen. Her aging is probably just beginning to slow. She'll be grown in a decade or so."

"That long?"

"More or less. It's a bit different for elves than for humans. Do demon children grow up faster?"

"We do not have children."

"Don't have children? What do you mean?"

"We are born of age."

She pulled back to stare at him. "Do you mean to tell me that you popped out of your mother at your current size? Gods bless that woman, she must have been massive!"

His mouth moved in an odd way that might have been his version of displaying amusement. "Mortal females grow children within their bodies, yes? And the children are still very small when they are torn out of the mother's body?"

Torn out? Sweet Astra, what a conversation. "I... Yes."

"My kind are not born from another's body. I do not have a mother the way you do. We are created by the eldresses when they see a need to increase our numbers."

"Created how?"

"A ritual. We are born fully formed, not small and weak like your infants."

"Then why do you have sex?"

"For power. For personal satisfaction. For enjoyment."

"I suppose I'm asking why you're built to have sex, if you don't need it for procreation. Why are you made with the same parts as mortals, if it's not a biological imperative?"

He shrugged. "There is not a reason for everything. Some things just are." He glanced down at her body curiously. "How many children have you made?"

"None, thank the Five."

"You don't want to?"

"No, I mean... Not with Nirlan, certainly." Suddenly morose, she looked into the fire, trying to listen to the music instead of thinking about Nirlan.

"It sounds very painful," Azreth said. He must have been very curious about this topic. Raiya hadn't seen him so talkative before.

"I hear it is."

He frowned a little. "But women are forced to do it anyway?"

"Not forced. I mean, not usually. I suppose many women feel that it's worth the sacrifice. My mother told me that when I was born, she knew immediately that she loved me more than she would ever love anything else in this world."

Azreth's frown deepened. Raiya's tone had grown a little wistful by the end of her sentence. She didn't long for children, but she did wish she could feel love that deep. She'd thought she felt that for Nirlan, a long time ago, but it was nothing like what her mother had described.

Jai announced her return with a loud sigh. "I'm back. I got the tea." She opened the lid of the tea kettle and dumped in a generous amount of dark tea leaves, then took it off the fire.

Raiya had been so fascinated by what Azreth told her that she'd forgotten to start eating. She quickly dug in.

Jai looked up at Azreth. "So what are you? Half giant?"

He looked dully at Raiya as if checking for approval. "Yes."

"I knew it. On your mother's side, right? It's got to be the mother's side. I dread to think how things would fit properly, otherwise."

Raiya choked on her food. Azreth, who didn't seem to be listening very closely, was reaching toward the tea kettle. Before anyone could stop him, he picked it up—not by the wooden handle, of course, no. He simply wrapped a hand around the scorching metal and then poured the boiling water directly into his mouth. Jai's jaw dropped. So did Raiya's.

When he noticed them looking at him, he stopped. Raiya saw him realize the mistake he'd made. He quickly put down the kettle and half-heartedly shook out his hand, feigning pain. Raiya barely held back a sigh.

"How did you do that?" Jai gasped.

"A good magician never reveals their secrets," Raiya said before Azreth could reply. He nodded slowly in agreement.

TWELVE

When they'd finished eating, Jai brought them to a small tent. The inside was empty except for the brightly colored carpet laid out on the floor, the furs set on top of it for warmth, and two neatly folded blankets. Whatever the outside of the tent was made of, it was thick enough that it was relatively warm and quiet inside. And it was big enough to stand in and even walk around a little. Raiya was impressed.

As soon as Jai left, Azreth dropped his glamour. The color ran off him as if rinsed by soap and water, revealing his empty eyes and horns again. Raiya hadn't forgotten what he was, but it was still startling every time. While he wore the glamour, it was easy to start to feel like he was just another person, just a man. He wasn't.

He checked that the tent was sealed, then turned to her expectantly. Raiya was stiff as he approached. Standing directly in front of her, she had to crane her neck to look up at him.

"May I begin?" he said.

She closed her eyes and ran a hand over her face. She'd

never had so much performance anxiety as she did with him. "Yes. You'll have to give me a minute..."

"To do what?"

"To try to get in the mood. It's not that easy to do, sometimes."

He frowned. "You do not need to do anything. I will take what I need from you, as you've requested."

"I know, but..."

Casually, his hand came up and gently cupped between her legs, as if he had every right to that part of her body. She froze. He was still looking her in the eyes as he did it.

"You may relax," he said, his voice soft. "We've established that I can bring you to completion." His long fingers undulated against her, and she drew in a tight breath, putting her hands on his arms to steady herself. She inched her feet farther apart, and Azreth's fingers delved deeper between her thighs.

"I enjoy touching you," he admitted.

Heat rushed through her. Moisture gathered at her entrance. Azreth's eyes glowed brighter.

Her face felt hot. "Do you?" She didn't know what else to say.

He brought her down to the floor, dropping to his knees over her. He pushed her robe above her hips and leaned down, touching his beautiful mouth to the lips of her sex through her trousers, as if even this scrap of her—just the scent and shape of her body through fabric—was worth worshiping on his knees. Sparks went through her as she watched him.

"I will feel your skin now," he said. His hand clenched in the fabric of her robe as if he wanted to tear it off. "I will slick my hand with what is gathering between your thighs before I make you come."

Raiya was trapped. His eagerness set fire to her, but also terrified her. She was afraid he would lose control, and she was afraid she would follow.

His movements reluctantly slowed, and he raised his head to peer up at her with heavy-lidded eyes—eyes of a hungry predator. He was waiting.

Perhaps it would help him absorb more power if he touched her there, skin-to-skin. Yes. Of course it would. It would be foolish not to allow it.

She nodded. "Remember the rules."

"I have not forgotten." With that, he slipped her trousers and underclothes below her hips and tossed them aside.

He flipped her over onto her hands and knees, and then his thighs were framing hers from behind. She felt his breath against the back of her neck as he bent low against her. His hand clenched in her robe again, and his other hand grasped her thigh, and another hand brushed through her hair.

His... *other* other hand? By her count, that was three.

Her head whipped around, fear spiking. There was no one else in the tent. Only herself and Azreth.

The mysterious third appendage dropped from her hair and moved in front of her. It was a disembodied hand, cut off at the wrist, made of the same transparent magenta magic as Azreth's prosthesis. The hand lightly grasped her chin between its fingers, pushing her to face forward again. It slid down her neck and grasped her breast tightly, and then another hand appeared to hold her other breast. Yet another appeared at her hip to pull her backside tighter against him, and then another grasped her jaw again. She lost count of them. It was overwhelming, too much sensation to think properly.

Behind her, Azreth's hips pressed against her, as if he couldn't touch her enough, even with half a dozen hands. Just as he'd promised, his hot fingers slipped between the lips of her wet sex, and she gasped, stiffening.

"I—" She wanted to protest again, but she couldn't.

She'd told herself that they didn't have to touch. There

was no reason for it. He could get plenty of power by touching her over her clothes. Anything else felt excessive, like they were crossing some barrier of intimacy that would make things awkward at best, and dangerous at worst. They weren't lovers. They were coconspirators. It was a mutually beneficial arrangement, and that was all. There was nothing personal about it.

And yet, in the span of a few days, she'd gone from touching herself quietly while he waited nearby, to this. All at once, he was claiming every part of her, holding her hostage with pleasure.

As the hands palmed her breasts, flicked over her nipples, and caressed the slick folds between her legs, she felt a thumb brush over her mouth. It pressed between her lips, and it felt just like real skin but tasted like lightning. Surprised, she let her mouth open, allowing the digit access to her tongue, and Azreth gave a satisfied groan, as if he could really feel everything that the hands felt. His pelvis molded tight against her, the outline of his cock nestled against the cleft of her backside. All the while, his single organic hand was coaxing soft gasps out of her with each stroke of his fingers.

A rising tide filled her, pushing her toward the edge. Liquid heat dripped from her sex and coated Azreth's hand, and suddenly a finger was pressing against her entrance, pushing past a soft barrier of flesh, sinking inside her and filling her, and then—

She gasped as she came. Azreth covered her mouth to muffle her moans, his finger still deep inside her as she rode out her climax.

He didn't release her until her body had gone lax and she was quiet. Gradually, the hands disappeared, except for the ones on her back and hip. Raiya stared at the carpeted floor, still perched on her hands and knees. Sweat dripped down her temple.

Gods, that had been too much. Too intense. Too enjoyable.

This was supposed to be a businesslike arrangement. She hadn't meant to lose herself like this. It was far more of herself than she'd ever intended to give him.

She wanted to cry. She shouldn't have—it was foolish—but she supposed that was how emotions were. Sometimes they arrived illogically, when they were unwelcome and inconvenient.

She wiped her forehead, breathing hard as she sat back on her knees. She waited for him to call her a whore, or laugh at her, or gloat.

He put an arm around her waist, gently pulling her against him as he knelt behind her. "Be at ease, Raiya," he said quietly.

His voice was like a soft blanket over her. Tentatively, she rested a hand on his wrist, taking perverse comfort in the heat of the demon's body against hers. She nodded jerkily. "I am."

She felt him hesitate, as if he sensed the lie.

"I'm fine," she assured him—and herself.

AZRETH LEFT and didn't come back all night. In the morning, she found him just outside the tent.

"Were you waiting for me?" she asked.

"Yes. We should go."

Raiya waited, tense. With Nirlan, there had been a near-instant change after the first time they'd had sex. He'd turned to her the next morning in bed, smirked, and said, *You're easier than you look.* Even now, she felt the same sick, sinking feeling she'd felt then.

Azreth just looked down at her impassively, waiting for her to lead.

Giving him another cautious look, she hefted her satchel and struggled to balance with it on her shoulder. It was heavy now, laden with the supplies the Roamers had traded to them. Without saying anything, Azreth took the satchel from her and easily slung it over his shoulder. Perhaps the glamour he was wearing made him easier to read, because she thought he looked tired. His eyes were heavy-lidded and dull. She had expected him to look energized from the previous night.

"How do you feel?" she asked.

"I am healthy."

"Yes. But are you... all right?"

He gave her a dark, suspicious look. "Why are you asking me this?"

"I thought you looked off. Did you not feed enough yesterday?"

He stared at her. Then, he slowly reached out and grabbed the collar of her robe in his fist. He pulled her closer, as if to remind her how easily he could overpower her. "I am strong enough to destroy you and half of this camp. You would do well to remember that."

Raiya's eyes widened. And then, she was annoyed.

"Only half?" she asked sarcastically.

Even if she hadn't been able to see the anger on his face, she would have felt it seeping into the air. Instinctively, she started to raise her hands to try to push him away, but then she thought better of it.

"If you betray me, I will make sure you regret it," Azreth said.

This time, she did not tease him. For the first time since they'd left the castle, she felt afraid of what he might do. And in retrospect, she should never have stopped fearing him. In her experience, men were most likely to turn on you just after you dropped your guard.

"I understand," she said quietly.

He regarded her for another moment, as if trying to see into her mind, before he released her. He looked over his shoulder suddenly. Jai was walking toward them. She frowned a little as she approached, but said nothing about what she'd just seen, for which Raiya was grateful.

"The clan matron told me to invite you to breakfast and then see you out of the camp, if you like," Jai said.

"That's all right," Raiya said. "We should be going. We're in a hurry."

"Oh. I'll take you to the road, then."

"Thank you." Raiya wondered if they were being escorted out of politeness, or so that Jai could keep an eye on them and make sure they didn't cause trouble. Maybe they were worried about theft.

They followed her toward the edge of the camp. It was early morning still, just past sunrise, and steam was rising off the dewy grass. Many people seemed to be just getting up, but Raiya spotted a dark figure standing atop one of the hills nearby. It was another night elf in dark armor. He looked too skinny to be very old—perhaps only a few years older than Jai. As he met their eyes, he pointedly rested his hand on the pommel of the sword at his side.

"That must be your brother," Raiya said.

Jai nodded, rolling her eyes. "Don't worry about him. He glares at everyone like that."

"I can relate," Raiya said, giving Azreth a sidelong glance. He glared back, apparently not noticing the irony.

Jai stopped by the road, turning to them. "Are you sure you want to go so soon? You could stay another day or two, if you want. I wanted to invite you to the campfire last night, but Fu-lon told me not to bother you."

"That's very kind of you," Raiya said sadly, warmed by the girl's interest in them. "But we've got something urgent to attend to, I'm afraid."

"Is there someone chasing you?" Jai asked bluntly.

"Was it that obvious?"

The girl shrugged. "A lot of people end up with the Roamers when they're running from something. For me and Madira, it was bounty hunters and Paladins. The Queen of Ardani still has a bounty on night elves, and Paladins hate us. The Roamers don't let those types into the camps, so we're safe here."

"I'm glad."

"So what are you running from?"

Raiya hesitated, not sure how much she wanted to reveal. In the end, she decided it would be useful to know if anyone had seen Nirlan nearby. "A man. He's Uulantaavan, like me. A little older than I am. Long hair. Slender and tall, though not as tall as my companion. Have you seen anyone like that pass by?"

Jai shrugged again. "Maybe. There are a lot of Uulantaavans around."

Raiya pursed her lips. "His name is Nirlan. He would have been wearing expensive clothes and riding a big horse."

Jai brightened. "The lord, you mean? Some people were just talking about him last night. They say the castle's been abandoned. The lord left in a hurry in the middle of the night."

"Has he been seen on the road, then?"

"I've got no idea." If possible, Jai looked even more intensely curious about them than before. "They say something awful happened at the castle. I heard something about dark magic."

Raiya shifted away from her, fussing with her hair. "That sounds terrible. I can only hope we don't encounter anything like that."

Jai nodded, still eyeing them closely. "Yeah. Me too."

THIRTEEN

They had been walking for several hours when Azreth suddenly pulled Raiya toward the side of the road. She followed his gaze, and far in the distance, she could just make out a few mounted figures in gleaming silver armor. She let him pull her to a rocky ridge beside the road, out of view of passersby. They crouched there, watching the figures approach.

More Paladins. It appeared that they hadn't seen Azreth, because they passed by without stopping.

Raiya glanced up at Azreth. She was surprised he was hiding rather than attacking. There were only five of them. He could have killed them if he'd wanted to. Perhaps he was growing more patient. Or perhaps there was something else stopping him.

He still looked tired. Earlier that day, she'd seen him stumble over a rock in the road. It had been bizarre, like seeing a mountain cat trip. Creatures as strong and graceful as Azreth didn't stumble.

They waited for the Paladins to move out of sight, then she confronted him. "What's wrong, Azreth?"

He looked over at her, scowling.

"You're unwell," she said. "And if something is wrong with you, it affects me, too. I am not threatening you. I'm stating a fact. So don't take out your frustration on me."

"I am half bound to your husband, and I would like not to be," he growled.

"There's something else. You're ill. Is it the binding? Is it hurting you?"

"No."

"Then what is it? Ash and blood. We're allies, aren't we? We need to be able to trust each other at least a little bit. Otherwise, what use are we to each other?"

He sneered. "Do you truly expect me to trust a woman who betrayed her own husband?"

A string in the harp of her soul, drawn taut, suddenly snapped. "I didn't betray him! *He* betrayed *me!* He betrayed me a thousand times. You have no idea what he's done to me, how he's tormented me, you could never understand..."

Azreth looked surprised by the outburst, but unsympathetic. "You pledged yourself to him. You were mates."

"Yes. I was an idiot. So I suppose I deserved it all. I'll admit that. It was my own fault for loving him. He fooled me into thinking he was someone he wasn't. And I've paid for it with the past year of my life. I've been humiliated and belittled and used in every way. Living with him has made me into someone I hardly recognize. I don't even know who I am anymore, or what the point of all this is." She clenched a fist in her hair, so angry that she wanted to rip it out.

Azreth stared at her, frowning slightly. "He tricked you?"

"Yes."

"How?"

Raiya rubbed a hand over her face. He was never going to understand. Even other mortals didn't understand, so how could he? "I thought he loved me." Did demons know what love was? She searched for another way to put it. "I thought he would protect me. That's what he promised to do. Instead, he treated me like... like he treated you. Like I was a bound thing for him to use as he wished."

She took a breath to calm herself. "Please tell me what's happening. If I can't depend on you because you're about to keel over, I'd like to know. I deserve to know."

He didn't look angry like he had when she'd asked that morning, but he said nothing. Raiya was about to give up and keep walking when he finally spoke.

"I need rest."

Was that all? "We can stop for a while. That's fine."

"No. I need sleep."

Raiya raised her eyebrows. "You said demons didn't sleep."

"I lied."

She paused, adjusting to this information. "How often do you need to sleep?"

"Once every seven days," he said, blinking slowly. "It has been twelve."

He'd been hiding this all along. He'd been afraid to tell her. Because sleeping would make him vulnerable. He couldn't *destroy* her or punish her for betraying him or make good on any of his other threats while he was sleeping.

"Did you think I would hurt you while you slept?" she asked, unnerved.

Azreth said nothing, but his silence was telling.

"I wouldn't do something like that," she said. "I would never murder someone in cold blood while they were helpless."

Azreth leaned against the rocks behind him, staring her down. She didn't think he believed her.

"You have my word," she said. She could see him slowly being persuaded—if not because he believed her, then because he was simply too exhausted to go on. "People on the mortal plane sleep every day. Sometimes multiple times a day. Very few of them die from it, I assure you."

"Mortals care for each other. They do not care for demons."

She couldn't argue with that. She didn't know what more to tell him. Impulsively, she started to reach for his hand, but then she recalled the violently negative reaction he'd had the last time she'd tried to touch him. She settled beside him, hugging her knees to her chest.

Azreth opened his mouth, and it hung silently for a moment before any sound came out, as if he still couldn't decide whether to speak. "I will sleep very deeply. You will not be able to wake me."

That meant that he'd be even more vulnerable than she'd thought, and also that she would be on her own if the Paladins —or anything else—happened upon them.

She disliked how defeated he looked. Like he was certain he was signing his own death warrant. "I'll make sure nothing happens," she assured him. "You'll be safe here."

There was nothing more to be said, it seemed, because Azreth finally stretched out on the ground, long and straight on his back, in the seclusion the little cliff offered above the road. He took off the enchanted bracelet and handed it to her as the glamour faded. He didn't seem to have trouble with spell fever from enchantment overuse like mortals did, but perhaps it was still too uncomfortable to wear it to sleep.

He closed his eyes.

Raiya couldn't help but watch him.

It took less than a minute. He slowly went dead still, his entire body going slack. She almost thought his breathing had stopped, but then she realized it had only grown incredibly slow, his chest expanding only three or four times in the span of a minute. His prosthetic arm disappeared as the spell lost power.

"Azreth?" she said quietly.

He didn't move.

She reached out and brushed her fingertips against his arm. He didn't move. Didn't even twitch.

Taken by an overpowering curiosity, she raised her hand to his neck, letting her thumb and middle fingers rest on either side of his throat. She squeezed slightly. His pulsed thrummed dully under her touch, but he remained limp and still, unaware.

Stunned, she sat back. He'd been telling the truth. He was dead to the world. It would really be up to her to protect him from any threats, and she had to hope she was up to the task.

"Nothing will happen by," she told herself, settling against the rock behind her. No one could see them from the road, and no one would have a reason to come this way. They would be fine.

She took the baton from her belt and laid it across her lap so it would be ready to use, nonetheless.

***

A couple of hours in, she realized that she'd forgotten to ask him how long he would sleep. By the time night had fallen and he still hadn't awoken, she was beginning to think it might be longer than she expected.

As the night went on, the cold crept through her skin and into her bones, and eventually she stowed her pride and curled up beside Azreth to leech his warmth. He still hadn't moved.

She'd been lying there for an hour or more, wide awake and alert, when she heard a footstep beside her. Something metal touched her throat, and when she moved, it nicked her. She took a sharp breath.

"Don't move," came a voice from the darkness.

She didn't. Her heart raced as she searched the darkness, blind. After a moment, a shaft of rune-covered crystal lit up in front of her, and she winced in the sudden light. The mage torch was in the hand of the young night elf male holding a sword to her throat.

Raiya's baton was still clenched in her hand by her side, but she wasn't brave enough to lift it. The boy looked twitchy. He'd probably slice clean through her throat by the time she raised it halfway.

"Lady Raiya, it's me!" whispered a familiar voice from somewhere nearby.

"Be quiet," the male hissed.

"What's wrong with saying that? I don't want her to be frightened."

He groaned. "By the Goddess, Jai. Don't talk so politely. This isn't how you threaten someone. She's not your friend."

"I didn't say she was."

The two of them had approached so quietly that Raiya hadn't heard them over the sound of wind in the grass. Amazing that they were suddenly so loud now. "What do you want?" Raiya asked.

The sword, which had drooped slightly during the argument, jerked up to touch her chin again. "Be still," the male commanded.

"Madira, you're hurting her! She's bleeding, look! Stop, just let her go."

"Are you joking?"

A hand reached over in the darkness and shoved him. With a frustrated growl, he moved the sword away from Raiya's neck and glared down at her.

Raiya dared to tilt her head to look over at Jai. She was on Azreth's other side, holding a knife near his throat. An iron blade. She smiled at Raiya.

"You followed us," Raiya said.

"We came to help you," Jai replied. She glanced down at Azreth, her brow pinching. "The demon's not waking up."

"He's in a deep sleep," Raiya said. "He told me he can't easily be awoken from it."

"Fantastic news," Madira said flatly. "Just kill him now, before he wakes."

Raiya was stricken with panic. "No! No. Please don't. Jai, I'm begging you, don't do that."

Jai looked surprised. "Why not?"

Madira sneered. "Because she knew what he was all along, and she's working with a demon voluntarily. I told you."

"No she's not." Jai looked at Raiya tentatively. "Are you?"

"It's not what you think. He's not dangerous." She'd never told a bolder lie.

Jai looked sympathetic. "I saw him hurt you."

Raiya shook her head vigorously. "He has never hurt me."

"He was threatening you," Madira said. "Jai told me what she saw."

She couldn't deny that. In a way, she was touched. Jai had been worried for her.

Raiya slowly sat up, laying a hand protectively over Azreth's chest. "He was afraid."

"He didn't look afraid," Jai said.

"He has been hurt before." He'd never said it outright, but she knew. "Have you ever seen a street dog who growls at anyone who comes near it, even when it's offered a friendly hand?"

Jai was frowning. She glanced up at her brother, and he looked conflicted.

Raiya considered reaching for her baton. Instead, she slowly reached out and put her hand over Jai's. The girl didn't resist as Raiya inched the knife away from Azreth's neck.

"I'm sorry for hiding this," Raiya said, "but most of what I told you was true. We're running from a man who almost killed me and tried to bind Azreth."

Jai's eyebrows went up. "A lord did that?"

"Of course he did," Madira muttered. "Human lords care nothing for their people." He shifted from foot to foot, indecisive. "But he's still a demon. It's irresponsible to let him go free. He's dangerous."

"I've heard people say the same about night elves," Raiya said. Madira scowled at her.

Jai slowly pocketed her iron knife. "He seemed perfectly nice when I met him. Maybe he really is. Maybe demons aren't as bad as people say."

"Don't be stupid," Madira muttered, but he lowered his sword anyway.

For a few moments, none of them seemed to know what to do. The elves had clearly been expecting a fight and were at a loss now that they hadn't found one.

"We need to remove the binding Lord Han-gal put on Azreth," Raiya said. "We're going to Ontag-ul to try to find someone who knows about these things."

Jai brightened. "You're going to speak with the people at the Temple of Moratha, then?"

Raiya had considered the temple, but that was where Nirlan had found Eunaios. She'd found Eunaios to be less than trustworthy. "You think followers of the dark goddess would help us?" she asked skeptically.

"There are some clever mages there. Some of them are a bit odd, but they're not like other humans. They don't discount people just because of their race. If anyone would be willing to help you, it's them."

Raiya looked down at Azreth's slumbering form as she considered it. The followers of Moratha didn't cling to the same moral standards that most of society did, and it was well known that they dabbled in dark magics like bindings and demonology. They might be Azreth's only chance.

She nodded. "I will go to them. Thank you."

Madira crossed his arms. "This isn't going to go well," he said, looking at Azreth.

"I'll be fine."

"It's not you I'm worried about. It's everyone else. How many people has he killed so far?"

"Not too many," Raiya said evasively. "Would it please you to know that it was mostly Paladins?"

Madira's expression was guarded, but his eyebrows went up a little.

Jai spoke for him. "Madira hates Paladins," she said, grinning mischievously.

"I'm finding that I don't particularly like them, either," Raiya said.

IT WAS NEARLY morning when Azreth finally awoke. Almost an entire day had passed.

He jerked awake with a sharp intake of breath. He looked up at her, his eyes aglow, and she was surprised by how glad she was to see him again.

"Good morning," she said.

He looked up at her blankly. As he slowly sat up, he looked down at himself, as if making sure he still had all his parts. His phantom arm reappeared, giving off a soft magenta glow as the magic threaded together.

He looked up at her again, and there was a strange expression on his face. He was surprised.

"Do you feel better?" she asked, arching an eyebrow.

He didn't answer, but looked her up and down. His eyes

locked onto her neck, noting the nick the night elves had left there—little more than a paper cut.

"What is that?"

She looked down. "Um. There was a small incident." She felt his pulse of anger and fear. At this proximity, it drifted off his skin like a perfume.

"What happened?"

She decided it would be best to tell the truth. She was having a hard enough time gaining his trust, and lying to him wouldn't help. "The night elves from the Roamer camp. I think they were suspicious of you, so they followed us."

His nostrils flared. "They attacked you?"

"No. It was a misunderstanding. Everything is fine now."

"But you're hurt."

"It's nothing."

He leaned in. "It is not nothing. If someone hurts you, you should punish them. If they think you will tolerate being hurt, they will do it again. You must learn to defend yourself."

She stiffened a little, because she sensed he was thinking of another person who had hurt her. *The* person. "Are you worried about me being hurt, Azreth?" she asked wryly.

"I take no pleasure in your pain."

He sounded far more earnest than she'd expected. She was taken aback for a moment. "I understand," she said. "But this is not like when Nirlan hurt me. They're young. And, frankly, they're night elves. They were trying to help, in their way."

He frowned like he still didn't understand, but he didn't argue.

She was starting to find that confused frown endearing. He didn't understand, but he was trying to. Before she met him, she would never have guessed that a demon would want to understand the perspective of mortals.

"I will follow your lead in this," he said reluctantly.

She smiled. "Thank you."

Fourteen

Raiya and Azreth passed through the gate to Ontag-ul without issue, though the watchman on the wall gave them a very curious look.

The town was fortified by a great wall all around its borders. The roads were paved with interlocking stones, the buildings constructed with neatly cut wood and topped with tiered, gabled roofs of dark tile. Night was quickly falling, and dark clouds were moving in to cover the moons, but flickering lanterns hung beside buildings and along bridges over the river that ran through the town.

Like much of Uulantaava, it was dark and mostly colorless, but it was beautiful in its own simple way. It gave the impression of being a part of nature, as if the landscape here had just happened to grow into the shape of a city.

"This city is not very defensible aside from the wall," Azreth commented. "These buildings are all wood. I could knock down their walls easily. And they would all burn with a single stray spark."

Raiya raised an eyebrow. "I hope you're not planning on setting anything aflame, Azreth."

"I'm not."

"Most cities have mages or sun elves who are responsible for dealing with fires." She kept her voice low as they passed other people on the narrow streets and paths. "I think it's very pretty."

"Pretty?"

"Yes. The architecture. The plants." She looked up at him. "Do you have artists in the hells?"

"What is an artist?"

She suddenly felt pity for him. She seemed to end up feeling that way whenever he talked about his plane. "It's a person who makes beautiful things for a living." She pointed to the elegant, curving slopes of the roofs and the intricate wooden lattices that covered some of the windows and doors. "These details serve no defensive purpose. They exist just to be beautiful. Because they're nice to look at, and they make you feel at home. Things like that are made by artists and artisans."

Azreth looked closely at the building she'd pointed to. He reached out and touched the latticework.

"Demons don't think about the beauty of things," he said quietly.

"What about you?"

He looked down at her blankly.

"Do you think about beauty?" she asked.

He thought for a long time.

"Sometimes," he said finally.

Rain began to fall.

They'd arrived in the evening, so they opted to stop at an inn for the night and find the Temple of Moratha in the morning. After speaking with a few locals—most of whom stared nervously over her shoulder at Azreth the entire time—Raiya located an acceptable establishment. The inn was busy enough that even someone as strange as Azreth would not attract too much attention, she hoped.

As they stepped through the front door and into the common room, she wiped rain droplets from her face. It was loud, bright, and warm, heavy with the scent of hot food and close bodies. It was not the classiest of places. Nirlan wouldn't have been caught dead here, which she supposed was a plus. All in all, it was a stark difference from the cold, empty halls of the castle. She and Azreth stopped at the edge of the room.

"There are armed people here," Azreth said tightly.

He was right. She could see a few people carrying swords. One group had a pile of quivers and bows leaning on the wall beside them, as if they'd just come back from a hunting trip. They were normal people. Many civilians carried weapons in Heilune. None of them looked like they would cause trouble.

"It's all right," she said. "Come on."

The innkeeper behind the counter was an older man, thickly built, wearing a large apron.

"We're looking for a room," Raiya said. Azreth stood like a statue behind her.

The innkeeper raised an eyebrow at Azreth. "It's half a mark for the night. But there's only one open. One bed."

She fished around in her bag for her small coin purse. People wouldn't think it proper for them to be sharing a bed when they weren't married, but that was the least of her concerns at the moment. "That's fine."

The innkeeper chuckled as he took the payment. He sounded like he'd dipped into his supply of ale a few times that night, and he eyed her for a little too long. "What? A fancy little lady like you with that big thing?"

Raiya stiffened. She held out her hand. "My change?"

He grinned lopsidedly at the other men drinking at the counter. The coins were in his hand, but he didn't hand them over yet. "Don't be coy. It's an inn. You're a traveler. Give us a story. Are you and him really an item?"

"Yes," Azreth said. Raiya looked up at him in surprise. She didn't know if he'd said it because he didn't know what it meant, or simply because he was trying to get through the interaction faster. The innkeeper and the other drunks laughed. One of the men clapped Azreth on the back in a congratulatory way, and Azreth gave him the most murderous look Raiya had ever seen, which went unnoticed by the other men. She found herself trying to become smaller.

"By the Five, I'd pay to see that," the innkeeper said. "Tell you what. I'll rent you the room for free if you give us a peek at you with the giant-spawn tonight."

Raiya glared at him, her face hot. The men laughed harder.

Azreth reached over her shoulder and took hold of the innkeeper's apron. He jerked the man up against the bar. Raiya held her breath. If he started a fight here, it would end badly.

"Be quiet," Azreth said. It was clear that he expected the command to be followed without further prompting. The innkeeper went a little pale. When Azreth released him, Raiya let out her breath.

"It was a joke," the innkeeper said. "Get a sense of humor, friend." He flopped a few coins into Raiya's hand, then gave her a key.

Raiya looked sidelong at Azreth as they went down the hall to their room. He stared ahead.

"Thank you," she said.

His gaze slid toward her. He held out his hand, showing her the runes still faintly glowing on his skin. "Tomorrow, you will fix this," he reminded her.

She nodded. "I will." She opened the door for him, peering inside to make sure everything was as expected. There was indeed a single bed. Raiya's mind was briefly filled with images of Azreth and herself on it together, doing exactly what the innkeeper had described. She cleared her throat. "Stay here. I'll be right back."

"Where are you going?"

"Just to order some hot food and a bath. It won't take long."

"I will go with you."

"I think it's best if you stay here. You attract more attention than I'd like."

He considered that, frowning. Then he nodded. "Return quickly."

She made her way back down the hall to the crowded common room. She spoke to the innkeeper again, ignoring the cold way he addressed her, then stepped back to wait for the food she'd ordered, rather than having it delivered to her room. She wasn't keen on the possibility of some maid popping her head into the room at an inopportune time and witnessing Azreth in all his demonic glory.

She leaned against the bar, surveying the crowd as she waited, and thought about that bed. Gods, she was looking forward to it, wasn't she? But how could she not? Those hands were surprisingly generous.

As she looked out at the crowd of mortals happily clinking glasses and laughing with each other, her stomach turned in circles. None of them would understand, if they knew. They'd happily kill Azreth and hang her for aiding him.

"What has you looking so unhappy, my dear?" came a smooth voice that made her freeze in place. "You look like you've seen a ghost." An arm curled around her waist, holding her against a slim body.

Nirlan smiled bleakly at her, the expression not reaching his eyes. "I've been looking everywhere for you."

She should have run. She should have called for help. She should have done *something*. But she couldn't move.

"Don't you have anything to say for yourself? Didn't you think you'd get caught? Don't you ever think ahead?" His lips curled with contempt, but his voice remained soft.

Raiya's heart pounded in her ears. She couldn't move. He was right—she was stupid. She was too cowardly and foolish to even speak.

Nirlan looked like he wanted to say more about what he thought of her, but he seemed to realize that this wasn't the place for it. He was good at controlling himself sometimes— when he was in public, and people might be watching. Raiya watched his expression smooth over.

"Where is he?" he demanded.

So he didn't realize Azreth was in the other room. He must not have seen him earlier. Perhaps he'd only just arrived at the inn. Perhaps Nirlan hadn't even guessed she'd made a glamour for him. As far as Nirlan was concerned, she was probably too stupid or lazy to think of something like that.

"I don't know," she said.

He reached toward her face, and she winced, but he only flicked a lock of hair out of her face.

"Who else aided you?" he asked quietly. "Did the Roamers shelter you?"

"No."

"The Paladins?"

"He killed the Paladins," she replied, deciding not to bring up the one he'd let go.

Nirlan cursed under his breath.

There were several other Paladins in the crowd, she realized. She caught glimpses of silver armor and scarlet cloaks. They were quietly searching the room, trying not to attract attention.

"You went to the Paladins for help dealing with the

demon?" she asked. "What happens when they realize you were the one who summoned him?"

"There's no point in tattling on me, wife. They work for me."

That gave her a chill. "The Paladins are a religious order, not mercenaries for hire."

"There's not a man or woman alive who won't sell themselves for the right price. You should know that." He shifted, and something prodded her in the side. He had a knife, and he was casually bumping the blade against her ribs.

Her heart stuttered, leaping into a panic. Gods help her. He was going to kill her.

"I'd prefer not to make a scene," he said. "And don't you dare touch that baton in your belt."

"What are you going to do?"

"Come with me without making a fuss, and I won't have to do anything at all."

Raiya didn't move. If she called for Azreth, he would come, and then all hells would break loose. Either he would end up dead, or everyone else would, or both.

Trembling, she pushed away from the counter.

Nirlan smiled. "Good girl," he said, like she was a dog. He slowly guided her through the crowd toward the door.

"What are you going to do?" she asked again.

"Don't sound so pathetic. You're not fooling anyone. This is all your own doing. If you weren't so impulsive, none of this would have happened, and we'd both still be sitting comfortably at home. You've forced me to go through a lot of trouble."

"What are you going to do, Nirlan?" she asked firmly.

"I'm taking you home. And after that, I'll do whatever I wish with you. You're mine."

As soon as they stepped over the threshold, Raiya grabbed her baton. Without drawing it out of her belt, she jabbed the handle backward into Nirlan's crotch. He shouted and doubled over, and she jerked out of his grasp. A sharp pain sliced through her hand. His knife had cut her. A rivulet of blood ran from the cut, but she didn't have time to examine it further. She drew her baton and sprinted down an unfamiliar path.

The rain had made the town muddy and slick. Raiya leapt onto the wooden boardwalk that curved through a maze of buildings, ducking under eaves as she ran. She flew by the entrance to another lively tavern, dodging through a group of people standing on the boardwalk in front of it. She didn't bother to ask anyone for help. Nirlan would find a way to spin it so they ended up turning on her.

It wasn't long before she heard his footsteps hitting the ground, rapidly gaining on her. She stopped in the middle of the walkway and whirled around, pointing the baton at him. "Don't come any closer!"

He stopped a dozen paces from her, but he was smiling. Two more men came running around the corner and stopped beside him. Paladins. The bystanders by the entrance of the tavern had looked up when she'd yelled. She realized how bad this looked for her. Paladins didn't chase innocent people. Everyone would assume she'd done something wrong.

She backed away from them, her feet slipping slightly in the mud. Drizzling rain was making her hair and clothes cold and heavy. The baton wouldn't do much good here. She didn't know how many shots it had left before it ran out of magic, but it wasn't many.

"Put down the weapon, Raiya," Nirlan said. He was still smiling. He knew he had her trapped. Raiya took a step back, but then she heard footsteps behind her. More Paladins had appeared at the other end of the path. She was surrounded. The people by the tavern backed away, huddling in the doorway as they watched the confrontation unfold.

"You're being foolish," Nirlan said, coming closer. "You've had your fun. It's time to come home now."

"I told you, we're done," she snarled.

"We're married."

With a frustrated roar, she discharged the baton. Sending a tendril of her will into the metal in her hand, the enchantment activated. The runes along the shaft glowed bright. Violent energy surged from the tip and shot outward in a beam of blinding light. It blasted into Nirlan's chest, and he shot back-ward. The baton's runes went dark as they lost power. It was out of magic.

A mass of metal hit her from behind, and then she was on the ground. A gauntleted fist struck her cheek. Something else hit her stomach. Someone grabbed her braid and yanked her head back, and then something heavy dropped on her, and she couldn't breathe.

"Azreth!" she cried, though he was much too far away to hear her strained voice.

One of the Paladins ripped her baton out of her hand. Another one took hold of her arms from behind her and hauled her to her feet. She struggled to pull away from him, knowing perfectly well that there was no point. People on the sides of the boardwalk were staring.

Another Paladin was helping Nirlan to his feet. He wasn't dead, but he looked much worse for wear. He remained doubled over for a long time before pushing away from the Paladin and coming toward her. There was a large burn mark on the chest of his overcoat, the fabric blackened and fraying at the edges.

He stopped in front of her. "It's a good thing the gods saw fit to bless you with beauty," he said. "Otherwise, no one would be willing to put up with you." With that, he leaned in and forced his mouth against hers. Raiya flinched away, but Nirlan followed her, grabbing the back of her head to hold her against him. He smashed his lips joylessly against her, just to show her that he could do as he wished with her. By the time he pulled away from her, she was crying.

"Tell me where the demon is," he said.

"Go to each and every hell and find him yourself."

Nirlan's eyes glinted with anger. Before he could respond, there was a rush of air above them. Everyone looked up.

A massive shape dove down from above. It collided with one of the Paladins, smashing him to the ground.

It was Azreth. An enormous pair of vibrant magenta wings, shaped like those of a dragon, had sprouted from his back, and the glow of his eyes lit his face in the darkness. He was snarling as he drove his fist through the Paladin's cuirass.

The Paladin holding Raiya released her, shoving her away as he drew an iron blade. Azreth whirled toward him, grabbing the man's arm before he could swing the sword. He yanked, twisting the Paladin's elbow at a stomach-turning angle before tossing him aside. The Paladin went flying across the path and sprawled against the side of a building, groaning in agony.

Chaos erupted. Bystanders screamed and ran. The Paladins backed away, scrambling for iron weapons. One of them threw a spear, which Azreth narrowly dodged. Another drew a bow and started to aim an arrow at him. Azreth simply picked up one of the other Paladins and threw him into the archer.

The remaining Paladins seemed to think better of facing him. They began to run.

Azreth turned to Raiya. Someone else's blood spattered his body, though the rain was already washing it away. Not long ago, she would have thought him a terrifying sight. But right then, she'd never been happier to see someone.

He looked her up and down, then turned to Nirlan, who had been surreptitiously backing away. Azreth strode after him, unhurried.

Nirlan made a desperate swipe toward him with his knife. As the point of the blade crunched against Azreth's skin, Nirlan slipped in the mud and fell. Cringing, he twisted to look toward Raiya. His perfect hair was soaked with rain, and his elegant cloak was twisted beneath him and covered in road muck. "Raiya! Help me!"

Azreth paused, glancing in Raiya's direction, almost as if asking her for permission. She raised her eyebrows. He was allowing her to decide Nirlan's fate.

Nirlan smiled nervously, as if they were old friends and this was all a simple misunderstanding. "For the love of Astra, call him off!"

She didn't even stop to consider the possible consequences, because she was furious and frightened and her blood was running hot.

Raiya looked at Azreth, and she nodded her approval.

Though he didn't quite smile, Azreth seemed pleased. He bent toward Nirlan.

Nirlan bared his teeth in fury. "You traitorous—"

Azreth's hand made contact with Nirlan's throat. And then, something went wrong. Azreth shouted and recoiled as if he'd been burned. He fell to his knees and clasped his own neck. Nirlan scrambled away.

Raiya ran to Azreth's side. When he pulled his hand away from his throat, there was a black mark in the shape of a hand in the same place he'd touched Nirlan. The runes on his palm glowed a violent red, and steam wafted off them.

Raiya could see Nirlan slowly gaining confidence as he came to the same realization she was coming to: the binding, even only half-made, prevented Azreth from harming him.

Nirlan ran to one of the dead Paladins and picked up the man's iron sword.

Raiya's hand clenched in Azreth's cloak. "Azreth—"

He picked her up by her waist and tucked her against his

chest, raising his enormous wings behind him. He paused long enough to pick up her fallen baton and press it into her hand as Nirlan approached with the sword. Then he flapped his wings, bent his knees, jumped, and suddenly they were airborne.

Raiya wrapped her arms tightly around his neck as the ground fell away. Wind rushed in her ears and rain pelted her as they shot into the sky. Below them, a crowd was staring up in awe and terror. She could see Nirlan at the center of it, sword in his hand as he watched them escape. He motioned to a few of the Paladins that were still nearby, and they started following in the direction Azreth was flying.

Raiya turned her gaze toward Azreth. His long arms held her close against his chest, and she felt surprisingly secure.

"You have wings," she said breathlessly.

"Yes."

She guessed it took a lot of magic to maintain them, otherwise he would have summoned them more often. "For how long?"

"Not long."

He flew in silence for a minute, his wings beating softly as he scanned the town. Then he tipped downward, speeding up and then slowing as he gracefully descended. They landed gently on the roof of a tall building. He set her on her feet, then studied her. The mark on his neck was already fading, but the runes on his hand were still inflamed.

When he found the cut on her hand, he frowned. Raiya's eyes widened as he lifted her hand and put his mouth over the wound. He sucked gently, his rough tongue dragging over the cut, stinging and then soothing. It was not exactly like when he'd licked her blood before, when he'd been starved and desperate. This time, it reminded her more of a dog licking a wound. Like an animal instinct. It was a sensual act, but also a caring one. She was surprised to find that it didn't disgust her.

Azreth seemed to realize what he was doing, and he paused, looking like he'd been caught in an embarrassing act.

Raiya swallowed. "Thank you. Again."

He covered her cut with his hand, casting a short spell that transformed the raw, red slice into a clean, pink line. Almost at the same time, his wings and right arm both disappeared as he abruptly ran out of magic. His entire body drooped, and his eyes were dim.

She held his massive shoulders, worried he would tilt sideways and fall off the roof. "Are you all right?"

"I am still strong."

She glanced over the edge of the roof. It was dark, but she could make out shapes on the street below, illuminated in torchlight. Paladins and other townspeople were searching the city for them. It wouldn't be long before they found them.

"How are we going to get down?" she wondered aloud.

Azreth didn't have an answer.

Trying to stay out of sight, she leaned close to a pillar beside them. Looking up, she realized it looked a bit like a steeple.

"Hello there!" someone whispered.

Azreth stepped in front of Raiya to put himself between her and the whisperer. Peering around his side, she saw a hooded figure beckoning them from a small window in the roof.

The person grinned, holding a hand above her face to keep the rain off. "The lady of darkness welcomes you," she said. "You are being pursued by the Paladins, yes? Come inside the temple. Hurry."

Azreth gave Raiya a questioning glance.

"Moratha cultists," Raiya whispered. "Like Eunaios."

Azreth frowned.

She took his hand, pulling him toward the open window. "Come on."

FIFTEEN

Azreth helped lower Raiya through the window, then started to climb through after her. It became clear that he was far too large for the opening, and his legs dangled through while his upper body was trapped outside. After a few seconds of contorting unsuccessfully, he simply punched the sides of the window, breaking out chunks of the frame until he fit.

The cultist just smiled as he stood up inside, unoffended by the casual destruction of the cult's building. She was human, past middle age, and her face was painted in unnerving black and white makeup that made her look rather corpse-like. "He is utterly magnificent," she said, her eyes traveling all the way down his body and then back up. "Truly a work of glorious, grotesque art by the dark goddess, praise her."

"Praise her," came an echoed chant. Inside the attic they'd dropped into were half a dozen women and men in black robes.

"What may we call you, young acolyte?" the woman said to Raiya.

"I'm Raiya. This is Azreth. I don't want to frighten you, but you might be in danger. The Paladins were on our tail. They'll be coming for him."

"You are both safe here," the woman said. "The wretched followers of Paladius, curse him—"

"*Curse him,*" echoed the others.

"—will not enter our temples. They know that to do so would be an act of war. Moreover, they are afraid to come too close because they believe our temples are tainted with evil. They are right." She smiled again. "The child of darkness and his human escort are welcome here, of course. I am High Priestess Gereg. We are happy to help in any way we can, and I would be pleased to offer you sanctuary from the Paladins."

Raiya hadn't expected such a warm welcome from death cultists. "Thank you. It's nice to meet you," she said, giving an uncertain nod. "I don't mean to keep going on about it, but the man leading these Paladins is... quite persistent. I'm not certain they won't be able to force their way in."

Gereg gave a signal to the other cultists, and half of them hurried downstairs. "Worry not, daughter of darkness. We arm ourselves just as heavily as the Paladins. I'll post extra guards at the entrances."

"Thank you."

"You must be tired from running. Would you like to rest here? You may stay as long as you wish. Let me show you our temple, and I'll take you to our sleeping quarters, if you like."

"You're too kind. We would appreciate that very much."

Gereg went to the stairs, and Raiya and Azreth followed a careful distance behind her. Azreth bent down to murmur in Raiya's ear.

"What is wrong with them?"

"What do you mean?"

He gave her a look.

She shrugged. She had a hard time arguing that they

weren't suspicious. "They're a little strange I suppose, but who isn't? They've done nothing to hurt us yet, which is more than can be said for a lot of people."

Azreth made a quiet, discontented sound as he straightened.

Priestess Gereg gave them a tour of the temple. It was larger than Raiya had expected, and appeared to be new construction, which made sense, considering that the cult of Moratha had been rapidly growing recently. The building was all rich ebony wood with vaulted ceilings and dark stained-glass windows, and smelled of incense. The beauty of the place was somewhat marred by its eerie inhabitants, though. They wandered about the temple like ghosts, many of them wearing the corpse-like face paint that Priestess Gereg sported, and even the ones who didn't wear the paint looked depressed or sickly. An unsettling chant could occasionally be heard throughout the building, though Raiya couldn't tell where it originated from.

They all stared at Azreth when they passed. They gathered in doorways and on balconies to get a look at him. Many of them bowed deeply, while others seemed too awed to react. Raiya looked up at Azreth to see how he was taking all this, and he gave her a tense glance. He was no more comfortable here than he had been in the Roamer camp or the inn.

As they entered the main hall of the temple, Gereg turned to them. "We have long awaited this day."

"What do you mean?" Raiya asked.

"For months now, there have been signs from the dark goddess that something is coming."

"Signs?"

"Dreams. I dreamed of a great awakening in Uulantaava. I dreamed of an otherworldly force that would come to help us spread the dark goddess's love far and wide. Now, it seems that this otherworldly force has finally arrived." She smiled at Azreth.

"I see," Raiya said. "And in your dreams, how was the... spreading of darkness accomplished, exactly?"

"I cannot say. But have faith. The dark goddess will reveal everything soon."

"Ah. Of course."

Gereg squinted up at Azreth. "Your companion doesn't speak much, Acolyte Raiya." Azreth frowned at Gereg.

"He is still new to the mortal plane. Our customs are unfamiliar to him, so he prefers to let me speak for him."

"How wise of him."

"Priestess Gereg, I hate to ask for more when you've already offered us so much, but there is something else we need help with. We've encountered more troubles than just the Paladins since Azreth arrived on our plane. Someone attempted to place a binding on him."

Raiya nodded to Azreth, and he reluctantly raised his palm to show Gereg the runes. They looked better than they had earlier, but they were still rather raw and red, like recent wounds.

Gereg raised an eyebrow. "A nasty bit of spellcraft."

"Can you help us undo it?"

She looked uncertain, and Raiya's hopes fell. But then Gereg nodded. "Many of our number are mages. We will help you find a way to fix it, with the Goddess's blessing. Worry not."

Raiya breathed a sigh of relief. "Thank you."

Gereg bowed to Azreth. "Please make yourself at home, beloved spawn of the dark goddess. We are eternally grateful to her for this gift. Praise Moratha."

"*Praise her,*" echoed some other cultists nearby.

Gereg bowed again as she left, and then they were finally

alone—except for the dozen or so people still watching them from around the cavernous room.

Azreth was bemusedly studying the display at the front of the room: a stone altar, a basin, and a lot of decorative skulls that appeared to have come from real people. For a moment, Raiya was afraid the liquid in the basin might be blood, but upon closer inspection, it appeared to be mere water.

"Is Moratha really the mother of demons?" she asked Azreth, keeping her voice down.

He shrugged.

"What do your people believe?" she asked.

"Our eldresses say nothing of gods. They kneel to the universe itself, to the forces of chaos, creation, and destruction."

"You worship the universe?"

"We don't worship anything."

"I see. Perhaps you should keep that to yourself for now. The acolytes will be sorely disappointed."

"I agree."

She was glad they had come to the same conclusion. It appeared that their welcome here was conditional upon their support of Moratha's goals. If they wanted the cultists' help, it would be best to play along for a while.

He rested a hand between her shoulder blades, grazing upward to the base of her neck. Her skin tingled at the touch.

"I am hungry," he said quietly.

"So am I," Raiya said, giving him a sly look. His eyebrows lifted slightly. She realized it was the first time she'd admitted she freely wanted him, and apparently he realized it, too. She cleared her throat. "Later. We should take care of some things first."

NIRLAN and his retinue of Paladins had the audacity to approach the temple and demand entrance, but were turned away by several cultist mages. Raiya watched the exchange from behind the curtains of a window upstairs. She didn't relax until long after he'd left. It appeared they were safe, for now.

That evening, Azreth sat stiffly in a chair that was far too small for him while a few of the cultists studied his hand. To Raiya's disappointment, even the mages seemed to know little more about the binding enchantment than she did.

"A pity Brother Eunaios isn't here," one of the cultists said. "He's been missing for some time. He was the most knowledgeable about summoning and binding of us all."

Raiya carefully didn't reply.

Predictably, Azreth drew a crowd of onlookers as he sat for the mages. The more people gathered around him, the more irritated he looked. Some of them began asking him questions about his purposes on the mortal plane and about the hells, which he answered mostly with noncommittal grunts.

Then people began making requests. Someone asked him to bless their ceremonial knife, a task which he surely wasn't qualified for, but merely being a demon seemed to be qualification enough to satisfy the cultists. Another cultist asked him to relay a request to the dark goddess.

When it got to be too much, Azreth got up and stormed out of the room, knocking over several cultists in the process.

"I dislike these people," he said to her later. "And this place is not safe. I can sense it. We should leave."

"I know. But they might be our best chance at fixing this."

He frowned, but didn't argue.

By the next day, she was starting to lose hope that this endeavor would yield any fruit. But then she found the temple's library.

It was not very large, but the selection of books was ideal.

The shelves were filled with an array of unusual tomes, including *Effective Methods of Murder, Sacrifice, and Embalming; The Nature of the Hells: A Noncomprehensive Study of Demonology; Confessions of a Blood Magician;* and various runic dictionaries and spell books.

Finding someone willing to help Azreth would be good, but being able to do it herself was even better.

There were no desks in the library, which struck her as odd. Perhaps, like Nirlan, the cultists were more interested in the idea of forbidden knowledge than in the actual knowing of it. So she worked directly on the floor, bent over a dusty book of demonic runes as she carefully copied them into her notebook. A small candle served as her only light, as the space lacked windows. Occasionally, one of the cultists would stop by to ask what she was doing and offer advice, most of which was unhelpful.

"Are you a mage?" one of them asked, crossing her arms as she looked down at Raiya.

"No, not as such."

"Too bad. You'd be a lot more useful if you were."

"I can't disagree."

"Perhaps the demon should have come directly to us instead of you." She smiled unkindly.

Raiya looked down at her work, though she was suddenly having a difficult time concentrating on it. "Yes, you're probably right."

After a few hours, she leaned back to stretch her shoulders, and she felt a presence at her side. She looked up, and Azreth was crouched beside her, watching her work. She had no idea how long he'd been there. He raised a hand over her candle, and the flame grew a little bigger and brighter, casting more light over her book.

She smiled and pointed to the book. "Look what I found. It was written by an Ysuran mage who lived in the fourth century. It's a study of runes found on enchanted artifacts from the hells."

Azreth looked at the page she'd pointed at, impassive.

She went on, too excited not to share her findings, whether he wanted them explained or not. "Look at these. They're very similar to the ones on your hand. And here—" She flipped to another page in the book. "This section has theories about reversing bindings. Most of it isn't relevant to you, but look at this set of runes. The runes on your hand appear to be a combination of several languages and spell types, but I think some of them use an old demonic language. We can use this as a basis for building a spell to reverse your binding. I've already made a few prototype enchantments for us to test."

Azreth studied the runes in the book she'd been reading, then looked over the enchantments she'd sketched out, his luminous eyes carefully passing over every pen stroke. At last, he looked up at her.

"You can read all these runes? These spells?"

"Yes, most of them. I've studied runic languages for a long time. Maybe longer than I should have."

"These languages can be merged?" he asked slowly. He looked at his hand, then back at the book. "What does this one mean?"

Raiya pointed out each rune on his hand as she explained their function in the spell while Azreth listened. When she'd finished, she sat back, waiting for him to react. He frowned. Raiya guessed he was going to point out how unlikely it was that her counter-enchantments would work, and she braced herself.

"You are very clever," he said.

Raiya raised her eyebrows. "Oh. Thank you."

"I thought you were a mere craftsman of enchantments, not an inventor of them. You have impressive skill."

Flutters filled her stomach. "I don't know about that. But I'm glad I can be of assistance."

"You offer more than just assistance," Azreth said. He lowered his voice, glancing up to look her in the eye. "If you were not with me, I would be trapped and without hope."

Raiya was startled. She swallowed back a lump in her throat. Without thinking, she found herself reaching out to touch his hand. He looked down at where she touched him, quiet and still.

"I'm glad I can help," she whispered. "No one should be trapped or hopeless."

His fingers slowly folded around hers.

A sad thought occurred to her—that he might no longer need or want her after this was done. She realized, rather suddenly, that she didn't want to leave him. Was it just because of the sense of safety that came from having a demon as a bodyguard? Or had she begun to appreciate his company?

"What will you do after you're free?" she asked. "You said you will not return to the hells."

"No. I will remain here with you."

She blinked, surprised. It seemed he'd already been thinking about this, as well. "With me?"

His gaze sliced toward hers. His eyes narrowed. "Yes."

Raiya watched him, and he watched her back. The warmth had gone from his aura. His expression was cool and unyielding.

Slowly, Raiya's pleasure drained and was replaced by confusion. "What do you mean by that?"

"You will stay by my side while I remain on your plane. That is all."

"That's all?"

"Yes."

She crossed her arms. "Perhaps you should ask me what I plan to do, instead of telling me."

He scowled. "What do you plan to do?"

"I don't know. I hadn't decided yet, and I was considering my options."

His lips twisted downward. He glanced away, and she could see the muscle in his jaw silently flexing before he returned his gaze to her. "You will remain with me, and I will feed from you."

"Is that a command?"

"If it must be."

It felt like a knife twisting in her chest. "You can't do that. You can't tell me what to do. You're not my master."

"There is nothing you can do to stop me. You are weak."

Raiya gaped at him. She shut her book and stood up. "How *dare* you talk to me like this?"

He stood up too, towering over her, unapologetically intimidating. "You give me no choice. I must feed, or I will grow weak and die. There is no other option."

"Perhaps I would have continued to help you if you had just asked me. Did you think of that?"

"You said you were considering leaving me."

"So you've decided to force me to stay?"

He waved his arm in a rare outward display of frustration, baring his teeth. "If you refuse, you will force my hand!"

"So if I tried to leave you, you would keep me against my will? And how will you feed from me? Do you plan to hold me down and torture me?"

"I do not want to hurt you."

That made her feel a little safer, but not much. "Then what is your plan, exactly? How will you feed from me if I'm unwilling?"

He had nothing to say to that, apparently. The silence was deafening.

"I thought you—I thought we were getting along." It sounded stupid now that she said it aloud. This was his nature. What else had she expected? It was only just recently that she'd started to think of him as a companion instead of an enemy, anyway. "You can't have it both ways. You can't have my trust and friendship while also holding me hostage."

"I apologize if I gave you the impression that you should trust me," he said sarcastically.

"You're right. That was my mistake." She shoved her notebook under her arm and shelved the book she'd been referencing before stalking toward the door.

Azreth grabbed her arm to stop her, and she stiffened, looking back at him nervously. His expression was hard but wavering slightly, like he was wrestling with several emotions. "Where are you going?"

"To my bed."

"It's only midday. You will not require rest for hours."

"And?"

"Aren't you going to try to undo my binding?"

"When I'm not feeling so exhausted, maybe." She glanced down at his hand on her. "Release me."

He hesitated, then let go. She left without another word.

Sixteen

When Raiya awoke very early the next morning, Azreth was not waiting outside the room for her like he usually was. She was relieved. She still wasn't in the mood to see him.

She ventured into the main hall, where she was alone except for one other solitary figure. She was surprised to see an elf with indigo skin and raven hair kneeling before the altar, bending so low that his forehead touched the floor.

"Madira?" she asked.

He started, jerking his head up, and he scowled when he recognized her. "You again?"

"I didn't know night elves worshiped Moratha," Raiya said, coming to lean against a column near the altar.

He looked annoyed. "We do not worship Moratha."

She glanced over at the altar, and at his position before it. "You'll forgive me for assuming..."

"We worship the night goddess, Ravi. The spirit of our homeland." He rolled his eyes, as if she was stupid for not knowing the difference. Or perhaps she wasn't the first one who'd asked, and he was tired of explaining it. "The Moratha worshipers are one of the few groups who won't attack my kind on sight. There are no places of worship for our goddess outside of Kuda Varai, so I come here instead. It is not Ravi's temple, but it is a temple nonetheless, built on a ley line that eventually leads back to the homeland. My prayers will reach the Goddess's ears, have no doubt."

He seemed very confident. Or perhaps it was wishful thinking masquerading as confidence. Kuda Varai was a very long way from northern Uulantaava.

"I'm sure you're right," Raiya said hopefully.

He nodded approvingly.

"Is there a reason you and Jai don't return to your homeland?"

He hesitated, a somber look crossing his face. "It's complicated," he said. "We can't go back."

"I understand the feeling."

He got to his feet, looking toward the door to the main hall. "Where is your monster? Isn't he with you?"

"Probably upstairs."

He smirked unkindly. "Getting weary of him, are you? I can't say that I'm surprised."

She didn't want to talk about it, so she just smiled blandly. "Where is your sister?"

"With the caravan. We arrived in town this morning."

"Did you come to the temple by yourself? Is it safe for you to be out alone?" Perhaps more importantly, was it safe for the townspeople to be alone while a night elf was around?

He grinned as if he'd read her mind. "I'm not the one you need to worry for."

Soft footsteps sounded from the doorway. They both turned to see Priestess Gereg entering, her hands folded into her black robe. She appeared to sleep in her makeup, because it was even more smeared and grotesque-looking than before. Perhaps that was the goal.

"I see you've met our other new acolyte," Gereg said to Raiya. "How lovely for Moratha to deliver us even more of her faithful. May her darkness shroud all of us."

Gereg seemed to think Madira did indeed follow Moratha, and he wasn't correcting her. In fact, he was glancing nervously at Raiya, his lips pressed together.

Instead of pointing out the misunderstanding, Raiya bowed her head respectfully. "Praise her," she said. Madira seemed to relax a fraction.

"Indeed," Gereg said. "You didn't tell me how long you'd been a follower of the dark goddess, Acolyte Raiya."

Raiya fiddled with the end of her braid, glancing at Madira. He raised his eyebrows.

"Oh. Well, it was fairly recent," Raiya said.

"Truly? When was your awakening?"

Raiya wasn't particularly good at lying. She told as much of the truth as she could. "I had an awakening about a week ago. I suppose I had reached rock bottom. But now I've found a way out."

Gereg nodded sagely. "The dark goddess often seeks us out when we are at our weakest, when we are most open to her wisdom. The assurance of death comforts you, does it not?"

Raiya stared at the old woman, trying to work out whether she expected an answer in the affirmative. Then again, this was the goddess of death they were talking about. "Oh, yes. Definitely."

Gereg smiled wanly. She took a breath, moving on to a new topic. "I have received another message from the dark goddess."

"Another dream?" Raiya asked, barely hiding her skepticism.

"Indeed." Gereg raised her hands as if making a grand pronouncement. "In my dream, the demon announced his purpose on our plane."

"His purpose?"

"Yes. He is here for a reason. Haven't you guessed?"

"I guess not."

"You will see." With that cryptic statement, she folded her hands behind her and walked smugly out of the room.

Madira frowned after her, fidgeting with the pommel of his sword. "That woman is creepy as all hells."

"On that, we can agree."

He looked her up and down as if reassessing her. "You shouldn't be here," he said. "The cultists are not as harmless as they seem."

"I appreciate the warning, but I can take care of myself."

"Whatever you say." He took a step back, and then his entire body faded until it was almost gone. He was still there in front of her, but he'd turned into a shadow, barely visible. It was the magical camouflaging all night elves were born with. She'd heard of it, but never seen it before now. "Give my regards to your monster."

"He's not a monster."

"Keep telling yourself that."

WHEN RAIYA WENT to find Azreth later that day, she had a harder time locating him than she expected. None of the cultists seemed to know where he'd gone. It wasn't until she went to the attic and craned her head out the window that her search came to an end.

Her demon was sitting on the roof in the shadows beneath the chimney, surveying the city. His knees were tucked up against his chest as if to make himself smaller. Somehow, it seemed to have worked. He'd avoided the attention of the townspeople below, and he observed them unnoticed. The sun was bright that day, and it was almost warm. If she'd been in a better mood, she'd have been tempted to join him. But when Azreth's eyes slid in her direction, she felt a flicker of irritation and apprehension that made her want to turn around and leave.

"I'm ready to try a counter-enchantment," she said instead. She still intended to free him, after all. Even if he was a bastard, it was the right thing to do. And besides that, she had started to think of it as a puzzle, and she would be annoyed if she left it unsolved.

He raised his head in interest. Then he unfolded his large body and followed her into the attic, squeezing through the broken window frame. Raiya set her satchel on the floor and turned to him. There was no point in delaying the inevitable.

"You'll have to provide magic for it," she said. "We should get that out of the way, first."

She had managed to get one of the mages at the temple to recharge her baton rather than going to Azreth for help. His artificial arm hadn't returned, presumably because he didn't have enough magic to summon it. He was going hungry, but he hadn't spoken to her since their argument.

She waited, hoping he would take the lead. It would be easier if he would just do it quickly without her having to think about it too much. That was her strategy for dealing with Nirlan's hunger, too. Sometimes, there was some comfort in being able to lie back and just let things take their course. She could close her eyes and pretend she was elsewhere.

"How shall I feed?" he asked.

"However you want to."

He seemed unenthused by that answer, which surprised her, considering how insistent he'd been that he would use her even if she tried to deny him. But after a long moment, he closed the gap between them. Despite herself, a little flush of attraction went through her.

He crouched so that he was not looming over her, and his hand went to the back of her thigh, pulling her closer. Raiya's eyes drifted shut as his hand slid further up her thigh and snaked between her legs. Instead of being quick like she'd hoped, his movements were soft and unhurried.

"It is more difficult without magic," he said, almost apologetically. He shrugged what remained of his scarred shoulder. "Without my hands."

"It's all right," she said compulsively, forgetting her anger for a moment. "It won't be a problem. We've never had a problem before."

He tugged on the waist of her trousers. She helped him pull them off, stepping out of her underclothes as well. Cold air caressed her bare skin.

"Will you help me?" he asked.

"Of course."

He took her hand and guided it between her legs. "Touch yourself."

Raiya felt her face heating.

His eyes stayed on hers as she slowly pressed her fingers into herself in the rhythmic motion she always found most effective.

He tilted his head a little. "You are good at this."

"At what?"

"Pleasuring yourself."

She stopped, frowning. "Are you making fun of me?"

"No."

"Isn't everyone good at pleasuring themselves? I mean, don't you ever...?"

His expression tightened a little. "No."

"You don't? Or can't?"

"I don't like to."

There was an uncomfortable pause. Azreth gently pressed

her fingers against herself again, urging her into motion. She resumed her steady rhythm.

Something about what he'd said troubled her. She wrestled with her thoughts for a few long moments.

"Do you like it... with me?" she finally asked. It wasn't that she wanted to soothe her ego. It was that she hated the idea of him being forced to perform against his will. What if he didn't even like sex? What if he only did all this out of necessity? The possibility of being party to forced intimacy, no matter the context, made bile rise in her throat.

Raiya's brow furrowed as the silence dragged on.

Finally, he looked up at her. "Yes. With you."

His hand caressed the soft curve of her buttock and pulled her closer so that he could drag his lips along her inner thigh. She felt his sharp teeth grazing her, and she tensed.

His mouth opened, and he licked along the angle between her thigh and her sex. She had never noticed how bizarrely long his tongue was. It was pointed at the end, and the color was a blue so dark it was almost black. Was that what his insides looked like? Was that what his cock looked like?

When he dragged his tongue along her slit, she gasped. She had already grown wet from the work of her own fingers, and his tongue on her bare, slick skin was heavenly.

He spread her legs further, burying his tongue deep within her. She groped for his hair, but her hands met his horns instead, and her fingers curled around them instinctively. To her surprise, the touch made Azreth give a satisfied sigh. His arm looped under her knee and lifted her leg over his shoulder, forcing her legs open. She gasped.

He licked her to climax expertly. Muttering an oath, she tightened her grip on his horns, pulling him tighter against her. His tongue obligingly undulated over her as she rode out the toe-curling waves of her orgasm.

"Gods damn you," she murmured breathlessly, shuddering.

His eyes flickered like newborn flames as he looked up at her, arching an eyebrow. He licked his lips.

Her gaze went to his horns again. More tentative now, she ran her hand over one of them. It was hard and keratinous, like a goat's. How did it feel to him when she touched them? Would it hurt him if she was too rough with them? She'd been fairly rough with them just now, but it seemed like he'd enjoyed it.

"I think that's enough," he said.

She paused, thinking he meant that she was touching him too much, but then she realized he was talking about his magic.

Right. The magic. That was the whole point of this.

She wiped the sheen of sweat from her brow and quickly dressed. She dug in her bag for the things she'd need for the enchantment: ink, a paintbrush, and her notebook.

"Take off your cloak," she said. He did so without comment, letting it drop to the floor. He settled onto his knees again, which put his face just below hers.

She held her notebook open in one arm, studying her runes and annotations. They were an ugly mixture of a few languages and odd combinations of spells. A few of the combinations were ones she'd used before and knew worked, while others were brand new, built from the components of other runes she knew and ones she'd found in the library's books.

A real enchanter would probably have fainted at the sight of her work. She was certain this wasn't the ideal method for removing the binding, but she hoped that it would still work, even if it was a little rough.

She'd never built an enchantment into a *person*, either.

Normally, they were put into inanimate objects. That added another unwanted layer of complexity.

"What are you going to do?" Azreth said. She heard a hint of apprehension tightening his voice.

She dipped the brush into the ink pot, dabbing off the excess on the rim before raising the point of the brush to Azreth's stony chest. "May I?" she asked. He nodded. "Eunaios painted the runes onto your skin. I've never done this before, but I don't see why I shouldn't use the same method." Azreth's chest rose and fell slowly as she slid the brush over his skin. "When I've placed all the runes, you'll activate them with your magic."

"That's all?"

"I hope so."

She painted a line of runes down his chest, branching over his heart, and then another down his arm and onto his palm, over the runes Eunaios had spelled onto his flesh. When she'd finished, she looked them over again several times, making sure not a single stroke was out of place. A mistake could be deadly.

It occurred to her that Azreth was putting a lot of trust in her. He did not read runes, and for all he knew, she could be enchanting him with something worse than what Eunaios had done. His eyes had followed her while she worked, but he seemed more curious than suspicious.

She set down her brush and plugged the ink bottle. She swallowed hard, mentally preparing herself for whatever would come next.

"It will work," she said.

Azreth just nodded.

"Go on," she said. "Charge the enchantment."

SEVENTEEN

Azreth didn't hesitate. Magic flowed into the runes Raiya had painted, illuminating them one by one until they all shone with a glittering, iridescent sheen. Raiya's heart leapt as she watched her work come to life. Azreth looked down at himself, studying the glowing runes covering his skin, and as he pumped power into them, the spell activated with an audible snap. The runes glowed so bright that Raiya had to look away.

And then Azreth cried out in shock. The air filled with a miasma of negative emotion, bright and sharp and violent. Raiya could feel it seeping into her skin, into her bones. Magic sparked at random around them as Azreth lost control of his power—or perhaps he was struggling to cast something in his desperation to make the pain stop.

"What's happening?" Raiya cried. "What's wrong?" She'd made a mistake. She'd expected that undoing the binding might be painful, but not like this. She was hurting him.

She rubbed furiously at the ink on his chest, but the runes wouldn't budge. The magic was helping to hold them in place. Azreth dropped to the floor, writhing.

Raiya spun to grab the bottle of ink, sloshing half of it out of the container as she rushed to uncork it. More of it spilled out when Azreth knocked into her as he shuddered. She climbed atop him to try to hold him still, which was a fruitless endeavor. It was all she could do to keep from being thrown off him. In sheer desperation, she dumped the rest of the bottle on him. She smeared it over the runes on his chest, marring the shapes of the lines, then rubbed her ink-soaked hands over the marks on his arm, too.

Azreth's movements slowed, then stopped. The runes stopped glowing. The terrifying atmosphere that he was emitting began to recede.

He slumped, breathing hard. When he held up his palm in front of his face, Eunaios's runes were still there.

"I'm so sorry," Raiya whispered, covering her mouth with her hands. "I didn't think it would be so bad if it went wrong. I've never tried enchanting a person before, and I didn't know..." There was a reason it was not usually done without the input of a healer. But she hadn't expected *this*.

Perhaps she had also forgotten that it was possible for Azreth to be hurt. He seemed almost too powerful to be damaged.

She raised her hands to touch him, and he recoiled a little. No one had ever flinched from her like that. Was that what she looked like to Nirlan? Or to Azreth? How could anyone live that way, having people recoil from them in fear and disgust?

She climbed off of him and knelt at his side. "I'm so sorry, Azreth." He didn't recoil this time, but he looked at her like he was still dazed, his eyes intense. Suddenly he sat up, reaching out to grab her by her chin. Raiya flinched, but he held fast.

"Why—" He shook his head, frustrated and perplexed, as his eyes bored into her. "Why are you this way?"

She stared at him. "What?"

"Why worry over me like a mother *nyra*? Why cry when I

am hurt? Why do you never use my weaknesses to your advantage? Do you not know what I am? Don't you know that I consume your kind for power? Don't you have any sense of self-preservation? Just yesterday, I angered you. I threatened you. But still, you worry for me. Still, you attempt to serve me. There is no logic here. I cannot understand it. You are the most baffling creature I've ever met."

She couldn't tell whether he was angry or grateful. "I didn't—I don't—"

"You should let me be bound. You should rejoice in my pain. It is a victory for you."

"I've never wanted you to be in pain."

"But why?"

"There will never be a better explanation, no matter how many times you ask for it. This is just how mortals are."

"No," he corrected her sharply. "It is how *you* are. Only you."

When he'd grabbed her, she'd thought he was going to hurt her. She'd braced herself the same way she did when she sensed Nirlan's temper rising, when she knew a blow was coming. She would not have blamed him for it. Instead, he gave her this softness, this rounded edge to his voice.

He searched her face. He had the look of a man peering over the side of a cliff and deciding whether to jump, and fearing the ground would collapse beneath him no matter his decision.

The door behind them slammed open. A male cultist barged into the room, followed by Priestess Gereg. "Praise Moratha!" Gereg said, which, from what Raiya had observed, passed as a greeting for the cultists, but this exclamation seemed particularly enthusiastic.

"*Praise her,*" echoed the others who lurked behind her in the doorway.

"Priestess Gereg," Raiya said, struggling to keep the

exhaustion from her voice. She tried to take a step away from Azreth, but he grabbed her arm to keep her in place. He was frowning at the cultists.

"We sensed your dark works from below," Gereg said, smiling. "You should have made us aware that you were ready to enact the dark goddess's will. We are eager to observe, and to aid, if we may." She gave a shallow bow.

Raiya started to reply, but to her surprise, Azreth spoke first. "There is nothing to observe. It was an anomaly, nothing more."

"Oh?" Gereg raised her eyebrows. The other cultists exchanged disappointed looks. "Then will you deign to give us any more information about your intentions here, demon? Can we expect your plans for the dark goddess's veneration to come to fruition soon?"

Raiya didn't know whether to be apprehensive or amused. They were getting bored, gods bless them. Like children on Lightbringer's eve.

"Yes. Soon," Azreth said flatly.

RAIYA WAS awoken from her bunk in the temple's sleeping quarters that night by the sound of the door opening. It let in a dim shaft of light from the hall, and the cultists in the other beds stirred. Raiya squinted toward the door.

Azreth stood in the doorway, his body a black silhouette with gently flaming eyes.

He walked into the room. It could not be called striding, exactly, because it wasn't quick enough for that. He had a graceful, self-assured way of moving that she always found beautiful, if a little intimidating.

"Get out," he said, looking at the cultists.

The cultists blinked at each other, half-asleep. "What?" asked one.

"Get out," Azreth repeated, jerking his head toward the door. The cultists very quickly evacuated the room without him having to repeat himself a third time. He shut the door and locked it, then sat on the edge of her bed. The mattress sagged so much that she worried the bed would break.

"Azreth?"

"I must speak to you."

"It's the middle of the night."

"I cannot wait." There was a pause, then he lifted his gaze from the wall ahead of him, looking over at her. "How do your people show remorse?"

That was not at all what she'd expected. It took her a few moments to mentally adjust. "What are you remorseful for?"

"Injuring you when Nirlan fed you to me. Taking you from the castle by force. Frightening you. Threatening you."

She stared at him. He'd been keeping a tally of all the times he felt he'd wronged her.

"Forcing you to serve me," he added.

"You didn't force me. This was a mutually beneficial arrangement from the beginning."

"I knew you had no other choice."

That much was true.

"I would never have hurt you. When I said I would, I was lying." His lips twitched, betraying some emotion on his otherwise impassive face. "I would not keep you against your will."

Raiya looked up at the strange, frightening being before her—a monster who, against all odds, was not monstrous.

"You're nothing like what they say, are you?" she said. "Demons are just like anyone else. You think and feel just like we do. You're just trying to live. You're not monsters. You're not evil."

"Are we not?" he asked tonelessly. "What is a monster? What makes something evil?"

"Hurting people. That's evil."

"I hurt people. I hurt you."

"Do you think you're evil?"

"I wouldn't know."

She felt a swell of warmth and sadness for him. "How do *your* people show remorse?" she asked.

"In the hells, penance is paid through submission and servitude. If I wished to align myself with someone I had previously offended, I would put down my weapons and prostrate myself before them so that they could punish me or feed from me. I would offer myself to them to use however they wished."

She arched an eyebrow. She had a difficult time imagining him doing something like that. "Have you done that?"

"Not willingly."

"I see."

"My people express regret when they want something from someone. Apologies are made for diplomatic reasons." He shook his head. "But that's not what I want. I feel regret because... I'm afraid I have been cruel."

She thought back to all the things she'd seen him do, to when he murdered Eunaios and Nirlan's guards, to when he spared the farmers and that Paladin on their way to Ontag-ul, to how careful he'd been with her body every time they'd come together. Dominating others was in his nature. But maybe he didn't want it to be.

"I don't think you're cruel," she said. She watched his shoulders relax. The crease between his brows disappeared.

"Tell me what service you require in order to forgive me," he said.

"An apology is enough on its own, as long as it's heartfelt."

"Then... I apologize."

"I accept your apology."

He searched her face. He looked like he didn't quite believe her.

"Do you really think demons can feel all the things that mortals can?" he asked.

"Why shouldn't they?"

"We are made different." He lifted her hand. "Look at you. Look at me."

She looked down at the massive, dark hand enclosing hers. He allowed her to turn it over. There were dark lines creasing his palm. There were whirling fingerprints. There were calluses beneath his fingers, freckles here and there, scars from old wounds, and faint veins beneath the skin.

"There are more similarities between us than differences," she said. She ran her fingers along his, and she felt him stiffen slightly. His skin felt normal enough—perhaps a bit less soft than a human's—but she knew it was impenetrable to most mortal weapons. But he was not invulnerable. His missing arm was proof of that.

He raised his hands to her face, holding her cheeks. She stared at him, taken aback by the touch. The skin of his flesh-and-blood hand was furnace-hot, and the other felt cold in comparison, pricking her with tiny tingles of energy. His luminous eyes darted around her face, studying her, searching for something. If he'd been any closer, it would have been a kiss or an embrace.

His thumbs stroked her cheekbones, just once. Raiya was frozen.

Azreth's eyebrows came together. And then he let go of her. Raiya watched as he got up.

"I'm sorry for disturbing your rest," he said, then left her alone in the room again.

EIGHTEEN

I n the morning, Raiya found Azreth waiting for her outside the door to her sleeping quarters. Had he been waiting there all night?

"Good morning," she said.

"Good morning," he replied perfunctorily. "I need to speak with you."

She held her breath, thinking of their meeting last night. "About?"

"When will you be ready to try another counter-enchantment?"

She relaxed. This was more familiar territory. It was easier to think about enchanting puzzles than to try to sort through her feelings toward him. She started walking toward the dining hall, and Azreth followed. "I didn't think you'd be so eager after what happened last time." Frankly, she was deeply embarrassed by the incident. The idea of trying again made her feel nauseous.

"I must be freed from the binding. There is no alternative."

"I'm not sure that enchanting is the way out of this. We might need a real mage who can cast real spells."

"Enchantments are real spells."

"It went very poorly last time, Azreth. It was irresponsible of me to even attempt it."

"Do you think I'm not strong enough to endure it?" He frowned, tilting his head at her. One of his horns scraped the ceiling as he moved, and he ducked, casting an irritated glance upward. "I have been in worse pain before."

She lowered her voice. "It's not that. All of this is just educated guesses. What if something worse happens next time? What if I... damage you somehow?"

"Another scratch on a broken sword is of little concern."

She frowned at him. "You're not a sword."

He moved to stand in front of her, blocking her path. "I would like you to try again," he said. He paused, then added, "Please."

Raiya gave him a skeptical look.

"Last time, I could feel something in your enchantment pushing against the binding," he said. "It didn't work, but it was close. We are on the right path. You will succeed if we keep trying."

"You can't be certain of that."

"I have paid more attention than you think I have. I know you know things. I know you're good at this."

She would have thought he was just trying to flatter her, but he said it almost accusingly, like he thought it was something she was trying to hide in order to get out of work.

"We will try again," he said firmly.

Raiya hesitated, still surprised by his confidence in her. "I'll... do my best, then."

Azreth nodded approvingly. "We must leave this place. You should get all the information you can now. Take whatever books you can carry from the library, and we'll leave tonight."

"That's stealing."

"Yes."

Several cultists appeared at the end of the hall. "Acolyte," said one of them, addressing her. "You and the demon are to come to the main hall immediately. The High Priestess has had another vision."

Raiya held back a sigh. They owed the cultists a debt for harboring them these past few days, but their visions and their refusal to address Azreth directly, as if she were his handler, were tiring. As was his custom, Azreth said nothing and waited for Raiya to deal with the intrusion. She suspected he would have completely ignored the cultists if left to his own devices.

She was too impatient for indirectness. "What does that have to do with us?"

"It's a message from the dark goddess herself, regarding the demon."

"Is the priestess quite certain it wasn't just a dream?" Or made up entirely.

The cultist scowled. "The priestess has requested your presence specifically. Come." He waited until Raiya headed toward the main hall. Azreth was a looming shadow on her heels.

Raiya stopped short in the doorway of the main hall. It was more crowded than she'd ever seen it, packed with cultists in dark robes and alarming black and white makeup. Dozens of eerie faces all turned to look back at them in unison as they sensed Azreth's presence. In front of the altar at the other end of the room was Priestess Gereg.

"Ah!" she said, smiling grimly. "Our guests of honor have arrived. Please, approach the altar."

Everyone in the room stared at them expectantly. Raiya felt a prickling of foreboding.

"My apologies, Priestess," she said, giving a slight bow. "Something urgent has come up. I'm afraid we have to be going. Please accept our most sincere thanks for your hospitality. You have been very kind."

"I'm certain you can spare a few moments more before you leave. It is a matter of greatest unholy importance. Come. Approach the altar."

She glanced up at Azreth, who was looking back at her for guidance. Reluctantly, she started down the aisle. She stopped a few steps from the altar when Gereg brandished a jagged knife.

"Take this," Gereg said, offering the knife to Azreth. "And make an offering to Moratha." She motioned to the basin on the altar, which was currently empty.

"What kind of offering?" Raiya asked.

Gereg gave her a heavy-lidded glance. "Blood. Life, drained and corrupted by death. The only kind of sacrifice the dark goddess accepts."

Raiya's blood pounded in her ears. Azreth glanced over at her as her fear spiked. Did Gereg mean for Azreth to kill her as an offering?

Her hand dropped to the handle of her baton. She hadn't reached for it since they'd first come to the temple, but she'd been careful to keep it always within reach. What would the cultists do if Azreth refused to do as they asked?

Azreth took the knife, but raised it to his own arm. He dug savagely into his flesh, bending the metal in the process of carving a small cut in his wrist. Raiya's stomach lurched, but Azreth never flinched. He held his forearm over the altar, and inky blood dripped into the basin. Gereg seemed satisfied.

"Last night, I had a vision," Gereg said. Her voice was not loud, but the other cultists were so still and silent that it filled the room anyway. "In it, I saw the demon before us. He spoke with the dark goddess's voice and proclaimed that he had come to fulfill Moratha's plans for Heilune. He is to be a reaper, come to bring her wrath upon our plane. He is her instrument of death, a weapon of unknowable destruction. The dark goddess's glory will follow him as he bathes the land in blood." Her voice had grown in volume gradually, and as she spoke these last words, she raised her hands skyward. "Praise Moratha!"

The room had been utterly, obediently silent up until now, but when the acolytes replied, it was with thunderous excitement that may as well have been cheering and applause. *"Praise her!"*

Azreth was frowning. None of them seemed to notice his displeasure.

"It begins tonight," Gereg went on. "There will be a massacre of epic proportions, starting right here in Ontag-ul. All will die. Humans and elves, children and animals alike. Death will rule the land, blood will flow like water, and Moratha will be pleased."

The room went even more quiet, as if the other cultists were as stunned as Raiya was. Many of the faces around the hall were grinning gleefully, but some looked perplexed or concerned. The priestess couldn't be serious, could she? This veneration of death was all a farce, wasn't it? They couldn't really want everyone to die.

"So, demon," Gereg said. "Thus begins the Goddess's reign. You are commanded to kill indiscriminately, whenever and wherever you desire, so long as it is often. You will rend flesh with your monstrous hands, tear bloody gashes with your terrible teeth, crush bones beneath your giant's feet. Go now and destroy; spare none. We will follow in your footsteps with our blades high." She bowed low, extending her hands toward him in a dramatic gesture.

"No," Azreth corrected her.

Gereg stopped, looking up at him. He arched an eyebrow at her.

"You are refusing her call?" Gereg asked tensely.

"I am."

Gereg raised her chin. "You were designed by the dark goddess to serve her will. You will obey her. It is your purpose."

Azreth gave her a withering look. "What do you know of my purpose?"

"You are a tool to be used as she decrees for the spreading of darkness and despair. You are death. This is your purpose, just as a stock animal's purpose is to feed, as a mother's purpose is to nurture, as a wheel's purpose is to roll. It is not a decision to make. It is already done."

Azreth raised a fist and smashed it down into the blood-stained stone basin, crushing it to pieces and cracking the altar beneath. Raiya jumped.

"What do you know of my purpose?" he snarled again, baring sharp teeth. The air wavered visibly with his fury.

The priestess remained admirably composed. "Do you deny your goddess?"

"I care nothing for your goddess."

There were gasps around the room.

"Blasphemy," Gereg breathed.

Raiya took Azreth's arm and started pulling him back down the aisle toward the exit.

"You *will* serve her," Gereg said. "If you will not do it willingly, then we will break you. You will obey."

On her command, half of the acolytes in the room raised weapons and chanted spells, as if they'd been prepared for this outcome. The surly acolytes they'd encountered in the hall were in the aisle behind Raiya and Azreth, blocking their escape. One of them was whispering words to a spell, her hands plucking at invisible threads of magic in the air.

"Get out of the way, or I will send you to your goddess," Azreth said, which Raiya thought demonstrated a vast increase in self-control compared to the first time she'd seen him interact with mortals.

"Submit, demon," snarled the one in front of them. All at once, all the mages' voices simultaneously reached a crescendo, and there was an explosion of magic.

A wall of vibrant reddish light rose up from the floor, encircling Azreth in a column of magic.

He pressed a hand to the wall, then pounded on it, to no avail. He was trapped inside, just as he had been in Nirlan's dungeon.

Horrified, Raiya kicked aside the long rug that spanned the aisle. Carved onto the wood just beneath where Azreth stood was a circle of runes, glowing with the power the mages had just imbued them with.

Fingers raked her sleeve as someone tried to grab her, and she jerked away. She drew her baton, spinning to point it at the cultists. "Stay back!"

The cultists surrounded her. There was not nearly enough power in the baton to stop all of them. Panicked, she turned the baton toward Azreth's cage and shot. There was an echoing blast and a bright flash as a beam of magic passed through the barrier, but the barrier was still intact, not even scratched. Inside the barrier, Azreth shouted something she couldn't quite hear. He pointed to the floor.

Fool, she thought. *Shoot the runes, not the barrier.*

She aimed the baton toward the circle of runes, but then someone grabbed her from behind, and her shot went wide, shooting a blast into the pews nearby. All at once, there were people all around her. As Azreth pounded on the barrier, a hand grabbed her wrist, and yet another grabbed a handful of her hair, pulling her away from Azreth. A wall of people formed between her and him.

She stomped down hard on the foot of the cultist behind her until he let go, then swung the weighty baton, clipping one cultist's jaw and smashing another one in the knee. Swinging the baton in an arc to ward them off, she backed away, then pointed the baton toward the ceiling. The baton's runes glowed brighter in her hand, and then a beam of energy shot into the roof above them. The baton's runes went dark again, spent.

There was a shower of dust, and then a loud crack as wood splintered and stone crumbled. People shouted and scrambled for safety as the roof in the corner of the room collapsed. A cloud of dust billowed from the corner.

Raiya turned and ran. In the confusion, she managed to shove her way to the door. She paused there, glancing back at Azreth. His hands were pressed against the barrier and his eyes were on her. With a grimace, Raiya ran out the door, leaving him behind.

NINETEEN

Raiya stumbled out onto the road and blinked in the thin morning light, still coughing from the dust. The temple was still mostly intact, showing no sign that it would continue to crumble, but it would take a great deal of money and labor to patch the enormous hole in the roof.

"There!" someone shouted, drawing her attention back to the door. A group of cultists were running through the doorway after her. All of them carried knives. They did not look like they meant to take prisoners.

She spun and ran down the road past bewildered bystanders. The cultists quickly gained on her. She hiked up her robe as she sprinted, slipping and nearly falling in a puddle of mud. Normally, she might have called for a Paladin. But in this case, she didn't trust them not to immediately turn her over to Nirlan.

Her heart was beating out of her chest as she zigzagged through narrow, winding pathways and boardwalks. She heard the cultists fall farther behind after she took several sharp turns, but then one of them appeared in front of her, having circled around to cut her off. She skidded to a stop and turned to run the other way down another side street.

A figure appeared out of thin air in front of her. She gasped, juddering to a stop. It was Madira. His brows came together as he looked her up and down, probably noting the mud and dust and blood.

"Hide me," she begged, gasping for breath. "Please."

Madira raised his eyebrows. But then he took Raiya's arm. Magic ran down her body, shrouding her in darkness. Madira pulled her to the side of the alley, and they stood motionless against the wall, two shadows. Raiya pressed her sleeve to her mouth to muffle her ragged breathing.

A few moments later, she heard footsteps coming near. The cultists ran by, coming within feet of them but never looking in their direction.

She and Madira waited until the footsteps had gone far down the road. Finally, Madira dropped his spell.

"I told you," he said, crossing his arms.

Raiya bent over, her hands on her knees as she tried to catch her breath. The seriousness of the situation was beginning to sink in.

She looked up at Madira. Suddenly her throat was sticky with emotion. They would have caught her and killed her if he hadn't stepped in. "Thank you," she said hoarsely. "Thank you."

His smug demeanor softened a bit. "What happened?"

"They have Azreth. They imprisoned him in a rune circle." She scraped her fingers through her mussed hair. They would make him a slave again. With him imprisoned and helpless behind that barrier, they could restrain him and bind him again and force him to do everything Gereg had demanded.

"Gods damn them," she hissed, shoving her inert baton into her belt.

"I told you," Madira said again, looking unimpressed.

He was right. Azreth had wanted to leave the very day they'd arrived in that place. He had stayed because Raiya wanted to. He'd trusted her judgment, and now he was paying for it.

This was her fault.

"I have to get him out," she said.

"You say that as if it'll be easy."

"It won't be. I can't do it myself. I'll need help." She glanced over at him.

He scoffed. "Why are you looking at me?" He leaned against the wall, crossing one ankle over the other.

She could go to the town guards, but they wouldn't help her set a demon loose. And if they were anything like the lawmen in other parts of Uulantaava, they would not be inclined to investigate anything involving the cult of Moratha. The cult held a lot of social and political sway lately.

"Can you take me to the Roamer camp?" she asked.

"WE CAN'T HELP YOU," the shepherd said. Raiya wilted.

It was the same stout woman Raiya had bargained with when she'd first encountered the caravan. It turned out that the woman was not only a shepherd, but the clan matron as well, named Fu-lon. Raiya had just given her a summary of everything that had happened since she'd met Azreth.

Fu-lon gave her a weary smile, puffing on a long pipe. She was seated on a plush pillow on the floor while Raiya paced anxiously. The smoke was filling the tent and making Raiya slightly dizzy. "I like you, girl, but your problems are not ours. What do you expect us to do about it?"

"I know there are warriors among you. Ex-soldiers and..." Deserters, pirates, rogue mages, ex-bandits. "...others. If I could just ask them—"

"If they would be willing to fight the entire cult of Moratha with you?" Fu-lon broke in, chuckling.

"I can pay. I'm an enchanter. I could make something for you. For the clan," she said quickly. Never mind that she could only carve an inert enchantment. "Anything you want."

At that, the woman tapped the end of her pipe to her lips, considering. But then she shook her head. "There is little that would be worth getting on the cult's bad side," she said. "We don't get involved in things like this. If we did, we would never have survived as long as we have. You understand. We have to protect our own."

Raiya clasped her hands nervously. "My mother was a Roamer," she said, her voice soft with embarrassment over her obvious desperation. "We're kin."

The woman nodded. "I guessed as much when we last met."

"You did?"

"I can see Roamer bones in your face. And not many outsiders would walk into camp so comfortably, the way you did."

"And?"

Fu-lon gave her another smile. "You know that doesn't change anything, don't you?"

"Yes, I suppose I do."

"Good." Putting out her pipe, she picked up her cane and held out her other hand. Raiya helped pull her to her feet. "If there's anything our people excel at, it's adapting. So, adapt. Move on."

Raiya frowned. "Move on?"

"Your alliance with a demon didn't work out. You can't pretend to be surprised. A partnership with a demonic entity is bound to end in tears one way or another. I suggest you pick yourself up and start anew. The caravan will be around if you need us, and your bastard of an ex-husband won't be able to touch you here if you wish to stay. My own husband was a bit of a bastard himself, before he died. I can sympathize."

Raiya pulled away from her. She couldn't just move on. Perhaps a week ago, she might have taken the shepherd's advice. But now?

She already felt Azreth's absence like a shadow over her heart. She missed having someone who understood everything she'd been through. She missed his tentative way of asking her questions or looking to her for guidance, the way he studied the world so curiously, and the hungry, oddly gentle way he touched her.

And gods, these were not things a mortal should feel about a demon. Of that, she was certain. The matron was right. A partnership with a demon was doomed to fail.

Tongue-tied, Raiya just shook her head. She bade the woman goodbye and stepped out of the tent into the bright midday sun. Madira and Jai awaited her, both squinting in the daylight.

"What'd she say?" Jai asked.

"She said no," Madira informed her. "Why do you think she looks so upset?"

Raiya was too frustrated to speak. She turned and started toward the road out of the camp. She heard Jai's quick foot-steps behind her, and after a moment, Madira's softer ones followed.

"What are you going to do?" Jai asked.

"I honestly don't know."

Jai ran around to stand in front of her. "We'll help you."

"That's very sweet of you," Raiya said. "I appreciate the thought."

"What's that supposed to mean?" Madira asked. "You don't think we can do it?"

"I can't ask you to come with me to fight through the cult of Moratha. Even if you weren't children—"

Madira's jaw dropped. "I'm not a child! The irony of a human calling *us* children. Everyone knows humans are the children of Heilune. I'm probably older than you."

"You look like a child to me."

"I'm twenty-five!"

Raiya thought he looked—and behaved, for that matter—about sixteen. She narrowed her eyes. "Isn't that still quite young for an elf?"

"That's irrelevant!"

Raiya considered them both.

"You'll never succeed without us. Those cultists would have killed you if I hadn't been there to save you," Madira reminded her.

"I didn't think you would be so eager to help," Raiya said.

Jai smirked. "Madira thinks he's a warrior, and he wants everyone to know it. He loves having a quest."

He gave her an irritated shove, which only made her grin wider.

Jai took Raiya's arm. "Let's go get something to eat, okay? You look like you need to catch your breath and consider your options. Your demon won't be going anywhere."

WITHIN THE HOUR, they were plotting Azreth's rescue. Once they had formulated a plan, they agreed to carry it out that very evening. Despite Jai's assumption otherwise, there was no guarantee that Azreth would be safe for even that long. Raiya was adamant that they needed to act as soon as possible.

She spent the hours before nightfall frantically flipping through pages in her notebook and carving runes as fast as she could, until her fingers went numb from gripping her stylus and her back got sore from hunching over her work. She'd carved the runes into a round, smooth stone she'd found in camp. The object chosen for the enchantment wasn't important in this case—it was just a canvas for the spell.

She didn't notice Jai watching over her shoulder until the girl spoke. She had a remarkable talent for sneaking up on people.

"Why do you keep wincing like that?" Jai asked.

Raiya tried to smooth the grimace out of her face. The runes she'd made were thick and jagged and ugly. In two cases, she'd even had to scratch them out and start over. There was no artistry to it, only function. Maybe not even that.

"It's not my best work," she said.

Jai looked worried. "You don't think it'll work?"

"Hopefully it will work well enough for our purposes." Finished, she tucked her stylus carefully into its small pocket in her bag. The stylus was specially made for enchanting, magically hardened to be able to carve into almost any material. It would be difficult to replace if she lost it.

There happened to be a mage in camp who had agreed to charge her baton and her new enchantment for a steep fee. The man took everything left in her coin purse, and it would take another hour for him to complete the charging. Raiya had to stifle the urge to complain. She'd been spoiled by the intense levels of raw power Azreth was capable of channeling. He could have charged them in seconds.

She looked up at Jai, wrinkling her brow. The girl's curious, jade-colored eyes met hers, crinkling as she smiled.

"Are you certain you want to do this, Jai?"

"Why wouldn't I be?"

"It will be dangerous. And you have no need to help us. You owe us nothing."

Jai pushed her dark eyebrows together. "Maybe we don't owe you anything, but we have plenty of reason to help."

"Not long ago, you were planning to kill Azreth."

"That was before we knew he was your friend. In a way,

that makes it even more important to help him, doesn't it? No one else is going to help a demon. I know what that's like. Before Madira and I found the Roamers, no one helped us, either. We had to fight our way through half the continent because of it. People were always either frightened of us, or just hated us. It must be the same for him."

Raiya smiled. Jai trusted easily. It was sweet. Madira was much more wary, but he was easily enticed by the promise of adventure and subterfuge.

"It will go perfectly," Jai assured her, taking on a self-satisfied tone. "If you'd seen night elves in action before, you wouldn't be worried. There's a reason the mere mention of us terrifies you humans."

THEY RETURNED to the temple just after sunset. Jai's hand was on Raiya's, the girl's magic shrouding them, while Madira walked ahead. He was only just visible if you waited for him to walk near a light and knew exactly where to look. Both of them were adept at blending in with shadows, avoiding the circles of light that dotted paths and shone from windows. The townspeople ignored them completely, too busy to notice a stray shadow or two.

"This is easier than I thought it'd be," Raiya whispered.

"I told you," said Jai and Madira in unison.

They came to a stop in the mouth of an alley. Across the road was the Temple of Moratha, a dark monolith rising above the rest of Ontag-ul. Raiya was surprised to see a group of steel-clad figures standing in front of it.

Paladins. They were speaking to the cultists standing guard at the front door. Above them, even more guards watched surreptitiously from windows above. Gereg hadn't been exaggerating the extent of their defenses.

Raiya heard a familiar voice, and her blood ran cold. And then she saw him.

"That's my husband," she murmured. There was a pause as the elves got their first look at him.

He was with the Paladins, animatedly arguing with the guard in front of the door. Just the sound of his voice filled her with dread. She hated that he had such an effect on her.

Could he know that they had taken Azreth? Was he trying to buy him? Would the cultists allow that?

Jai gripped her hand tighter.

"That's him?" Madira said. "What a priss. He looks like he's never touched a sword in his life."

"He probably hasn't. He'll never need to lift a weapon as long as he can get others to do it for him."

It seemed that the guard at the door had grown tired of the Paladins, because he raised his voice and waved them off. The Paladins backed down, and Raiya was relieved when Nirlan strode away furiously. His anger meant that he hadn't gotten whatever he wanted.

The Paladins lingered in the street. Raiya realized there was another civilian among them, a young man with ash blonde hair tucked behind his ears. It was Adamus, the Paladin she and Azreth had encountered on the road.

Strangely, he wasn't wearing his uniform. He wore no armor at all, and he seemed to be having a debate with a few of the others.

"I know that one," she said. "He's one of the Paladins. We saw him with them a few days ago."

"What's he doing?" asked Jai.

"I'm not sure."

Madira turned to Raiya. She could just barely make out the features of his face. "We'll wait for them to leave, and when the coast is clear, we can move in," he said.

Jai and Raiya nodded. Raiya reached into her pocket and

closed her hand around the stone she'd enchanted. The enchantment was the key to her escape from the temple. All they needed was to get in and find Azreth. That alone would be a challenge. There were no doors other than the ones in the front, and the windows were tall and narrow, too small for a person to fit through. There were more guards than they'd anticipated, too, and Raiya's confidence was shaken by the ones lurking in the windows above the door, who were probably armed with arrows or spells.

The Paladins drew her attention again as the volume of their argument increased. Finally, the one arguing with Adamus waved his hand dismissively and walked away. Adamus looked dejected. The others left to follow Nirlan down the road the other way.

Raiya pressed herself closer to the wall as Adamus came toward their alley. He was going to pass right by them. Madira and Jai were silent and motionless as they watched him approach, like trained assassins. At times like this, it was hard to remember that they were actually still children.

As Adamus passed within arm's reach, Raiya held her breath. But to Madira, it appeared it was like dangling a mouse in front of a cat—he pounced. He revealed himself suddenly, grabbing Adamus by the collar and pinning him to the wall. Madira drew his sword, resting it just below his chin.

"Keep your mouth shut or I'll put my sword in it, Paladin," Madira said, a little too gleefully. Raiya put a hand on his arm, fearing he'd run the man through. Jai released the spell shrouding them, and Adamus looked around at them all. His eyes focused on Raiya.

"You!" he said, and seemed more surprised than angry. "Strange company you keep. First demons, now night elves?"

"I said keep quiet." Madira jerked the blade against his neck, making him wince. "What business do the Paladins have at the temple? Tell us what they're planning."

"Do you want me to keep quiet, or do you want me to answer questions?"

"Don't get smart."

"I'm not a Paladin any longer," Adamus said. "I've hung up my sword."

Madira glanced pointedly down at Adamus's hip, where his sword still rested.

"I mean that I don't fight for the Paladins," Adamus amended. "What they're doing has nothing to do with what Paladius wants. I want no part of it." Raiya raised her eyebrows, and Adamus shrugged at her. "My father always wanted me to join the family trade and become a lawyer. I'm starting to think I should have listened to him." He studied her, and Raiya could sense him piecing together what he knew of herself, Nirlan, and Azreth. "Where is your demon?"

Madira and Jai were looking cautiously between Raiya and Adamus. Suddenly, Adamus punched Madira in the stomach. Madira gasped and doubled over as Adamus shoved him away. Madira clutched his side, struggling to breathe. Raiya jumped back, pointing her baton at Adamus, but he hadn't drawn his sword.

"You're trying to get into the temple, too, aren't you?" he asked her, eyes wide. "I want to help you."

Raiya was dumbfounded. "What?"

"The demon is with the cultists, isn't he? If there's a choice between having him with you and having him working for the cultists, I'd prefer the former."

"F-fuck you, Pa-aladin," Madira wheezed. Jai was at his side, trying to comfort him. Adamus gave him an almost-but-not-quite-sympathetic look.

"You seemed to have the demon under control, at least," Adamus said. "I would rather he returned to the hells where he belongs, but I cannot abide having him in the hands of the cult. Gods know what they'll have him do."

"You're not a member of the Paladins anymore?" Raiya asked skeptically.

"Not those ones," he said, jerking his chin toward the others. "We are supposed to be holy seekers of justice, not mercenaries."

Raiya was surprised she was considering his offer. She was even more surprised to find herself saying, "Okay. Come with us."

"*What?*" Madira hissed.

"We could use the help," she said. And she believed Adamus would protect the siblings if they needed it, even if they might not return the favor.

Adamus smiled and nodded. "You won't regret it. What is your plan?"

"We barge in quickly and get out before they can stop us."

His smile wilted slightly. "That's... refreshingly simple, I guess."

"As if you had a better idea?" Madira snarled.

"No, I don't," he admitted.

"Make nice, Madira," Jai said under her breath. "I'll go with the Paladin. You go with Raiya."

"Absolutely not." Madira strode forward to grab a wary Adamus's hand. "I will go with him. You stay with Raiya, Jai."

They moved toward the temple. The street was empty, and their path to the door was clear.

"He didn't go with the cultists willingly. They abducted him," Raiya whispered to the Paladin as they padded across the street—because she felt it was important he knew. She felt Adamus looking at her for a few moments before he replied.

"I understand." He was probably humoring her, but it made her feel better anyway. She wanted them to understand that this wasn't Azreth's fault.

When they came close to the light of the torches at the

front door, Madira turned to Raiya and Jai. "Are you ready?" he whispered. "There's no backing down after this."

Raiya felt a sharp pang of anxiety in her chest. She was not a fighter or a spy. She wasn't made for things like this. But lately, she'd been doing a lot of things she had never thought herself capable of. She could do this, too.

"Ready," she whispered before she could change her mind. She squeezed Jai with one hand and clutched the handle of her baton in the other.

There was a beat, and then Madira and Adamus rushed the cultists at the door. The guards didn't even have time to draw their weapons. Madira and Adamus quickly and quietly beat them over the head one after another with the hilts of their swords, and they dropped. Raiya couldn't tell whether they were still alive, but at this point, after getting a glimpse of the cultists' true beliefs, she didn't care. One of the guards in the windows above gave a shout, sounding an alarm.

Madira shoved open the door and slipped inside, and the rest of them followed. Madira scanned the entrance, then nodded to Raiya. "Go. We'll delay them."

Raiya pulled Jai down the corridor to the main hall. They peered through the doorway into the room. Azreth wasn't there. The spot where they'd imprisoned him was empty, the carpet smoothed over the runes on the floorboards again.

And yet she was certain he was still inside the building. She could feel him. His misery was seeping through the walls like a bad odor. They were getting closer.

They continued down the hall. Nearby shouts rang out periodically and rushed footsteps pounded on the floor above them. Behind them, Raiya could hear the clashing of blades.

There were only so many places in the temple that would be adequate for securing a demon. She doubted they would keep him in the sleeping quarters or the kitchen. The attic, perhaps?

She closed her eyes and listened past the footsteps and voices. She listened to the fury and darkness that scented the air and thrummed across her skin like a pulse.

She opened her eyes. It was coming from the floor.

"Cellar," she whispered to Jai. "There must be a cellar."

"Through the kitchen?" Jai suggested. Raiya turned and pulled her back toward the kitchen. They ducked into a dark alcove when a pair of cultists ran by, then continued on until they reached the darkened kitchen.

Raiya scanned the room, looking past a smoldering hearth, worn table, and neatly stacked dishes.

In the back corner of the kitchen was a trap door.

Raiya turned to Jai. "This is far enough. Go back to Madira."

"But—"

"You need to get out. I can't take both you and Azreth when I leave. Go on."

Jai hesitated, then nodded. As she let go of Raiya, her spell left Raiya's body, rendering her visible again. Jai disappeared back down the hallway.

TWENTY

Raiya was alone. She stared at the cellar door, her heart racing.

She could do this.

She pulled on the door. It was heavier than she expected, and it didn't budge. Planting her feet, she heaved, and it opened with a creak. The stairs down into the earth were dimly lit by mage light coming from somewhere farther down. She stepped down, her feet quiet, both hands on her baton.

She had never thought of a cellar as a place that required decorating, but the earthen corridor was lined with alcoves containing skulls, candles, eerie violet mage lights, and statuettes of the goddess of death herself, who was always depicted with a veil covering her face. Raiya had to give the cultists credit for committing to the theme.

At the bottom of the stairs, the cellar fanned out before her. It was a sprawling space filled not with food storage but with more altars and statues—places for worship or rituals. She passed a long slab that she at first thought was dark wood, but then realized was actually pale stone stained by massive amounts of blood. The walls were lined with neat rows of suspiciously ornate jars. It wasn't a cellar after all. It was a crypt.

A distant voice came from somewhere on the other side of the room. Raiya clutched her baton even tighter, though her fingers were already aching and sweat slicked her palms. She crept toward the voice. As she rounded the corner, the other half of the room came into view, and she sucked in a breath.

Azreth knelt on the floor, sagging and bent over. There was no magical barrier holding him, but his body was wrapped in chains. Before him were two cultists, one holding a sword and the other wielding only her hands. The woman waved her hands slowly in the air, gathering magic for a spell. Raiya watched as lightning crackled through the air and then bolted into Azreth. He barely reacted. His body stiffened and convulsed for a moment, but he didn't seem conscious enough to feel much pain.

"Wake up!" the woman snapped at Azreth. He didn't respond. His head was drooping, his eyes on the ground. "Pitiful, useless creature," the woman spat, then motioned to the other cultist. The man brought his sword up and pressed it lengthwise beneath Azreth's chin, where—though the metal looked cold—it sizzled against his skin like a brand. Iron.

Raiya broke into a run. She raised her baton above her head and brought it down on the male cultist with a furious roar. The man stumbled, bleeding heavily from the head, then dropped to the ground. Raiya spun toward the mage, who was staring at them in shock. The woman quickly whispered words to a spell, but Raiya was faster. An enchantment didn't need words or weaving—it only needed her will.

A bolt of energy burst from the baton and hit the cultist in the chest, sending her flying backward. She slammed into the wall, then went still.

Raiya turned to Azreth, who was swaying, not looking up. She shoved the baton through her belt and took his big face in her hands, forcing him to look up at her. "Azreth?" she said, her voice hoarse. The flesh on his throat was dark and raw—a magical burn from the sword. Beneath the iron chains wrapped around his torso and arm, his skin was peeling and covered in welts.

"Azreth?" she said urgently, needing to know that he was still alive. What would this much iron do to him? What if it was too much for him to heal? What if it had poisoned him beyond repair?

His eyes flickered. His lungs seemed to flutter in his chest, his breathing hitching. "Raiya," he murmured.

She squeezed his cheeks. "It's okay. I'm here. You're safe."

She had half expected that he would be suddenly invigorated now that he saw he was saved. She had pictured him standing up and shrugging off the chains. But he didn't.

When she began pulling at the chains, she realized they were merely wrapped around him—there was no lock. The iron weakened him so much that none was needed. Raiya began unwinding them as quickly as she could, but she struggled under their weight. Azreth jerked in pain occasionally when the metal dug into him, but mostly he remained still, even as the iron seared his skin.

"Azreth, please stay awake," Raiya begged as she worked. Chain clanked to the floor as she successfully unwrapped a short length of it. "Stay with me. Can you hear me?"

He said nothing.

She heard shouting above them. The door to the cellar creaked, and footsteps pounded on the stairs. She gave up trying to unwind the chains and just grabbed Azreth's arm. Thrusting her hand into her pocket, she curled her fingers around the enchanted stone, feeling the etched runes. She channeled her will into it, activating the spell.

A group of cultists came around the corner. Raiya urged the spell to work quickly as the cultists ran toward her. She felt the enchantment coming to life, the magic taking hold of her and then crawling along her arm to where she clutched Azreth. One of the cultists raised his hand. A stream of fire burst from his fingertips. Raiya watched the flame as it shot toward her face. And then, just as the fire was about to reach her, it faded away. Or rather, she and Azreth faded.

The world spun around them and then turned into a messy, gray limbo laced with flashes of color, images of other places that went by too quickly to make out. Raiya's stomach did flips, and she got the distinct sensation of moving very quickly, though she was standing perfectly still.

They collapsed to the ground in a heap, Raiya on top of Azreth. Her head spun. It was too dark to see much, but they were outside. Grass tickled her palms.

The enchantment had worked. They'd been transported outside of the temple, outside the city, far from anyone who would harm them.

She let out a shaky breath. "Azreth?"

He exhaled softly.

She cursed, pulling the unwieldy chains off him. It took longer than she would have liked. When she pulled away the last of them, she threw them as far away as she could—which wasn't far, given how heavy they were.

Azreth would need magic to heal himself. Raiya climbed up to straddle him, thinking to... to what? Thinking about sex while he was in his current state made her feel ill, but what else could she do? Would he die if she didn't find a way to force-feed him?

She gave a frustrated sob. "I'm sorry. We should have left when you wanted to. I let this happen. I'm so sorry." She reached for his hand, one of the only parts of his body she was certain wasn't hurt by the iron. "Please tell me what to do. Tell me how to help you."

His fingers slowly closed around her hand.

"Azreth?"

His eyes glowed very faintly, barely there. He was looking up at her. Slowly, his arm circled around her waist and pulled her against him until her head rested against his pectorals, his soft breath puffing against the top of her head.

She lay still as his breathing grew deeper, sharper. His palm moved up her back to the base of her neck, holding her close as his nose pressed against her head. He opened his mouth, breathing her in greedily.

Like magic, his entire body slowly began to move. He was regaining energy. And the more he woke up, the hungrier and more desperate he seemed to become. He sat up, tipping her forward. Before she could find her footing, he'd tipped her fully onto her back on the ground. He moved over her, one knee on either side of her, and seized her throat.

"Azreth?" she gasped. He didn't answer, and she wondered if it was because he wasn't there. As she tried to pry his hand off, he bent low, pinning her with his body as his mouth went to the crook of her neck. She saw the gleam of fangs.

Pain exploded in her shoulder. She screamed.

She shoved against his chest, which only made him hold on tighter. Four bright points of pain appeared in her neck and shoulder where his teeth had pierced her skin.

For a terrifying moment, she thought he had really, truly lost his mind and was going to tear into her the way she'd seen him tear into Eunaios. But he only held her there, like a dog with a toy. He made a low growl in his throat, and Raiya stayed very still, held in place by those four anchor points.

Another hand appeared at her wrist, and then another at her ankle to restrain her further. He moved his real hand up to her jaw, tipping her head sideways to expose more of her neck. His teeth slowly withdrew from her skin, and a tremor went through her when she felt blood spill from the wounds. And then she felt the soft, slick lick of Azreth's tongue lapping at the blood, his mouth closed over her.

Raiya closed her eyes and shivered. Something that felt a lot like pleasure went through her.

Azreth paused, as if listening. And then he continued. His tongue swept across her shoulder in a gruesome kiss as he drank her blood. Out of the corner of her eye, Raiya spotted flares of white magic glowing across his body, where the iron had burned him. Healing magic.

More hands appeared. They moved down her chest, over the dip of her waist and the curve of her thighs, squeezing and feeling and grabbing and bruising her like he couldn't get enough, like he wanted to be utterly overwhelmed by her. It reminded her very much of the first time Nirlan had fed her to him, when he'd been out of his mind with hunger.

"Azreth, say something," she said.

His mouth pulled away from her shoulder to hover over her throat, and then her chest. He breathed so heavily against her that she could feel the heat from his mouth through her clothes.

"I want you," he said, his voice impossibly two-toned and reverberating with an alien resonance. Every part of her body was alight, aware of him, fearing him, desiring him. His eyes were like suns as he looked down at her. She was breathless with awe.

The disembodied hands hiked her robe over her hips. All at once, they lifted her up and turned her over, dumping her onto her hands and knees and pulling her trousers off to bare her to him. She struggled to catch her balance on her forearms as the hands took hold of her ankles, calves, and thighs, then lifted her knees off the ground again, positioning her to his liking. More hands clasped her wrists and throat as if to be sure she stayed where he liked, beneath him.

He grasped her waist tightly and pulled her against him,

pressing his hard cock against her. It was thick and weighty between her thighs—an impossible, alarming size, and she nearly asked him to stop. She was almost certain that a mere mortal couldn't take him, but she needed to know what would happen if she tried.

There was no more preparation. She felt the tip of him against her entrance, and then he pushed inside. A sharp pain followed, and she cried out in surprise. His hips met the back of her thighs as he bottomed out, stretching her beyond what she could take.

"*Az*—" she choked, her hands grasping at the dirt. The hands on her waist and ankles lifted her, spreading her legs wider, and he slid in even deeper. She gave a moan of mingled pain and desire.

He bent over her, reaching around to palm her sex, and she felt the familiar tingle of a spell being cast on her. Heat spread from his hand, penetrating deep into her flesh, and she was surprised to feel herself slowly opening beneath his touch. Her channel softened around him, growing hot and slick, pliable and eager, and suddenly she found it not so difficult to accommodate his body. Still a jaw-dropping stretch, but no longer breaking her.

It was all she could do to hold herself together as he gripped her waist and ground his hips against her. He withdrew and slowly thrust into her again, and it felt like he was filling her entire body. It took the breath from her lungs—there was no room for it—and she couldn't think, could only feel. The world narrowed to that point of union between their bodies and to the hypnotic sensation blooming therein.

Her climax was so explosive that she might have blacked out for a moment. As her body clenched around his cock, she felt him grow even larger inside her, pulsing as he came with her. He thrust deep, holding himself at her farthest depth.

Raiya's head pounded, her senses overwhelmed. The air

was saturated with their desire, just as it had been saturated with Azreth's anger before. She already wanted more of him.

Azreth's arm looped around her waist, holding her against him. He panted, nuzzling her neck, and she smiled, reaching back to comb a hand against his scalp.

"You came back for me," he said.

"Of course I did."

He set her down slowly in the grass, turning her onto her back. She tipped her head up to try to check his injuries, but it was too dark to see them. He was kneeling over her, his eyes bright. He seemed to have calmed somewhat.

His hand brushed her shoulder where he'd bitten her. She stiffened as his fingers passed over one of the wounds. Light poured from his palm, and the pain began to dissipate as he healed her.

"Thank you," she said quietly. She touched her shoulder. It no longer hurt, and the punctures had healed, but blood still dampened the collar of her robe. Azreth's expression tightened.

"I lost myself. I did not mean to hurt you." He bowed his head until it touched the ground. "I beg your forgiveness."

"Forgiveness?"

"I have broken the terms of our agreement. Strike me," he said, glancing toward the chains on the ground nearby. "And I will lie still while you pay the hurt back."

She scoffed. "I don't want to hurt you. I will never hurt you."

"I cannot say the same."

"I don't believe you." She sat up on her knees, pulled him up to face her, then pressed her lips to his.

He froze. Raiya savored the unexpected softness of his lips. They were hot, not too dry or too damp, not resisting but not particularly inviting. He waited passively while she kissed him, and she had to wonder if he'd ever been kissed before. Maybe it was not done in the hells.

TWENTY-ONE

Raiya awoke to the sound of gentle birdsong.

Heavy, warm arms enclosed her. She was tucked against Azreth's body beneath the blanket he normally wore, comfortable and secure. Tilting her head, she blinked up at him sleepily. He was already awake, of course.

"Are you well?" he asked.

She curled her body into a smaller shape against him. He radiated heat, but the air was frigid. She felt a twinge of soreness between her legs. "Yes."

"You're cold," he observed. He got up, wrapping the blanket around her before he left. She shivered, her breath clouding in front of her.

Azreth piled fallen wood together and then lit it with a wave of his hand. Fire burst from his palm and quickly blazed high, eating through the wood and casting out waves of heat.

"Thank you," Raiya said, moving close to the fire.

He picked up a rather large log and dropped it beside the fire, making the ground shudder beneath her feet, then gestured for her to sit. She did so gratefully, and he sat beside her. She peered over at his bare chest, aghast. There were still dark marks wrapping around his arm and torso where the iron had touched him. She put her hand to the marks—slightly raised patches of discolored skin. They were subtle, but they were there.

"Does it hurt?" she asked.

"No."

That was hard to believe. "What does the iron do to you, exactly?"

"The burns alone cannot kill me."

"But it weakens you? And causes you pain?"

"Yes," he admitted.

That was almost worse.

He leaned down. She was surprised when he lowered his mouth to hers and carefully, gently, kissed her. By the uncertain way he moved, she was sure it was the first time he'd kissed someone, but evidently he'd liked it enough when she'd done it to him that he wanted to try it again.

"Thank you for coming back for me," he said.

She gave him a wobbly smile. "I'm sorry for what they did to you."

He exhaled softly, glancing at her shoulder again, as if checking how it was healing. His expression darkened. "I should not have done that to you. I will not do it again."

"I'm not hurt."

"You screamed in pain."

She raised an eyebrow, giving him a suggestive glance. "I was... surprised. I told you: I am not weak."

He gave her a long, thoughtful look.

"I'm curious," she said. "Is this common among demons? Have you... bitten someone before?" She imagined his previous couplings, and she mentally recoiled. Thinking of his hypothetical previous lovers was unpleasant.

"I think it is common. But I haven't done it before."

She frowned. She hadn't expected that. "Do you only have the urge to bite mortals, then?"

"No." He was being evasive, not looking back at her.

"You don't want to tell me."

He lifted his gaze cautiously. "No. You can ask me whatever you want."

She smiled. "So?"

He took a long moment to organize his thoughts, staring at the fire. "Others have done it to me," he said finally, turning to show her his back. There were scars on his shoulders and the back of his neck that she had noticed before but only now realized were bite marks. "These were put here when others subdued me and fed from me."

Raiya's eyes widened. She had known he had suffered in the hells, but seeing this evidence of it on his body made her want to do terrible, violent things to whoever had put those marks there.

She swallowed her outrage. "Haven't you—surely there are times when demons make love consensually?"

"Yes, sometimes. If it's agreed upon as a mutual exchange of energy. But my people never truly trust each other. It's done quickly and fearfully and we hurry to part ways before one of us can turn on the other. There is no passion."

"And that thing you did to make me... more receptive?" she asked. "What was that?"

His expression dulled. "It's a simple magic to help a receiver ready themselves. Most of my kind know it."

Raiya's skin crawled. It made sense. Apparently, it was common for people in the hells to be forcefully prepared for intercourse.

"It will not hurt you," he said, "and it will not alter your thinking or make you desire anything you did not desire before. It only opens your body. But I deeply regret using it without your permission."

"It's fine."

"No, it isn't. You should be angry, Raiya. You should not allow anyone to treat you poorly. You should have struck me. I have betrayed you, just as your husband did."

"You're nothing like Nirlan. You would have stopped if I asked."

He was still frowning. "If I had hurt you, would you tell me?"

She smiled ruefully. "You know, Nirlan would always get angry when I told him he'd hurt me."

"Why?"

"He didn't want to be reminded that he is the sort of person who hurts people."

"When you first freed me from Nirlan's dungeon, you said that you didn't care if I killed you, as long as I killed him as well."

That seemed so long ago now. She'd been so desperate. "That was the truth."

"You were brave to sacrifice yourself in order to destroy him."

She wrinkled her brow. "It was suicidal, not brave."

"I disagree. You were strong, even at your weakest." He put a hand on her shoulder. "I still owe you a death. When we find a way to remove this curse from my hand, I will kill him."

She felt a rush of excitement and apprehension at the idea of destroying Nirlan, of turning all the pain he'd inflicted back on him. She had a blood thirst. It was probably what had drawn her to Azreth in the first place.

"You know," she said slowly, "we could just leave the binding alone. As long as it's incomplete, I don't think it will harm you. If you keep away from Nirlan, you could just ignore it."

The glow of his eyes intensified, but his voice was calm. "I don't want to keep away from him. I want to tear out his backbone so that he will be as spineless in body as he is in spirit."

She smiled. "I will keep working on it."

"Please do."

The fire went out, reduced to embers. She shivered.

"We must find shelter for you," Azreth said.

Shelter, he said, as if he was accustomed to living in the rough. She wondered if he was imagining a lean-to or a cave somewhere. "We need to go back to civilization. I can't just wander the wilderness."

"Why not?"

"I just can't. Nobody does that."

He frowned. "There are too many people in the cities. Here, away from others, we are safe."

She actually considered it. In a way, being alone with him, far away from cultists or Paladins or any of Nirlan's minions, was tempting.

"I've lived shut away in a castle for the better part of a year. I want to be a part of society. I want to see other people. I left Nirlan so that I could grow, not so I could go back to the same miserable life I had."

Azreth conspicuously said nothing. She realized that she'd forgotten something obvious: he was thinking of himself, too, not just her. He was destined for a life of isolation if he remained on the mortal plane. She might be able to return to civilization, but he never could.

"Do you still have your glamour?" she asked.

He held up his hand. The bracelet was on his wrist, its tiny runes glowing faintly. The glamour would allow him to change his appearance as much as he wished, as long as he had the magic to power the enchantment. It would protect him well.

"I'm not going to ask you to return to the hells," she said, "and I'm not going to leave you. But things aren't going to be easy for you here, no matter how many enchantments we have."

Something passed behind his eyes as he looked at her. He nodded solemnly. "I understand."

He reached behind him to pick up her baton, which must have fallen from her belt at some point during the night. "Make it stronger," he said. "Make a weapon worthy of your hand. I will provide however much power it requires."

Raiya took the baton from him. The greatest limitation on enchantments was the amount of magic energy required to power them. But with the amount of magic a demon could generate... there were few boundaries on what she could create.

"Before we do anything else, you must arm yourself properly," he said. "Finish your weapon, and then we will do as you wish and—" he frowned with distaste, "—go back to civilization."

She clutched the baton to her chest, already smiling as she thought about how she would modify it. "Thank you."

"We are allies," he said simply.

"No," she said, and he looked up at her suspiciously. "Allies are merely people with a common goal. You are a friend to me, not just an ally."

She hoped he would voice his agreement, but he just frowned, contemplative.

She got up to put her back to the smoldering embers, studying him. "You know, there was... one other thing I was curious about," she said awkwardly. "About last night."

"Yes?"

"You... finished inside me. But I didn't notice any... ah... remnants, afterward."

He tried to parse that for a moment, then said bluntly, "What?"

Raiya pursed her lips. "You know that in order for mortals to procreate, a man must... plant his seed in a woman."

To her astonishment, Azreth still showed no recognition whatsoever. She hadn't thought she'd ever end up giving a sex education lesson to a demon, but life was full of unexpected turns, wasn't it?

"It's... sort of a fluid?" she said. "When a mortal male climaxes, his body releases his seed into the woman's womb."

"Oh." He arched an eyebrow. "No. I don't have that."

"Strange."

He seemed faintly amused. "I'm strange? I would argue that your 'seed fluid' is strange."

"Fair enough."

TWENTY-TWO

"I don't like this," Azreth said. They were walking down the road toward the Roamer camp, which had just come into view beyond the hill ahead of them. Raiya had decided it was safer than Ontag-ul, and she wanted to check on Jai and Madira, too.

She smirked up at Azreth. He wore his glamour, and his face was a familiar shape wrapped in unfamiliar beige skin. "You know, I wasn't alone when I rescued you from the temple. The night elves and a Paladin were with me, too."

He looked down at her sharply, his lip curling. "A *Paladin?*"

"Yes. I wouldn't have gotten you out without their help."

"That does not mean you can trust them. If they helped you, they had their own motivations for doing so. They would not have done it if they did not see a benefit for themselves."

"For some people, doing what you feel is right is a benefit in itself."

He looked down at her, his brow knitted. "Do not assume others feel the same as you. Keep your baton within reach."

Raiya brushed her fingers over the handle of the baton

tucked into her belt—not because she was worried, but because she liked the feel of it. She had begun adding runes to the shaft and more in the handle, as many as she could fit. It was the most self-indulgent thing she'd ever made, ridiculous and impractical by most standards, but not when you had a demon to power all those runes. It was not finished, but already the baton positively glowed with latent power, and she was intoxicated by it.

Soon after they entered the camp, Fu-lon greeted them—though that may have been overstating things.

"So you got your creature back," she said to Raiya. Raiya was tense, waiting for her to tell them that he wasn't welcome in the camp. Azreth glowered at the woman. Fu-lon puffed on her pipe as she thoughtfully looked Azreth up and down. "I didn't expect that. Well done."

"Thank you," Raiya said.

"You'll be looking for those troublemaker elves, I suppose?"

"I was, actually."

"Jai won't stop talking about you." She heaved a sigh, breathing out a cloud of smoke. "You can stay, but if an army of Paladins come to get him, I'm not going to get in their way. I've got nothing against you, but I'm not going to defend one of his kind. You're on your own. Understand?"

Raiya was stunned. It was more of a welcome than she'd expected. "I understand. Thank you, Matron."

Fu-lon nodded. "Go talk to Jai."

Predictably, Jai found them before they found her. She grabbed Raiya's arm and dragged her toward her tent, practically bouncing with excitement.

"You could have told us you were alive. We thought the cultists might have gotten you," the girl said as soon as the tent flap closed behind them. Madira was sitting on the floor inside. Startled, he looked up from the bowl of salad he was eating and the book he'd been reading, and his entire body flickered into shadow for a moment—apparently a fear reflex.

"Ash and blood, Jai, you can't just barge in here with whomever," he said. "What if I was naked?"

"You're not," she said, giving him a withering look.

"I could have been."

"Shush! Raiya and her you-know-what are here."

Madira set down his bowl, looking up at them both warily. "So you're alive, demon?"

"Not so loud!" Jai hissed.

"My name is Azreth."

Raiya looked up at him. It was the first time she could recall him introducing himself without being prompted.

Madira seemed to hold his breath for a moment, nervous. But then he shrugged. "I did not want to upset Raiya by saying this, but I was certain you would already be dead by the time she got to you."

"The cultists did not want to kill me," Azreth said. Everyone went still. His presence commanded attention, but more than that, he had the benefit of being one who rarely spoke. It made people want to listen on the rare occasions when he did. "They coveted my strength. They wanted to make me their servant, force me to be a weapon. They thought they could coerce me with torture. They were wrong."

"Gods," Jai murmured.

"I doubt you'll be welcome at the temple again after this," Raiya said to Madira. "I'm sorry."

He shrugged again, though Raiya thought he looked dejected. "It's not important."

"What isn't?" Azreth asked, surprising Raiya again.

"He was using the temple as a surrogate space to pray to the night elf goddess, since she has no temples of her own in Uulantaava," Raiya said. She wasn't completely clear on the details of how it worked or what sort of worship their goddess demanded, but she knew that the night elves' goddess was deeply important to them. "The cultists allowed him access for a time, but I don't think they'll welcome him back after what happened yesterday."

Azreth sat down on his knees in the center of the carpet. "Tell me what happened."

They all took turns telling him the story. Jai told most of it, very animatedly. Raiya and Madira had to remind her to keep her voice down multiple times.

"Why did you come?" Azreth asked them. Raiya had seen the question coming.

"I had nothing better to do that night," Madira said coolly.

"No, it's because we wanted to help," Jai corrected him.

Raiya saw a crease form between Azreth's eyebrows. He glanced over at her. She imagined the blue glow of his eyes beneath the brown-eyed human facade.

"I am indebted to you," he said to the elves. Jai and Madira exchanged raised eyebrows.

"You're welcome," Jai said, giving him a tentative smile.

"And the Paladin?" Azreth asked. "Where is he now?"

Jai shrugged. "We got separated after the cultists chased us out. We went in one direction, and he ran off in the other." She turned to Raiya. "The good news is, your husband left town. I overheard some people talking in the market today. Him and those Paladins were seen going north last night."

He wouldn't give up so easily. He'd be back. She and Azreth had defied him, and he'd never let them get away with that. But the farther he was from them, the better off they were. She could finally rest for a moment.

"Please don't talk to anyone else about all of this," Raiya said to the elves. "The other Roamers might be open-minded, but even they wouldn't knowingly allow a demon amongst them."

"It took them months to get used to Madira and me being here, you know," Jai said, crossing her arms. "It's a good thing I'm so likable. If Madira was alone, they would've kicked him out a long time ago."

Madira scowled at her.

***

THERE WERE no tents free this time, so Jai and Madira—mostly Jai—invited them to sleep under theirs. They put up a curtain dividing the space in half, and Raiya arranged a bed using a pile of blankets and furs while Azreth watched. The elves were out, but they'd likely return soon to sleep.

While she prepared their space, rain began to fall, hitting the outside of the tent in a lulling rhythm. The smell of wet earth and moist air joined the smell of camp fires, and Raiya was grateful they'd been allowed a space inside.

Azreth hovered beside her as she stripped to her underclothes and settled into the bed. She couldn't pinpoint what it was that tipped her off, but she sensed he was unwell.

"It's been a while since you slept," she realized. "You must need rest."

"Not here."

Raiya pushed herself up onto her elbows. "No one will hurt you here. And I'll be with you."

He hesitated, glancing up toward the door flap and then back at her. "I can't." She heard a tinge of regret in his voice.

She smiled at him, gathering her courage. It had been a long time since she'd asked a man for platonic touch. She feared rejection. "Then... will you just hold me while I sleep?"

"Are you cold?" he asked, frowning at the blankets, as if questioning their quality.

"No."

He paused, considering her.

Then he crept closer. "Does it not frighten you to have my arms around you? Does it not make you feel... trapped? In danger?"

"I like having your arms around me."

He let his glamour drop away. He waited, as if questioning whether she would feel different when the illusion was gone. Raiya took in his dusky skin and elegantly curving horns, the many scars crossing his skin, and the soft glow of his prosthesis.

"Do you know that you're beautiful?" she asked softly.

He tilted his head at her.

"I suppose you must know that you're impressive," she said. "And I suppose demons are designed to seduce mortals, so maybe it goes without saying. But you're beautiful. I'd bet that you're uncommonly beautiful even among other demons." She put her hand on his arm. Corded lengths of muscle moved under her palm as his hand curled into a fist. "You are a marvel to look at. To touch." She ran her fingertips along his forearm, tracing a vein. Goosebumps appeared in the wake of her touch. Raiya looked up at him. He was frowning faintly.

His hand closed over hers. Hot, rough fingers engulfed hers, but they did so slowly, with caution. He leaned down, his dark hair draping to obscure her view of the tent as his face neared hers. He halted there, inches from her skin, like he'd almost lost his nerve, and then he touched his lips to hers. He did it so lightly that it almost wasn't there, like a feather brushed across her lips. But he lingered there in absolute silence that was broken only by the pattering of rain outside. There was nothing confident or seductive in this kiss. It was tentative and fearful, and filled with longing.

He pulled away hesitantly. "I am happy to do as you ask," he murmured, still close.

It took Raiya a few moments to remember what she'd asked of him. To hold her. "Happy?" she echoed.

"Yes."

Raiya didn't know if she'd ever seen him happy before.

He unclasped the blanket-cloak hanging over his body and set it aside. Then Raiya's heart sped up as he removed his sarong, too. She studied his entire body, all his curves and angles and points. He was art. He was perfectly formed, and even the imperfect parts, they were perfect too. He was exactly as the gods—or the eldresses, or the universe, or whomever—had made him. Exactly himself.

Looking at him now, she was filled with an intense desire for him. Not to make love to him, exactly, but to have him, keep him, see him, protect him. The feeling filled her chest in a pleasant and unpleasant bundle, like lead and tiny fluttering birds.

Azreth went still. "What is that?"

She grew self-conscious. "You can feel that?"

"Yes." He put an arm around her waist as he leaned close, breathing her in.

"Can you feed from it?"

"Yes." He sounded as surprised as she. "It smells sweet."

She had thought demons only craved hatred and fear and lust. She knew he felt deeper emotions than those, but she had not thought they would appease his hunger.

He settled in beside her, beneath the blankets. Wrapping his arm around her, he pulled her against him, tucking her head beneath his chin and conforming his thighs to hers.

She slept better than she had in months.

TWENTY-THREE

After a few days in camp, Azreth seemed to run out of things to do. He followed Raiya around as she helped Jai and Madira with their chores, and he sat and watched her in the evenings while she drafted new counter-bindings or worked on her baton, which didn't bother her, but she could tell something was on his mind.

"What's wrong?" she asked him, working her stylus into the tricky curve of an Auren-Li rune.

He put his chin in his hand. "Nothing. I have everything I need. We are not hungry or cold. We are not in imminent danger. But I don't feel content. I am restless."

"You mean you're bored."

He looked thoughtful, as if that possibility hadn't occurred to him. "Yes. Bored," he said, rolling the word around in his mouth like it was deeply unfamiliar.

"Have you never been bored before? When mortals have free time, we socialize or play games or create things."

He silently contemplated that. That night, he abstained from sleep yet again, though he must have been exhausted.

In the morning, he disappeared while Raiya was in the

bathing tent with Jai and some of the other women. Later, she was surprised to find him fully glamoured and hauling water from the nearby river, holding several large buckets on each arm. A group of Roamers lounged nearby, watching him with amusement. Raiya gleaned that they were the ones responsible for carrying water that day, and he'd relieved them of that task. As Azreth went back for a third trip to gather another six bucketsful, the group clapped and cheered him on, bemused but clearly won over. Azreth wrinkled his brow at them.

After they assured him that he had brought more water than they could possibly use, Madira introduced him to his friends, a group of young men and teenage boys. They were chopping wood for the fires that night, so Azreth joined in. He kept going long after the others had tired, and even when he had a neat stack as high as himself beside him, he seemed like he could have carried on.

He seemed to come to a realization that night, because the next day, instead of chopping logs into wedges, he went into the woods to do the hard work that the others couldn't. He felled trees and carried them back to camp, slinging entire tree trunks over his shoulders. Bystanders stopped and stared as he passed. A few trees in, Raiya spotted him wiping sweat from his brow. Finally, he had found something that required effort.

He quickly became quite popular, and people began asking him for help with other things. When a carriage on the road became stuck in a ditch near town, someone came to ask him for help putting it back on the road. When a group went hunting, they asked him to come along as protection from the bandits and monsters that roamed the wilderness. He always obliged. And no one asked too many questions about his origins.

Raiya spent the first day helping Jai with her chores around the camp, but then Fu-lon suggested that her skills might be better spent elsewhere. Raiya took the hint and asked her if there were any enchantments she might benefit from. She spent that afternoon weaving a heating enchantment into a pair of gloves.

Word got around, and people began asking her for other small items. Heating devices were popular, as were water purification and anti-conception enchantments.

When they'd been in camp for a week, Raiya saw Azreth begin to change. His shoulders became less stiff. He stopped looking over his shoulder so often. He became comfortable moving around the camp on his own without having Raiya nearby.

They slept together every night, but didn't have sex, even though Raiya craved him constantly. It was difficult to find a private place in the camp.

On the seventh night, lying in bed, she felt him go still and lax in her arms, and when she looked over, his eyes were closed. She didn't think she'd ever been so pleased by the sight of someone sleeping.

One day, she found him painstakingly carving a long piece of wood with a small knife.

"I didn't know you did woodworking, Azreth."

He gave a noncommittal hum. Later that afternoon, she saw him present a small, rectangular wooden object to Madira.

Madira gave it a disinterested look as he took it. "Why would I want this?"

"It is an incense burner," Azreth said flatly. "It is small, so you can take it anywhere with you. You can make an offering to your goddess even if there is no temple nearby."

"I know what it is. The Goddess doesn't care about incense. I don't see when I would use this."

Azreth shrugged.

That night, Raiya caught the unmistakable scent of resinous incense burning somewhere nearby.

Later, Azreth came to her in their tent and showed her another result of his efforts. He'd made a bow. It was made of dark wood, smooth and polished, with little geometric designs carved into the limbs that reminded her a little of her rune-covered projects. It was beautiful, though it looked smaller than what she would have expected a man of his size to use.

"I made this for you," he said, making her look up at him in surprise. He'd divested himself of his glamour, as he always did when they were alone. She was getting used to these two very different versions of him, but she would always prefer his true appearance. She regretted that he had to hide himself.

She took the bow in both hands. "You made this for me?"

"So you can stay practiced with a weapon other than your baton," he explained, answering the question she hadn't asked. "So that you can defend yourself and hunt your own food if you ever need to, when another weapon isn't close at hand."

Raiya looked down at the bow helplessly. She didn't even know how to hold it properly, let alone shoot it.

"Do you know how to use it?" Azreth asked, cocking his head.

"I've never tried," she admitted, feeling very sheltered. She struggled to draw it. She wasn't strong enough.

"I will modify it to make it easier for you," he said.

"You're very kind."

"If you don't know how to shoot, someone should teach you. You are clever. You'll learn quickly."

"Will you teach me, then?"

He pretended to think about it, then nodded and said, "If you wish," and it was fairly obvious that he'd been hoping she would ask. She suppressed a smile.

He pointed to the carved details he'd made in the wood—unusual patterns of lines and squares. "This part is art," he said, glancing up at her. "Like the lattices on the windows in town. It serves no purpose but to be beautiful."

She grinned. "It is beautiful," she agreed.

Beneath his stony expression, he looked pleased.

A runaway wife and a demon could, in fact, make a peaceful life in Heilune. They'd found a place where their talents could be of use, where they weren't being driven out with torches and pitchforks, where they were actually starting to get along with people. And the runes on Azreth's hand weren't hurting him, much as it dismayed her to see the permanent reminder of Nirlan's attempt at enslaving him.

Madira had taken it upon himself to go on several scouting missions at the temple, and he had seen nothing suspicious—at least, not more suspicious than the cultists usually were—except that Gereg was missing. Raiya doubted they would try to capture Azreth again without a significant advantage on their side. Trapping him in a rune circle had been lucky for them, and would be a difficult maneuver to repeat.

The only thing that still worried her was Nirlan. She'd seen no sign of him since he'd left town over a week ago. It was almost enough for her to hope he might have gotten tired of chasing them.

AFTER AZRETH HAD FINISHED MODIFYING her bow, he took her to the edge of camp to practice shooting into the woods. He demonstrated how to draw it, then handed the bow and an arrow to her. Taking the smooth, elegant pieces of wood in her hands, she raised the bow. He reached over to reposition her arms, then nodded. She planted her feet, snug in their fur-lined boots, and her slow exhale clouded in front of her.

She released the arrow. It flew into the woods and struck a tree. It was immensely satisfying, even if it wasn't the tree Azreth had told her to aim for.

"I'm sorry," she said, fearing he would consider it a waste of time to try to teach her. "I'm not very good at this."

He arched an eyebrow. "It was your first attempt." He didn't chastise her for apologizing, but she sensed his disapproval. She was apologizing for nothing. Most people who were not Nirlan would not be angered over such small failures.

"Do it again," he said. "I want to watch you."

She kept shooting until her back and arms were too sore to continue, but by the end of the session she was consistently hitting the correct tree.

"Did you use bows in the hells?" she asked him.

"Sometimes. There are many dangerous things in the hells. Many of them fly."

"Really? I've never seen you use a weapon here."

"I've never needed one. Mortals are easy to hurt."

"Of course. How could I forget?"

"You would do well not to. I have told you that."

She turned to him, serious. "Isn't it more... unpleasant to use your bare hands to kill someone?"

He cocked his head. "Unpleasant?"

"People are naturally averse to killing. I think Astra made us that way. People prefer weapons like bows because they put you farther away from your victim. It means you can't see the fear on their face so vividly. You can't smell their blood, or feel it on your hands. It makes the horror of killing... less horrific."

Azreth's dark, illusory human eyes stared at her. In that moment, she was sure that anyone could have seen through his glamour. There was something demonic about his eyes as he contemplated the idea of murder.

"I like to feel blood on my hands," he said. "I enjoy the sensation of it slicking my skin, and the metallic taste of it on my tongue. I want to smell my enemy's panic as their insides spill from their body."

Raiya wasn't quite breathing as she listened to him.

"The people here have good reason to fear me," he said. "I long for destruction and bloodshed. I am dangerous."

For once, it didn't sound like a boast. He sounded almost unhappy, and Raiya wondered if, perhaps, he didn't want to be who he was. Maybe he didn't believe he could be the sort of person he wanted to be.

"When I killed that mage in your castle, you felt that bloodthirst, too," he said. "I could feel your terror, but I could also feel your fascination. Your triumph." He raised a hand to her cheek. "You were lovely."

She wanted to deny it. But there was no point in lying to him or to herself. Both of them held darkness deep inside them. The fury of a person wronged. A craving for violent retribution.

But she shook her head slowly, denying it anyway. "If you really felt such a desire for bloodshed, you would act on it. You would have done as the cultists wished. You could kill me and all the others at the camp. You would enjoy it, and it would strengthen you to feed on us. What's stopping you?"

He blinked slowly, studying her. His fingers stroked her hair.

"Nothing," he replied. "I am either a poor example of a demon, or a poor attempt at a goodly mortal."

"Then I must be, as well."

The ground shook, interrupting them. Azreth's eyes widened.

Raiya blinked, startled. "Was... Was that you?"

The earth shook again, a shivering vibration and then a distant screech that rent the air. Raiya spun, trying to identify the source of the sound. It echoed everywhere, and it was difficult to tell which direction it came from. Azreth put an arm around her, keeping her close.

"We should return to the camp," he said. "Come."

TWENTY-FOUR

A crowd had gathered at the edge of the camp by the time they returned. Fu-lon and a dozen others were watching a hill nearby.

"Did you hear that, too?" Raiya asked as she approached.

Fu-lon gestured toward the hills with her cane. Raiya followed her gaze. After a few moments, a faint orange flash lit up the horizon—the kind that only came from magic or fire.

Fu-lon turned to one of the other shepherds. "Make sure the herd is secure. They'll spook and run." The shepherd nodded and hurried toward the grazing behelgi.

There was another screech, and then a large shape came over the hill. It was high in the air, flapping batlike wings.

It was unmistakably demonic, looking like a cross between Azreth and a dragon. Black scales and plates dotted a vaguely humanoid body, and horns and spikes tipped its reptilian head and tail. A gout of fire burst from its mouth into the air.

The group drew back, gasping in unison. "A demon?" someone asked.

"A vythian," Azreth corrected them, his expression dark. "Another creature from the hells."

"Astra preserve us," someone said.

The vythian turned its head in their direction. It studied them from a distance, and then, as if it had found its target, it accelerated toward them, its wings shaping it like an arrow in flight.

Fu-lon turned to the others. "Take shelter in the city. Leave the behelgi."

Raiya was startled by the command. The behelgi were the Roamers' livelihood. Losing them would mean losing everything. It was not a command that would be made lightly.

"The vythian will set fire to them if you leave them," Azreth said to Fu-lon. "They will all die."

The shepherd gave him a solemn look, her lips tight. "I know."

Azreth's brows twitched. He watched the others help Fu-lon hobble back toward the city.

Raiya grabbed his arm. "We need to make sure Jai and Madira are safe."

He nodded, following her to their tent. The vythian was gliding rapidly closer.

"How could it have gotten here?" Raiya asked.

"Vythians are not intelligent creatures. It is unlikely that it found a way out of the hells on its own."

So who had brought it here?

"Where are the Paladins when you need them?" Raiya muttered.

"The Paladins would all fall before a vythian. They would be no help."

They found the elves in front of their tent, huddled together and staring up at the sky with horror. Madira had drawn his sword, though what he planned to do with it against that thing, she had no idea.

Jai grabbed onto Raiya as she arrived. "There you are!

Didn't you see there's a fucking giant demon in the sky? Come on, let's get out of here."

Madira scowled at her. "Jai, don't curse. It makes you sound stupid."

"If there was ever an occasion for cursing, it's when a demon is about to kill you." She pulled on Raiya's sleeve, tugging her toward town, where everyone else was running.

There was a blast of heat and light, and all of them flinched. The vythian had released a jet of flame from its mouth, engulfing several tents in fire. Even from several dozen yards away, Raiya could feel the heat on her face. By the time it stopped, the tents and their contents were smoldering ash. Raiya reached for Azreth without thinking. He took her hand reassuringly.

"We must get to the city and behind something solid," he said.

"And when it sets fire to the town?" Raiya asked as they ran. Azreth didn't reply.

They were halfway to the city wall when there was a screech behind them, so close and loud that Raiya had to stop and cover her ears. Azreth's arm wrapped around her and held her against him to shield her with his body. Powerful gusts of wind buffeted her as enormous wings flapped above them. Up close, she realized the creature was nearly the size of a small house.

The vythian swooped down on them and then glided away, seemingly for fun. It made a series of short screeches that sounded almost like laughter, and she had to wonder whether Azreth was certain that it wasn't intelligent.

They ducked behind the stables outside the town gate, all of them breathing hard from the sprint. Raiya could hear the behelgi and horses inside the stable stomping nervously. As the vythian circled above them, its head turned toward the

Roamers' behelgi, and its gaze lingered on the animals. Then it turned and started flying toward the herd.

Azreth straightened. Sparkling, magenta wings sprouted from his back.

Raiya raised her eyebrows. "Where are you going?"

He flapped twice and then leapt into the air. Raiya stared after him, gaping. He was heading toward the vythian.

She turned to the elves. "Into the stable. Stay out of sight." They all crept inside. Jai patted the noses of nervous horses, whispering to soothe them. Raiya couldn't keep her eyes off Azreth and the vythian. When the vythian arched its back and drew a deep breath, its mouth aglow with the promise of death for the herd, she stopped, frozen.

Before it could release its fire, Azreth slammed into it at high speed, grabbing it around the neck. The vythian screeched, tumbling through the air. With a powerful flex of its body, it shook Azreth off. There was black blood oozing from the vythian's neck, and Raiya realized Azreth must have used his teeth.

He dove and righted himself, coming at the creature again. This time, he attacked its wing, ripping at it with his bare hands as he flew past. The vythian roared. Azreth had torn a hole in the webbing of its left wing, and now it was flapping erratically as it spiraled. As it fell, its heavy tail lashed out and hit Azreth across his middle. His wings disappeared, and he dropped like a stone. Both of them hit the ground, sending tremors through the earth.

The vythian scrambled onto its hands and feet, its posture hunched and inhuman. Azreth was still shakily trying to rise as the vythian galloped toward him with its jaws agape and razor teeth flashing.

Raiya jumped up, raising her baton. The runes glowed bright as she took aim at the vythian, and just as the monster's teeth were nearing Azreth's head, a bolt of magic energy exploded from the baton. It shot clear across the camp to blast the vythian in its side. The creature stumbled, giving a hoarse cry, and Azreth's head jerked toward Raiya. Even from this distance, she could see his look of disapproval, but she'd just saved him from having his head bitten off, so she returned the look. The handle of the baton was hot and prickling with energy, and her hair felt like it was standing on end. The baton didn't make her feel like a fearsome elven warrior princess the way her bow did, but it was certainly effective.

The vythian's scales were blackened and cracked where the attack had hit, but it seemed to have done little real damage. The thing was even sturdier than Azreth was. She needed a stronger weapon.

She turned to Madira and Jai. "Iron. Find some iron. Quickly."

"Like an iron knife?" Jai asked. "A spear?"

"I don't know. Anything. Whatever you can find."

The elves exchanged a skeptical glance, then began searching the stable.

In the distance, Azreth backed away from the vythian, teeth bared in a grimace, and the vythian followed, circling him. Azreth waved his hands around him. He was weaving magic into a spell.

From nothing, a bright light burst forth and shaped itself into an enormous, shining, magenta sword, big enough to match the vythian's size. It hung in the air above him, as if wielded by an invisible hand. Azreth swung his arm, and the ghostly sword echoed the movement, swiping toward the vythian. The vythian screeched again as the sword struck it, but it wasn't bleeding. It couldn't have done more than bruise the thing.

Raiya kept one eye on them as she scanned the room for metal. There were hinges on the doors. Stirrups on the row of saddles hanging on the wall. Bits of something silver on the bridles and Madira's armor and on her own shoes. Much of it did not look to be pure iron, but other metals or alloys. She grabbed anything that looked promising, prying up loose nails and grabbing horse shoes from hooks on the wall. Madira handed her a knife so she could cut the stirrups from the saddles.

A long-handled broom leaned against the wall. She grabbed it, then found a roll of twine. She dumped out her satchel and shoved all the clanking iron bits inside, then began winding twine around and around the bag to attach it to the end of the broom handle, her hands moving like a madwoman's.

"What are you going to do with that?" Jai asked.

She knotted the twine over and over to be sure it was secure on the broom. Gods, she must have lost her mind. "Kill the vythian?" she asked.

"Is that a joke?" Madira asked.

Raiya chose not to answer as she hefted the broom in both hands. She looked across the fields to where Azreth still fought. Just as she looked up, the vythian cocked its head back and breathed a massive jet of fire. Azreth flung his arm in front of his face defensively, and the blaze of fire engulfed him completely. Raiya's breath caught in her throat.

It was only then that she realized there was a crowd watching the fight from near the city gate, because all of them screamed and gasped as the flames overtook Azreth. The blaze seemed to last forever. Raiya wondered if the vythian would ever run out of breath.

But finally, it did. The jet shrank and then died, bits of flame and sparks spiraling away as it shut its jaws. And Azreth was still standing there, his arm over his eyes. His body steamed and smoked, his cloak was gone, burned to nothing, and only his demon-crafted sarong remained. But he was unharmed. He slowly lowered his arm to look defiantly at the vythian, and the vythian gave a screech that almost sounded irritated.

Azreth must have finally decided there was no more point in maintaining any pretense about what he was, because his glamour flickered away, baring his cobalt skin and horns to the world. There was another concerned murmur from the nearby crowd.

But the fight wasn't over. The vythian darted for him again, its damaged wing dragging beside it. Azreth jumped back, bringing his floating sword down to knock the vythian aside. Raiya could see Azreth tiring. His movements were becoming slower.

She started running toward him. Toward a fight between a vythian and a demon. She had definitely lost her mind.

The duel went on as she ran, until Azreth's floating sword disappeared. He'd run out of magic. The vythian saw its opportunity and dove in, teeth bared.

Raiya screamed as the vythian grasped Azreth in its jaws and bit down, teeth piercing his shoulder and chest. Azreth contorted to reach up and jab his fingers into the creature's eye, raking it viciously. The vythian dropped him, shaking its head. Its eye was a ruined mess of gore. Azreth staggered, leaking black blood everywhere.

"Hey!" Raiya screamed at the beast. It ignored her until she waved her broom in the air, the attached iron-filled satchel swinging, and then the vythian turned to look at her. "That's right," she said. "Leave him alone. Come here."

It did.

The vythian stalked toward her at a frightening pace, and Raiya's knees threatened to collapse beneath her. She forced herself to run toward it.

It drew back its head and opened its mouth, its throat filled with pent-up heat. The scent of boiling metal and burning flesh singed her nose, and hot wind from its maw blew back her hair.

With a shout, she raised the broom above her head and jabbed it forward, shoving the satchel of iron into the vythian's mouth. The end of the broom stuck deep in the back of its throat, and the vythian recoiled, choking.

The broom was ripped from her hands as the vythian withdrew. It backed up, trying to dislodge the stick from its mouth. It was too deep, possibly stuck in the flesh of its soft palate. And then the iron began to take effect.

The vythian panicked. It heaved and retched, foul-smelling steam erupting from its mouth. The broom remained stuck, the iron burning it from the inside out.

Its struggles didn't last long. The vythian collapsed, heaving a few last labored breaths before it went still. The metallic poison had done its job more effectively than Raiya had ever imagined.

She turned to Azreth, who was kneeling nearby, clutching his wounds as he watched her in disbelief. Punctures on his shoulder and stomach were bleeding freely. Raiya ran to him, pressing her hands against his shoulder to try and stop the worst of the bleeding. He grimaced at her touch.

"Azreth," she gasped. "That was foolish of you to fight that thing alone. Damn you, that was foolish."

"Are you hurt?" he said.

"No." He was practically bleeding out, but he was worried about *her*. She wanted to hug him, but she thought it might cause him pain. "You saved everyone. The whole camp. The whole town."

"The behelgi?" he asked.

Raiya choked on a laugh. Perhaps he cared more about the welfare of the animals than the people.

She looked over at the herd. The fires hadn't touched them. They were frightened, but were being calmed and corralled by a few shepherds who had lingered despite Fu-lon's orders.

"They're fine," she said. "They're all fine."

Azreth nodded. He allowed himself to slump a little, as if it was an effort to even hold himself upright. His gaze moved toward the crowd in front of the city. They were staring. None of them had moved yet.

Raiya noted that Azreth's prosthetic arm had disappeared. "Do you have enough magic to heal yourself?" she asked.

He slowly shook his head, then tried to stand. "Help me," he said, reaching for her. Raiya's eyes widened. She wrapped an arm around his back and let him lean on her as he stood up. She staggered under his considerable weight.

"You need to be healed," she said.

"I will survive as long as the people do not attack," he said. Given the amount of blood streaming down his chest, she wasn't too sure. "I can't fight them. We must go. Please."

She nodded rapidly. "We'll go. I have my baton. I won't let them hurt you."

They started moving away from the town, but he couldn't manage more than a slow walk. Soon, people were breaking off from the group to approach the vythian, and perhaps to follow her and Azreth. She kept moving and tried not to look back.

TWENTY-FIVE

They had not gone more than a dozen yards before Raiya realized they couldn't go any further. Azreth did not even have the strength to straighten up. He leaned on Raiya, his head drooping so that his blood-dampened hair obscured his face.

"We need to stop," she said.

"No."

"You're still bleeding." His weight was growing heavier, his arm crushing her shoulders. She couldn't carry him like this, and even if she could, she didn't know how much blood he had left to spare. "Lie down."

He looked like he wanted to protest, but then he dropped to his knees. Raiya urged him onto his back and pressed her hands against the hole in his shoulder again. He winced silently.

"Get your baton," he said.

She pulled it from her belt and placed it in his hand. "You're going to be all right," she told him. "You're safe with me. I promise."

His hand curled around the baton's handle. "A poor excuse for a demon," he murmured.

"Azreth," she said firmly. "You're not a poor excuse for anything. You're just as you should be. You've done everything just as you should have. And I will fight anyone who says otherwise, including you."

His bright, hollow eyes looked at her, blinking slowly.

She lowered her voice. "Do you trust me?"

His chest rose and fell beneath her blood-slicked hands a few times. "Yes," he said.

"I'm not going to let any of them harm you. I will die before I let that happen. So worry about keeping still and conserving your strength, not about them."

His brows twitched down, perplexed, and Raiya felt her face heating.

When she heard footsteps in the grass behind them, she spun. It was only Jai. The girl knelt beside them, holding a hand to her forehead to protect her eyes from the daylight.

"Here." She handed Raiya a small bundle. "Some things to stop the bleeding. Is he going to be all right?" She stared, horrified, at the sight of Azreth's body stained with blood. Raiya couldn't blame her.

Raiya took a thick cloth off the bundle and pressed it to Azreth's shoulder. "He's going to be fine," she insisted. "Thank you, Jai."

"The humans in town are all in shock. They mostly just seem confused, but some of them are discussing taking weapons to confront you both."

Raiya's jaw clenched. Azreth had saved all their sorry lives, and they still planned to kill him.

"What was that thing?" Jai asked quietly. It was the sort of tone one might use in a hospice sickroom—soft and reverent and a little nervous.

"Azreth said it was a creature from the hells." She turned to him. "Have you fought them before?"

He shook his head slightly. "I've seen them before. I have never approached one. Only a fool would pick a fight with a vythian."

"A fool, or a hero," Raiya said.

Azreth's brows pinched together. "We must find the person who brought the vythian here."

"Maybe no one brought it here," Jai said with a shrug. "Heilune is full of monsters. It's not that uncommon to encounter them."

He shook his head again. "Not monsters from the hells. It is too difficult to escape the hells alone. The vythian was summoned here by mortals. Someone is responsible for this." He looked up at Raiya. "What is the likelihood that this is a coincidence? Another creature from the hells? Why here? Why now?"

Jai and Raiya exchanged dark looks.

Raiya peeked under the corner of the cloth she was holding to his shoulder. She couldn't tell whether the bleeding was slowing.

Azreth stiffened, his hand tightening on the baton. Raiya looked behind her. A group of people were approaching: several men and women whom she recognized as members of the Roamer clan.

She got to her feet. "Stay back." She was surprised at how firm and confident her own voice sounded.

A tall, ochre-skinned sun elf woman, whose name she didn't know, approached with her hands raised in front of her. "We wanted to help." She looked uncertainly at Azreth, and her face paled. Azreth was baring his teeth at her. In an instant, he'd hidden all his pain and fear, unwilling to let this new threat think he was weak. The elf looked like she wanted to turn back. She looked at Raiya for support. "I'm a mage. Not the best mage, but I can heal a little."

Raiya was stunned into silence for a moment. "Yes," she said. "Yes. Please. Help him."

Azreth's eyes darted to Raiya's, mistrustful. She gave him a look that was half reassuring and half reproachful. "Stop glaring like that," she said under her breath. "You'll scare her off."

He continued glaring, albeit a little less intensely.

The elf warily approached, raising a hand that glowed with healing magic. "This may be a bit of an experiment. I'm not sure about how your biology compares to ours."

Raiya looked at Azreth, who just shrugged slightly. Evidently he didn't know, either.

One of the men who had accompanied the elf leaned down to rest his hands on his knees as he watched. "So... You've been a demon in disguise all this time, huh?"

"Yes," Azreth said.

No one seemed to know what to say after that, and an awkward silence followed.

With the Roamers' help, they patched Azreth's wounds. He still lacked the magic to finish healing himself completely, so Raiya wrapped him in gauze and cloth to help keep his wounds closed and clean—a practice he seemed bemused by, but she insisted.

She felt proud seeing him wrapped in her inexpert but careful handiwork. She wanted everyone to see the proof that he was taken care of, that he was worth caring for, and she wanted them to know that she had done it. And, a part of her wanted them all to see that he had suffered in the process of protecting them, too.

By the time they'd finished, they still had not been accosted by a group of angry villagers, though Raiya could see the crowd still there, watching. The other Roamers had calmed the behelgi and were rapidly breaking down their camp.

Madira eventually found them. "The caravan's moving on," he said. "The matron just announced it. If you have anything to pack, you should do it now. The clan moves quickly and it doesn't wait for stragglers. Ask us how we know."

"Why would they wait for us?" Raiya asked. "Surely they won't welcome us among them, after..."

Madira shrugged one shoulder. "She would have said something if the elders had decided to keep you out. She's not shy about these things."

Hope bubbled in Raiya's chest. "And the other Roamers?" she asked, looking around at the people packing up the camp. "Won't they be angry?"

"Perhaps. Some people objected when we first arrived, too. But they'll adjust. Roamers are nothing if not adaptable."

She retrieved her things from the stable, making sure she still had her bow and her notes and stylus in particular, because those were the only things she could never part with, and decided to find another bag later. She was a little curious about what had happened to the one she'd shoved down the vythian's throat. Had it melted or burned or somehow remained whole? Perhaps the vythian's saliva was acidic, or as hot as lava. She decided to ask Azreth later. But either way, she wasn't interested in trying to retrieve it.

The clan packed up quickly and left Ontag-ul behind as the townspeople slowly descended on the dead vythian. Raiya spotted armored members of the town watch as well as a few Paladins at the front of the group. She frowned when she saw a familiar face in the distance.

"Is that Adamus?" she asked, nudging Jai.

"That's him," Madira said. His tone was flat, but lacked the hatred he'd expressed for the man previously. Maybe he was slowly learning to get along with others.

"For someone who claims not to be a Paladin any longer, he still spends a lot of time with them," Raiya said.

"Do you think he'll come after us?" Jai asked.

No one answered. Perhaps this was what it was to be among the Roamers—knowing that there was always a chance someone from your past would come calling, and accepting that running was a part of life. It helped that they had the clan at their backs, more or less. They were stronger together than they were alone.

Raiya put her hand into Azreth's as they walked, squeezing it. He looked down at her, then squeezed back gently.

RAIYA WAS NOT PARTICULARLY surprised when she heard a quiet argument at the entrance to the camp that night, and was even less surprised when the source of the argument turned out to be Adamus and the guard on watch, who was denying him entrance. His eyes locked onto her when she came into view.

"Lady Han-gal," he said, dipping into a shallow bow. "I've been looking for you."

The guard held out an arm to block his way. "I've told you, you're not welcome. Leave before we make you."

"You should listen to her," Raiya said. "Nothing good will come of chasing us."

"I need to speak with you. It will only take a few minutes. It's about the monster at Ontag-ul. I saw you and your companion kill it."

"So?"

"I think there are more of them coming."

"More?" It sounded just like what Azreth had been suggesting. This wasn't a random attack. But she hadn't thought there would be more monsters.

She turned to the guard. "Will you give us a few minutes?"

The guard raised an eyebrow, but she nodded. Raiya reluctantly guided the ex-Paladin aside.

Adamus bit his lip, looking torn. "Ontag-ul is my hometown," he said somberly. "I am indebted to you for saving it. I was at the gate when it happened. The battle was impressive to behold."

"He is impressive," she agreed.

"You were, too," he clarified. "Although I thought you were mad to run at it like you did."

"Thank you."

"Where's the demon?"

"He's resting," she said vaguely, not sure she wanted him to be aware of just how injured Azreth was. "As he deserves."

Adamus flashed a friendly smile. "You'll hear no arguments from me."

Raiya came to a stop in a secluded section of the camp and turned to Adamus. "What do you want?"

He cleared his throat, his expression growing serious. "There have been other attacks," he said. "Along the road to the north, I heard."

Raiya stiffened as she imagined more of those beasts. How many more could they possibly take on? Just one had almost killed them.

"There have been at least two," he said. "I don't think they were demons, like your friend, but there's no doubt they're hellspawn. The rumors I've heard said they were smaller beasts, but fearsome nonetheless. If there have been three already, you can bet there will be more. They're killing people.

Destroying houses and farms. It's only a matter of time until they get into the cities and cause even greater harm."

"They came from the same place Azreth did," Raiya said. "My husband brought them here. I don't know how or why, but he did."

Adamus looked both relieved and dispirited to hear her say it. "That was my suspicion, as well."

The only other person she might suspect was Gereg, but she hadn't seen any evidence that there was anyone at the temple besides Eunaios who had the knowledge to summon demons.

What was Nirlan's goal? Why set monsters loose on his own land? Was he that desperate to get to her and Azreth? Was all this destruction her fault?

She could not run away with the Roamers and forget their troubles, as much as she wished to. They had to deal with this. There was no one else who would.

"I have to do something," Adamus said. "But I don't know if I or the other Paladins can handle this. This, ah, is the part where I humbly ask for your help."

"You want the help of a demon and his mistress?" she asked dryly. "Are you certain?"

He smiled. "Not even a little."

"Then why are you doing this? Why trust us?"

"To tell you the truth... it's just a feeling I have. I think Paladius is telling me to believe in you. Even if I don't understand it, I trust him to guide my heart."

"And why are you so personally invested in this? None of the other Paladins care so much."

He raised his eyebrows a little. "It's why I became a Paladin. To help people. To try to, anyway. I don't know if I'm doing a very good job."

She looked him over. She saw no sign of deceit. There was something about him—he completely lacked bitterness.

Somehow, he'd avoided becoming jaded like her as he'd grown into adulthood, and he'd held on to a childlike sense of hope. "I'm not sure whether I envy your optimism or pity your naivete."

"That makes two of us, lady."

TWENTY-SIX

When the caravan stopped for lunch the next day, Azreth went off on his own while Raiya ate with Jai and Madira and some of the others. When she went to look for him later, she found him near the herd. The sun was bright and cold that day, and he was a vibrant spot of alien blue in the landscape of green and brown. He was still wearing her gauze bindings, though she guessed he'd probably healed quickly enough that he no longer needed them.

She watched from a distance as he approached the behelgi. He hadn't attempted to get close to them since that first time he'd seen them, when they'd encountered the Paladin riders.

The behelgi watched him closely, their heads raised, eyes angled toward him. As soon as he came near, they darted away.

Raiya sighed quietly. Azreth didn't try to approach again, but contented himself with observing them quietly. Animals were sensitive to magic. Behelgi were sturdy, even-tempered creatures, but even they shied away when approached by a demon.

This was the way it would always be. Azreth was not of

their world. He couldn't change what he was, but she wouldn't have asked him to even if he could.

"The caravan is moving again," she said softly. "Are you hungry? I haven't seen you eat anything in a long time."

"The Roamers don't like the way I eat."

She thought about how she'd seen him eat, ripping into raw meat like a wild, ravenous carnivore, and she couldn't help but be amused. The Roamers who had witnessed it must have been as unnerved as she had been.

"So I eat in private," he added.

"You don't have to do that. Eat with me next time you're hungry."

"You were sleeping last time."

"Wait until I wake up, then."

"Why?"

"Eating is a social activity for mortals. We like to gather and talk and enjoy our meals together. It's important."

He tilted his head in that curious, interested way he often did when she explained the intricacies of mortal life to him. "All right," he agreed.

They kept away from the other Roamers, for the most part. Some of the people in the clan were surprisingly accepting of his presence, but many still had mixed feelings about him. It probably helped that he had shown he was willing to protect the clan from threats. Even if people didn't like him, they liked having the extra muscle around.

Raiya had no desire to cause tension between any of them, and it appeared Azreth didn't, either. They walked at the very back of the group, almost out of sight of the others, where their presence was less obtrusive. She was content there. Azreth was the person in the group she most wanted to spend time with, anyway. Sometimes, Madira and Jai dropped back to walk with them. Other members of the clan also approached occasionally to ask if Azreth was healing well, or just to say hello. Raiya got the impression they mostly just wanted to get a closer look at him, but they were polite enough.

"What are you thinking about?" Raiya asked after they'd been silent for half an hour or so.

"Your husband."

The mood instantly soured. "I would rather think about anything else," she said.

"I think of him often. I imagine tearing off his limbs or burning him until he is blackened and crisp. I dream of his screams."

Raiya gave him a sidelong glance. "I am not sure even Nirlan deserves those things," she said carefully.

"Does he not? Even after what he's done to you? What he's done to me?"

She didn't know what she wanted anymore.

She had once thought she wanted Nirlan dead, but the more she was confronted with the reality of killing him, the more she feared it. She imagined his body broken the way Azreth had described, and it made her sick. She wanted him dead, and she didn't.

"I'm not sure I can go through with it," she admitted quietly. "I'm not sure I can just... kill him."

Azreth studied her, his eyes sharp. This must have felt like a betrayal to him. It *was* a betrayal. Her palms began to sweat, and she balled her fists into the fabric of her cloak.

"I spent every day with him for the better part of two years," she explained. "We were a part of each other's lives for so long. I thought I would spend the rest of my life with him, for better or worse."

"Do you still care for him?" Azreth asked, his tone even.

Gods, no.

Did she?

She went too long without speaking, and she feared

Azreth's judgment. He was conspicuously silent, hiding whatever he was thinking.

"I hate him," she said. "I hate everything he's done to me, and how he makes me feel, and how much of my life he's taken away. Everything about who he is disgusts me."

She sniffed. Azreth was silent, and something heavy hovered between them.

"Was he never kind to you?" Azreth asked after a while.

He was backing her into a corner. "Of course he was, sometimes. Or, I thought he was. I wouldn't have married him otherwise."

He hummed his agreement.

"Just say what you want to say," she said.

"You love him and hate him."

She was surprised he'd identified the feeling so accurately.

"I don't love him," she said. "Maybe I loved the person I thought he was. That person was never real, but I still miss the way I felt with him in the beginning."

"You mourn the future you thought you would have together."

Tears pricked her eyes. "Yes."

"But you will never have that future you imagined. He destroyed it. There is nothing left for you to love."

A tear fell down her cheek. She gave a heavy sigh, rubbing her face. "I'm sorry. I don't know why I'm..."

Azreth stopped. He knelt down and put a hand on her face. He held her there for a moment, looking alarmed, and it seemed that he didn't know what to do next. He'd wanted to comfort her, but didn't quite know how.

"Think of a future with me, instead," he said.

Raiya stared at him. Was he being serious?

He was very still, his jaw tense.

He *was* serious.

"I do think of that," she said. Azreth's eyes brightened,

almost imperceptibly. As impossible as it was, she did. She thought about it every day.

There were raised voices ahead. The caravan had stopped. Raiya and Azreth both squinted down the road.

The road sloped gently downward, giving a clear view of someone coming up the road from the opposite direction. They were moving fast, their wagon bouncing unsteadily on the rough road. A swarm of large birds followed.

The birds were like none she'd ever seen. They were as big as grown men, and so black that they seemed to consume all the light around them, but their eyes glowed like green fire. One of them swooped down, talons extended, and ripped into the shoulder of the woman in the wagon. The woman screamed, clutching the wound and ducking her head.

"Do you have your bow?" Azreth asked, moving quickly toward the approaching wagon. She handed it to him without comment.

He quickly strung it and took the arrow she offered him. They weaved through the crowd of Roamers until they reached the front of the caravan, where Azreth stopped and took aim. The bow looked comically small in his hands, but his shot was perfect. The arrow arced gracefully, piercing the chest of one of the birds just as it dove toward the wagon.

The rest of the creatures continued circling, watching Azreth as he took another arrow from Raiya's outstretched hand. He rested the arrow against the bowstring, but didn't draw it yet.

The birds seemed to think better of their choice of targets. They turned and flew back the way they'd come. It appeared that lesser creatures of the hells knew better than to try to fight a demon.

As the wagon rolled to a stop, the riders turned their attention to Azreth. He met their gaze as he handed the bow back to Raiya.

Then a man in the back of the wagon stood up. "Lady Han-gal?" he asked, eyebrows raised. "Is that really you?"

She realized she recognized the man. He was a baker in Frosthaven. They were not close, but her stall had been next to his in the market before she'd married and closed her business. She knew he'd lived in Frosthaven all his life. She hadn't expected he'd ever leave, but the wagon looked like it had been packed up with everything the family owned.

She hurried closer. "What are you doing here? Are you all right?"

He climbed down from the wagon, his limbs struggling a little. He looked a decade older than she remembered. Perhaps it was just nerves from the attack. "We all thought you were dead," he said.

Raiya blinked at him. "What?"

"Lord Han-gal said..." He waved a hand. "Well, who cares what he says? Apologies, lady, but your husband is mad."

Nirlan was surprisingly well liked in town. She'd never heard anyone talk that way about him. "What's happened?"

The woman driving the cart, the baker's daughter, spoke up, still cradling her bleeding shoulder. "You don't know?"

She looked behind Raiya suddenly, stiffening. Raiya looked up to see Azreth approaching, wearing his human glamour.

"Your wound needs to be sealed," he said pragmatically. Healing magic swirled across his palm. He knew they had already seen his true form, so Raiya knew he wasn't trying to deceive them. He must have decided that this form would frighten them less when he approached.

The woman paled, but said nothing when Azreth moved closer to her. Raiya wasn't sure if her silence was consent or just fear, but when Azreth had finished and the wound had closed, she looked cautiously relieved. "The lord has gotten involved with dark magic," she said. "Involved with the cult.

He and that priestess have done something awful up at the castle."

Raiya exchanged a dark look with Azreth. The priestess had to be Gereg. "How many other monsters have you seen?" Raiya asked.

The baker shook his head. "Dozens?"

"They've been pouring out of the castle gate and into the streets," the woman said. "There are those flying ones, and tiny, angry, ratlike ones with too many legs, and pale, eyeless creatures that almost look like humans, but they crawl around on all fours at night..." She shuddered.

"What about others like me?" Azreth asked.

"None like you," the baker said. He seemed hesitant to actually say the word *demon* aloud, as if by not saying it, they could pretend that wasn't what he was. "We're heading for Ontag-ul. Lord Han-gal has doomed Frosthaven." He glanced at Raiya nervously. "No disrespect intended, lady. There's no point in staying. The town is done for. Everyone with a good head on their shoulders is leaving now, while they still can."

Raiya was in disbelief. This was the worst thing Nirlan had ever done, and he'd done a lot.

But in a way, she wasn't surprised. Nirlan's father had lived in Frosthaven for much of his life, but Nirlan had hardly stepped foot in the town until just before his father's death. He'd grown up in boarding schools in the big cities to the south and abroad. His heart wasn't in Frosthaven. He didn't care if the place she'd lived her whole life was destroyed. He didn't care if the tiny temple and the lively market and the cheery lamps that lit the streets during the long, dark winter all turned to dust.

She took personal offense to it. It angered her more than when he raised a hand to her alone.

Azreth put a hand on her shoulder. She realized her anger had been steadily building. She took a breath.

"No offense taken," Raiya assured the baker. "Thank you for warning us. You should get to Ontag-ul. Astra keep you."

"And you, lady." He gave them an appreciative nod as the caravan parted to let him go by.

The caravan erupted into chatter.

"Azreth." Fu-lon, who was driving a wagon at the front of the caravan, beckoned him. "What do you know about this?"

"The birds are of the hells," he said.

"Color me surprised."

"There will be more like them. They are fierce, but they are not invulnerable, as you have seen. You should keep your weapons in hand. Keep your eyes open, especially at night. But if you see one that looks like me, run."

The chatter quieted to nervous murmurs as he spoke. Many of them were already stringing bows and drawing swords.

The road they traveled headed north before it curved east, where the caravan was going, meaning that they would have to move closer to Frosthaven before they could move away from it.

Azreth turned to Raiya, his expression grim. "I will not have such an easy time fighting off another of my own kind."

"Then Nirlan needs to be stopped before he summons another demon."

Azreth said nothing, waiting for her direction.

"Do you think he and Gereg could perform another summoning without Eunaios's help?"

"They have his work to build from. The remnants of the spell are still in that room where they imprisoned me. And I have begun to wonder if the priestess was holding back some of her knowledge from us. Perhaps she never wanted to help me. Maybe she had an idea of how to dissolve the binding all along, and she hid it from us because she wanted to bind me herself."

Raiya felt sick. "We can't wait until after we find a way to remove the binding. We don't have time. If he's found a way to loose monsters all over the countryside, people are in danger right now. We have to stop him."

Azreth nodded. "We are in agreement."

"But what will we do when—if—we get to him? You can't touch him while the binding still marks you."

"I know," he said darkly.

That meant it was up to her.

She began unbraiding her hair, only to comb it out with her fingers and braid it again. "What could he have to gain from this? He really has gone mad."

"Maybe he is like me," Azreth said, earning an arched eyebrow from Raiya. "Maybe he is naturally filled with anger and a desire for destruction."

"Maybe he is filled with anger," she replied. "But don't ever think that you are anything alike."

Jai appeared at her side, Madira trailing after her. "What in the name of the Goddess is going on?" the girl asked, nudging the dead demon-bird's wing with her toe. She wrinkled her nose. "How many more of these things are there going to be?"

"This is only the beginning," Raiya said.

"Not if we deal with it," Azreth replied.

TWENTY-SEVEN

The caravan set up camp when night fell. After they'd raised their tent at the back of the group, Azreth started to head for the center of the camp until Raiya grabbed his arm.

"Where are you going?"

"They're setting up a watch rotation. I'm going to help."

"It's been too long since you've had a decent feeding. We'll reach Frosthaven soon. We should make sure you have as much power as possible before then."

He paused, then relented. "You're... right," he said, oddly hesitant.

She motioned to the tent. "Shall we?"

There was a tiny crease between his brows, but he nodded. Giving him a lingering look, Raiya lifted the flap of their tent and slid inside, then waited to let her eyes adjust to the dim light.

One of the shepherds had gifted the tent to them after the day with the vythian. The small space was insulated by furs and heavy cloth bedding, and a lantern filled it with amber candlelight. It was humble, but it was their own, and it was private. She had consciously set it up away from the others.

She was grateful to Jai and Madira for sharing their space, but it had grown a tad tiring living in such close proximity to a pair of bickering teenage siblings.

She pulled off her robe and her warm trousers, bare except for her underwear and a thin undershirt. Suddenly cold, the peaks of her breasts hardened against the fabric. Goosebumps formed on her exposed arms and legs.

Azreth didn't blink during the entire process. His eyes never left her.

He bent forward, and his nose came close to her head as he inhaled her. Prickles went up her spine. "I have craved you," he said softly.

A tiny shiver of anticipation went through her. "A minute ago, I almost thought you didn't want to…"

"I have never wanted anything as much as I want you."

Her heart fluttered. Watching his face, she reached up and unclasped his cloak from around his shoulders. His expression was soft, but somehow seemed tired.

Wearing nothing except his armored sarong, he was stunning. In the low light, his skin was dark and his eyes were bright, like candle flames. The swells and tucks of lean muscle binding his limbs were powerful but not bulky—his supernatural strength far surpassed whatever power they should have reasonably granted. He was perfection.

Even the prosthetic arm seemed to have been intentionally made with an eye-catching, almost ostentatious color. Was that just the natural color of his magic? Or had he picked it specifically out of a rainbow of choices?

Her eyes went to the spot where magenta magic met what remained of his shoulder. "May I ask you a personal question?" she said.

His eyes shifted and refocused, as if he'd been thinking of something else. "Yes. Whatever you like."

"How did you lose your arm?"

His eyebrows twitched. She held his gaze.

"It was taken at birth," he said.

Raiya frowned. She had assumed he'd lost it during a battle. "What do you mean?"

He sank to his knees, tilting his head to look toward the side of the tent as he recalled old memories. "Something went wrong when I was made. All the sacrifices were made, the sacred words were said, the ritual was performed correctly, but when I walked through the veil, my right arm was misshapen and weak. There was no magic that could fix it. The eldress conducting my creation was offended by my ugliness and weakness. So she removed it and banished me."

Raiya felt the blood run from her face.

"After that, she said that my fate was in my own hands, and that I would live if I was strong enough." He shrugged, arching an eyebrow almost cockily. "I lived."

Azreth had never been a baby, so his memories wouldn't have faded, would they? He must have recalled every agonizing second of the process. "How long ago was this?"

"I was made ten years ago."

Raiya stared at him. He'd only been alive for ten years?

"And the others just let her do this?" she asked.

"I was weak. It was the most practical course of action. Even if it hadn't been, they had no reason to fight her on my behalf." He cocked his head at her. "Don't be angry, Raiya. It was long ago."

"They shouldn't have done that to you. You didn't deserve that. You hadn't done anything wrong. You'd only just been born, and your first experiences in the world were pain and loss."

"She could have killed me, instead. I know she wanted to.

She was angry because of how I'd turned out, because I wouldn't make a good servant to her. She was generous to spare me even though I was worthless to her."

"That's not generosity. You know it's not. You wouldn't do that to someone, because you know it's wrong."

He didn't answer.

"What happened after that? You said you were banished. What does that mean?"

"It means that I was without a house. The fourth hell is dominated by a number of houses, each ruled by an eldress, that are eternally at odds with each other. Most of my kind belong to one of those houses. We roam alone for most of our lives until we are recalled by the leaders of our house when we are needed. The houseless are outcasts. They are beholden to no one, and no one is beholden to them."

"But you didn't have anyone to guide you, or teach you things? How did you learn to... to live? To speak? To use magic?"

He shrugged one shoulder, uncertain. "I just knew. We are born knowing many things. The rest, I learned on my own."

"It sounds lonely."

He said nothing, but reached up to take her hand. Despite everything they'd already done, touching him this way still made her heart race. She curled her fingers tighter around his hand, cradling it in both of hers.

"I shouldn't have brought this up," she said. "I'm sorry." She must have been radiating sadness and pity. Perhaps he disliked that. Maybe depression tasted like something that had started to rot.

"You have been alone, too," he said.

She raised an eyebrow. "What makes you say that?"

"I can see it. There is a deep unhappiness in you that never completely goes away."

"That's—that's not true. I'm fine."

"You were alone in that fortress with the man who you loved, who hated you. If you'd had anyone else to help you, you would not have turned to me for aid."

He was right.

Was it true that the unhappiness had never left her? Was it trapped inside her, marking her like a scar? Would it ever go away?

She put a hand to his sternum and idly slid her fingers down his body, watching his chest rise and fall heavily beneath her fingers.

"Have you ever been intimate with someone just... for fun?" she asked. "Not for feeding?"

"...No. But I have enjoyed spending the nights beside you."

She smiled at him. She didn't often hear him talk about enjoying things. Bringing him out of his shell and bringing him happiness felt like a herculean accomplishment.

She grazed her lips against his cheek, and he leaned into the touch.

"I like it when you touch me like that," he said, his voice almost inaudible, as if it had taken some effort to say it.

"Like what?"

"Softly."

She recalled the rough, almost animalistic way he'd taken her last time. That hadn't been very soft at all. Not that she'd minded. "Do you remember when you told me never to touch you?" she asked.

"Yes." He thought for another long moment, his hand rising to cup hers. "I like... how gentle you are. No one else has ever touched me the way you do. I had never seen anyone touch other people like that before I came here." He looked faintly amused. "You are so unlike me."

"We're not so different."

She wanted to take her time touching him. She wanted to

run her hands over every part of his hard, smooth skin, exploring his entire body one bit at a time, watching the subtle ways he responded with little twitches or breaths.

He was incredibly seductive when he wanted to be, and yet she wondered if it had never occurred to him that someone might long to touch him, not just to be touched *by* him.

She was going to take her time. Sleep could wait. Feeding could wait. She kissed him, then pushed on his chest with both hands, but he didn't move.

"What are you doing?" he asked.

"Lie back."

He gave her a careful look. Then he slowly leaned back on his elbows.

"All the way," Raiya said.

There was another noticeable hesitation before he did as she asked. He tilted back until his head touched the threadbare blanket that made up the base of their bed, then stared up at the ceiling, waiting for her to show him what came next. He looked a bit like a prisoner awaiting execution.

"Are you all right?"

His eyes flicked toward hers. "Yes."

She placed herself on his waist, straddling him. "Are you sure?"

His hands settled on her waist, just above the flare of her hips. "I will do whatever you like." His hands gave her a careful, loving squeeze.

Her voice kept getting quieter, as if to match the gentleness of her touch. "I'm honored. But I don't want you to do anything. Just let me touch you." She leaned forward, pressing a barely-there kiss to his cheek, brushing the corner of his beautiful lips.

He was unnaturally perfect, inhuman, a being made of magic—and yet sometimes, he seemed so perfectly mortal. Like now, as she weaved her hand through his hair, brushing the spot behind his horns, and he arched slightly, his breath catching. When she rubbed him there, he hissed a pleased sigh.

There was a soft spot hiding there. Who would've guessed that his horns were guarding something sensitive?

As she touched him, he didn't moan or say any appreciative words, even though his body betrayed his enjoyment. It didn't seem like he was trying to hide it—more like he didn't know how or when to express pleasure.

She worked her way down his body. His eyes grew heavy lidded and distant, and she'd hoped his body would relax as she worked on him, but if anything, he grew more tense. She slid her hand over his sarong, feeling the hard length beneath it. It jumped as she took the thick shape in her hand and lovingly outlined it with her fingers. Azreth hissed in the back of his throat, his hips rolling. She squeezed up and down the length, teasing him slowly.

"What are you doing?" Azreth murmured after a while.

"What do you think?"

"This is pointless," he said, his voice hoarse.

She raised an eyebrow, watching him suppress a shudder as she stroked his length. "What?"

"I can't feed from this. I've told you, it's only you—"

"I don't care about feeding. I want you."

He stared at her. "It is not necessary."

"It is to me." She rubbed her hand over his cock, and it pressed up against her from beneath the fabric of his sarong, hot and eager. "Tell me you want this."

He looked at her for a long moment, his hips lifting slightly in time with her strokes.

"I do," he breathed.

Her hand left him just long enough to undo the ties holding his sarong closed, letting his cock spring free. She gingerly ran her fingers over the velvety skin, admiring the gentle pull and stretch as she drew it down to reveal the slick head. Gods, he was beautiful. Was it lewd of her to find his cock beautiful? The flesh was dark blue and vibrant at the tip. It was as tall and blunt and intimidating as the rest of him, but it was sensitive and needy, and it was making him shake with pleasure as she touched it.

He groaned, powerful hands grasping at blankets as his hips strained toward her. "Raiya," he sighed, the word like a protest, like a prayer, like a poem.

"Azreth," she replied placidly. She used both her hands on him, putting all her heart into her strokes. "You are so beautiful like this."

His hips bucked involuntarily, thrusting into her hands. He threw his head back, gasping as he climaxed.

Just as he'd said, he had no ejaculate, but his cock pulsed and strained with his orgasm anyway, mimicking a mortal's body in every other way.

How odd and fortuitous that the gods had given them the gift of sexual pleasure even though it wasn't necessary for procreation. It was a kindness done simply to give them a little more joy in their lives. To Raiya, it felt like further evidence that demons were not inherently evil, the way mortals believed. They were intelligent individuals, capable of desire and happiness independent from feeding and survival, though it seemed like even Azreth hadn't quite believed that about himself.

Azreth let out a sharp, harsh breath. His gaze slanted toward her, and glittering swirls, like faraway galaxies, filled his eyes. Raiya pushed a lock of hair away from his forehead, then found herself running her hand through his hair. She couldn't stop touching him.

He closed his eyes blissfully. He was unbelievably lovely when he was soft and relaxed. It was an entire new dimension to him that she'd not seen before.

"There is something I must confess," he said.

He sounded serious, and she stiffened.

"What's that?"

"In the hells, there is an illness of the mind—a rare and deadly kind of madness that befalls some of us." He took her hand. "I have felt the change coming over me for some time. I am not myself. I can no longer think properly. I can no longer reason. I care only for one thing. It occupies my mind every waking second. I have tried, and I cannot escape it. The obsession consumes me."

Raiya's heart thumped hard. The world had gone still, narrowed to only him. "What are you talking about?"

"I have let myself become addicted to you," Azreth said. "I think of you always. I crave the feel of your skin and the sound of your voice constantly. Every moment I am away from you feels empty. Where I once would have cared only for myself, I now care for you. It's torture, and bliss. In the hells, the people who fall victim to this curse are called Enthralled. Once the madness takes hold, it rarely lets go."

Raiya's head was swimming. "Are you describing love, Azreth?"

He nodded slowly. "Yes. This is what mortals call it."

The sadness and fear in his voice sent Raiya's soaring heart crashing to the ground.

He sensed her mood. "Don't be afraid," he said, clutching her arms. "This means I'm yours. Your servant. Your slave. Be anything but afraid."

A madness. He considered love a madness.

She could not know what happened to demons in the hells who contracted this "madness," but she could imagine it. Were they taken for all they could give, used and then thrown aside, like she had been with Nirlan?

And it was no wonder he considered it madness if he saw no middle steps between being someone's enemy and being their slave. To proclaim that you loved someone was the ultimate vulnerability. It was the equivalent of prostrating himself before her, opening himself up to whatever wounds she might intentionally or unintentionally inflict on him. And he was doing it willingly.

"I can't return to the hells," Azreth said. "They will take me to an eldress to be exorcised if they find out I am Enthralled. They'll force me to be cured."

Raiya's eyes were wet. She took his face in her hands. "There is a difference between the devotion of love and the devotion of a servant, Azreth. Love isn't about power and submission and fear. When you're with someone who loves you back, like I do—" Emotion filled her throat, and she swallowed hard. "When you're with someone who loves you back, it's about mutual affection and trust and selflessness. It's the greatest thing in the world. People live for that kind of love. People kill and die for it."

"It scares me."

"If you are mine, then I'm yours, too." She leaned in and kissed him.

He kissed her back. It was chaste at first, and then it wasn't.

His arms wrapped around her. It was enough to make the breath wheeze from her lungs, and yet she felt him holding back, using only a tiny fraction of his strength.

The world turned as he flipped her onto her back and knelt between her spread legs. Magenta light glowed around her as summoned hands appeared in the air.

"That isn't necessary, Azreth," she offered. "You alone are enough."

"But one hand alone is not enough to touch you. Even a dozen is not enough."

"Oh," was all she could say before the hands took away her breath. They stroked down her sides, tickled her thighs, and caressed her breasts. Ghostly fingertips scraped over the palms of her hands and the arches of her feet, brushed over her lips and plucked her tight nipples.

Azreth's own flesh-and-blood hand found the sweet spot between her legs and dipped into her warmth. His fingers came away dripping.

She writhed beneath the touch of his summoned hands. "Yes," she whispered.

The hands smoothly removed her underwear and her shirt, and then he was spreading her legs with his knees as he positioned himself above her. He did not touch himself except to grasp the base of his cock to put himself at her entrance. She looked down, drinking it in. The size of it was in proportion to the rest of him. She normally would have found such size off-putting, but on him, it seemed correct and lovely. Maybe it was also because he didn't seem overly proud of it, the way some well-endowed men might have.

He placed his hand just above the soft triangle between her legs. "I want to help you."

Raiya realized what he meant, and she nodded rapidly. "Yes. Do it."

Magic flowed from his hand. A tingling, opening sensation spread through her core, making her insides numb and hypersensitive at the same time, and her sex was suddenly hot and relaxed and achingly empty. She felt wetness dripping from her, and she was drunk on pleasure.

"Oh gods, Azreth," she gasped. She felt the broad head of him pushing against her, and she sucked in breath. She couldn't reach his flesh-and-blood hand, so she grasped the magenta one at her hip. It turned over obligingly to interlace its fingers with hers.

His body bowed over her as he pressed into her. She choked out a soft cry as he seated himself within her and his hips came flush with hers. Whatever that magic was, it made it all so much better. It opened her for him, but it also made everything more sensitive, more hungry. Her body pulsed with need, and the twitch of his cock inside her sent waves of satisfaction through her.

His body was hard and hot and heavy, inhumanly massive and smelling of heat and fire. He was familiar now, and all of these things were comforting rather than strange. He was hers. She was his.

"More," she murmured, her voice shaking. She felt almost feverish. "Please."

He panted as he thrust into her in a steady rhythm. The hands, which had been stroking and teasing her, grasped her tighter now, greedily clenching handfuls of flesh, or tightening their grip to hold her still. She felt her climax rapidly approaching.

"Azreth."

"Raiya," he groaned, his voice reverberating with multiple impossible pitches at once.

"Bite me," she said.

He looked down at her, startled. "What?"

She paused to consider her words. They came through a haze of arousal that made speaking feel like running through tar. "I know who you are. What you are. I want all of you. The sweet parts, and the vicious ones."

Hunger brightened his eyes.

"I would never hurt you," he said.

"I know."

"I am yours."

"I know."

He gripped her hair to gently pull her head back, exposing her neck. He pressed deep into her, then lowered his mouth to her throat. She felt his teeth on her, and she tensed.

His lips sealed over her skin, and his teeth pierced her, taking her blood. She climaxed in a flood of pleasure as sharp pain burst across her throat.

Azreth moaned, his hips rolling against her, luxuriating in her clenching heat. His teeth released her, and she felt trickles of blood drip down her skin, which were quickly caught by his tongue. She lay still and allowed him to lick and suck her as her limbs trembled with exhaustion. She felt his teeth scraping her, as if some part of him was imagining taking more than just a little of her blood, but his touch was careful and restrained.

Suddenly he moved up to kiss her cheek, a stark contrast to the pleasurable violence they'd just been engaging in. One by one, the hands disappeared. Azreth wrapped an arm around her waist, pressing her body against his in a desperate, hungry embrace. It was an awkward gesture, not exactly sexual. She realized he did not exactly know how to express love or nonsexual desire. Those feelings were new to him. She said nothing, but put her hand behind his head and touched his hair, content to be held by him.

His tongue caressed the wounds on her neck in long, sweet strokes, and she sensed a spell sealing the punctures.

"I love how you taste," he said.

"What do I taste like?"

"Like life."

Her hand wandered behind his horns again, rubbing him the way she might rub behind a cat's ears. His eyes fluttered closed.

Something invisible and magical was warming the air around them. It had been slowly growing in intensity since she first began touching him, and now she could feel it permeating her skin, entering her with every breath. It was the polar opposite of the heavy, oppressive rage and despair and fear she'd felt when she'd first met Azreth in Nirlan's dungeon. It was light and effervescent, bright and energizing.

It was Azreth. It was his joy. And it was the most beautiful thing she'd ever felt. She had never expected that his happiness would be as palpable as his anger was, but it was, and more.

"I am yours," he said again.

She replied with a different wording of the same sentiment —her preferred wording, which declared devotion without subservience, as they both deserved. They were each other's, and they were free. "I love you."

He pulled back to look at her, a small crease of concentration between his eyebrows.

"I love you," he said carefully, testing out the words. There was something uncertain in his voice, but there was nothing uncertain about his emotions, which had unfolded to fill the space between them.

TWENTY-EIGHT

When the road forked and the caravan veered east, Raiya and Azreth parted ways with them to continue north to Frosthaven.

Raiya wasn't particularly surprised when Jai insisted on accompanying them, and Madira insisted on accompanying Jai. Raiya told them they should have stayed with the caravan where they would be safe, but privately, she was pleased. She enjoyed their company. Even Azreth seemed to brighten a little when he saw them following.

Clouds moved in as the day went on, darkening the sky and hastening the oncoming night. At this time of year, as fall came on, the sun set in late afternoon. When it became too dark to see well, Azreth conjured a ball of mage light to float above them as they walked. Raiya hugged herself to ward off the chill.

"I spy something that begins with *S*," Jai said after there had been silence for a while.

Madira sighed. "Not this again."

"It's not like there's anything else to do."

"Sword," Madira guessed impatiently. "Steel. Sparrow. Stream."

"Snow," Azreth said.

Everyone looked up. It had indeed begun to snow. Tiny flakes fell here and there. Azreth held out his hand to catch one and then lifted his hand to peer at it, only to find it had instantly melted on his skin. He looked disappointed.

"Back home in Kuda Varai, snowfall is said to be a sign of bad things to come," Madira said. No one replied, but the tension in the group was obvious. Everyone grew quiet.

Raiya was the first one to spot Frosthaven on the horizon. Dark shapes of walls and roofs rose up in the distance. It looked darker than she remembered, with only a few scattered lights dotting the town.

She reflexively gripped the handle of her baton beneath her cloak. It was filled to the brim with power, so much that it felt hot to the touch. They were as ready for this as they could be, but that didn't stop her heart from drumming an anxious beat in her chest.

She glanced up at Azreth. Finally, something good had happened to her, and she couldn't help but fear that the universe was conspiring to take it away.

As if he'd sensed her unease, he looked down at her, reaching over to put his hand on her shoulder.

She just nodded reassuringly, not trusting the steadiness of her voice enough to speak. Azreth bent to kiss her cheek, and warmth flooded through her. He must have noticed the bloom of emotion, because he smirked conspiratorially at her before he straightened.

As they entered the town, a new chill came over her, quelling any warm feelings she'd had. The town was silent. Eerily so. Normally, there would have been people bustling about even after dark, but today, the streets were empty. Still-burning lanterns swung in the wind, snow swirling around the soft, golden balls of light. With no one to disturb the snow, untouched drifts were gathering in doorways.

She'd half expected to find it overrun by screeching hellspawn. She was relieved that was not the case yet, but she was not particularly comforted by the odd quiet. Even less so by the smears of what looked like blood that she occasionally saw beneath the thin layer of snow, and the torn awning here and broken lamp post there.

She spotted a face in a dark window of a house before the curtains quickly closed. A while later, she saw another. So everyone was not gone, just hiding. At least they were not all dead.

"This is your home?" Jai asked, gazing around at the empty streets. Her voice was low but clear. The snow dampened any echo that might have otherwise carried through the stone streets and buildings.

"It was," Raiya replied.

"Not anymore?"

"I'm... not sure."

"Home is where your friends are," Jai said, looking up at her encouragingly. "A real home is wherever you choose to make it."

"That's not true," Madira said. "Kuda Varai will always be our home, no matter how long we spend away from it."

"Well, maybe Raiya doesn't want this to be her home anymore," Jai pointed out. "The place where you were born isn't always the place that feels like home. Especially not when you're no longer safe or welcome there."

"You're both right," Raiya said, glancing up at Azreth.

The sound of flapping wings drew her attention. Down the street was a group of the same large black birds they'd seen on the road. They were gathered around a misshapen form that, after a few moments of scrutinizing, Raiya realized was a corpse. The birds were pecking at cold bits of flesh.

They passed the corpse and the demonic birds without comment. The birds never looked up from their morbid meal.

Raiya led them to the northeast, where she could just see the dark outline of the castle on its hill outside of town, illuminated by the half-hidden moons and shrouded by snowfall.

She blinked rapidly at it. Through the haze of snow and darkness, she could see a red glow suffusing the castle, almost like a magical fire burning the stone.

"What do you want to bet that's where they're coming from?" Raiya said, nodding toward the castle.

"I wouldn't take that bet," Jai said.

A distant screech split the air, and Raiya stopped short. They all waited, listening, and another screech followed.

"What's that?" Raiya asked, looking up at Azreth.

He'd cocked his head toward the sound. "A thresher, or a winged nyra. Stay close."

When they reached an intersection of paths, the source of the sound became clear. Down the street, armored men were battling a nightmarish creature that scrambled around with alarming quickness. Raiya recalled the baker's daughter describing this thing—like a pale human on all fours. Long, needle-like teeth protruded from its jaws, dripping with saliva.

It lunged at one of the armored men, sinking its teeth into the man's throat.

Raiya drew her baton, but she didn't know if she could hit something that moved that fast.

"Thresher," Azreth confirmed absently. He held out his hand, and a length of magenta light appeared in his palm. A spear. In one quick, powerful motion, he raised the spear and hurled it, looking like a champion gladiator. It flew at blinding speed and tore through the thresher's neck, stopping its movement abruptly. The spear disappeared, and the thresher dropped to the ground.

All the men spun toward Azreth. It was only then that

Raiya saw their red cloaks and the sword emblems. Paladins. They raised their swords as they moved their attention to their next threat: Azreth.

"Wait!" someone shouted. "Stop, damn you!" Adamus pushed his way to the front of the group. He was wearing his armor again, but it looked like he'd scraped the Paladin emblem off the breast of the cuirass—certainly a statement, though Raiya questioned whether it made any real difference.

The other men hesitated. They looked less eager to attack Azreth than they had last time. This time, they had other enemies to deal with, and they seemed exhausted already. If they could barely handle that thing Azreth had just killed, it was doubtful that they wanted to try their luck against a demon.

"Lady Han-gal," Adamus said, a note of relief in his voice. He glanced up at Azreth as if he was considering greeting him too, but he didn't.

"You're with the Paladins again, I see," Raiya observed.

"They needed my help." He shifted his weight from one foot to the other. "Have you come to help, too?"

"Obviously," Madira said.

Raiya gave Adamus a sympathetic look. "We're going to the castle. I'm going to fix this."

As a few of the Paladins went to tend the dead man's body, one of them looked suspiciously at Raiya. "You must be joking. You expect us to trust a demon?"

"Whether you trust us is of no importance to me," she said. "Just don't get in our way."

"The castle is where the beasts are coming from, as far as we can tell," Adamus cut in. "I don't know how or why. We've been too busy fighting the ones already loose in town to investigate it."

"I thought you were all working with Lord Han-gal. Now

you're working against him?" Raiya asked. To her surprise, the Paladins looked a little sheepish.

"There was a... misunderstanding," one of them said.

She realized she recognized the man who'd spoken. He'd been there in Ontag-ul when Nirlan had attacked her. "It didn't seem like a misunderstanding when you all were mashing my face in the dirt."

The man's face reddened. "Your husband told us you were a witch. It looked like he might not have been wrong." He jerked his head at Azreth. "That monster of yours killed half our team."

"After you attacked us!"

There was another distant screech. Some of the Paladins broke off from the group to hunt the source of the sound, swords and torches raised. The rest of the Paladins began murmuring to each other behind Adamus. They were eyeing Azreth as if they were still formulating a plan of attack.

"Right now, we both want the same thing," Raiya said. "Can we make a truce? Don't stab us in the backs, and we'll return the favor."

"I didn't agree to that," Madira said under his breath. Jai elbowed him.

There was some murmured discussion between the Paladins before one of them turned to Raiya. "We'll honor your request for the sake of overcoming this greater evil. For now."

"How generous of you," she said, unable to hold back the sarcasm. Azreth could have killed all of them. Their cooperation was merely a convenience. "Keep yourselves safe. We're going to the castle."

"I'm coming with you," Adamus said. "We have to stop whatever is bringing them here if we want to finish this. Otherwise, they'll just keep coming."

Raiya glanced up at Azreth to see if he would object. He frowned deeply, but said nothing.

"Very well," Raiya said, starting toward the castle. "We could use the help."

"What is your plan?" Adamus asked.

"There isn't one, other than to find Nirlan, find out how he's done this, and see if we can undo it," Raiya said. "We can't be sure what we'll find when we get there."

"Ah. Good," Adamus said. "Walking into a den of demons with no plan and only three swords. Again." She shot him a look, and he gave her a wan smile. "Kidding. Sort of."

"Not just three swords," Raiya said. "I have a weapon. And Azreth has..." She waved to all of him demonstratively.

"Raiya knows the layout of the castle," Azreth said. "She knows the rune magic used for this kind of summoning, and she knows our enemy. She will lead us to victory."

Raiya blushed, not certain she deserved his confidence. She could imagine Nirlan's voice very clearly, suddenly. *You? You couldn't be relied on to lead a household, let alone to lead anyone into battle.*

Adamus nodded. "I'll do whatever you think is best."

She took a few deep breaths as they started up the path out of the town, up the slope to the castle. "I am grateful to have you with us." She turned to Madira and Jai, too. "All of you."

She could not have done this without them. The thought of seeing Nirlan again, even now, made her want to turn back. Facing demons was one thing. Facing him was another.

The iron portcullis on the outer wall was up. They passed beneath it and stepped into the bailey. An awful, rotting scent hit Raiya's nose, and she covered her face with her hands to try to block it out. Adamus put his hand over his heart in the way that worshipers of Paladius did, murmuring a prayer.

There were bodies lying here and there on the ground, half covered in snow. Some of them were new, but the source of the smell was likely the ones that had been there longer—the guards Azreth had killed when they'd escaped. Nirlan had been in such a hurry to chase after her that he'd left them here to decay. Raiya stopped to stare at them.

"Raiya?" Azreth said quietly.

"What kind of person just leaves the corpses of their own men to rot in their garden?" she asked.

It was not even the lack of respect that bothered her, although that was also concerning. It was the bizarre decision to prioritize chasing her over cleaning dead, rotting flesh out of his own home.

"There's something wrong with him," she said. "He's not normal."

"Did you just realize this?"

Perhaps she had.

Maybe madness was harder to see when it was wrapped in a clean-cut, well-mannered package. With someone as calm and confident and well-dressed as Nirlan, someone who knew how to flatter and charm and use clever words... People assumed that someone like that knew what they were doing. Someone like that couldn't be wrong. Even Raiya had believed it. She'd believed the illusion of his competence over her own.

She turned to Azreth. "Let's go."

He put a hand on her cheek. "We will succeed. Don't worry."

His little sweet touches always surprised and pleased her. "Are you so certain?" she asked.

He hesitated, betraying his own fear. "I am certain that I will do whatever it takes to keep you from harm."

She squeezed his hand. "I'll do the same for you. Come on."

They met the others at the entry to the castle proper. The doors were different than the last time she'd seen them. A circle of glowing runes covered the old wood.

"Some kind of dark magic," Adamus said.

"It's locked," Madira explained, turning to Raiya.

"It's not dark magic," she said. "They're just runes. An enchantment to block the doors. But I think I can devise a counter-enchantment. Let me see if..."

Azreth put a hand on her shoulder to stop her. She stepped aside. Without further prompting, he kicked a booted foot through the wood, sending both doors crashing across the room inside.

Madira snorted. "I was going to suggest stealth, but I suppose you think showing off for your woman is more important?"

Raiya smirked up at Azreth, who just looked confused by the comment.

"You're a night elf. Of course you were going to suggest stealth," Adamus said. He gestured into the castle, looking up at Azreth. "After you."

TWENTY-NINE

As they stepped through the broken doorway, a rush of memories assaulted Raiya. The last time she'd stepped over this threshold, she'd been with Azreth. She'd been terrified of him, but more terrified of her husband. She'd felt so helpless, so filled with misery and desperation, that she'd seen no other way out.

So much had changed in only a few weeks.

She had strung her bow and hung it over her shoulder beside her new satchel, placed her small quiver of iron-tipped arrows on her hip, and she held her charged baton in her hand. She was prepared this time. She was ready to face whatever would come.

From the moment they entered, she sensed something off. The castle was always dark and cold and quiet, but now there was a heaviness to the silence. The air was dead, no breaths disturbing it, and no flickering, lively candlelight breaking up the shadows. She was thankful for the moon slicing through the narrow windows, and Azreth's ball of mage light.

They had only taken a few echoing steps into the large entry hall before they encountered another corpse sprawled on the floor. It was a woman with a dark robe and a ghostly pale face marked with black. Her hood had fallen back to reveal silver hair.

"It's Priestess Gereg," Raiya said.

"She's dead?" Azreth said. He seemed as surprised as she, his brows dipping down in a deep frown.

Raiya stepped closer and found the reason for the woman's death—several deep punctures in her belly. A short trail of bloody footsteps was smeared behind her, as if she'd managed to wander for a few steps before bleeding out. "Quite dead."

"Well. She's with her goddess now."

Sensing the irony in his voice, Raiya raised an eyebrow at him. "Was that a joke, Azreth?"

"Maybe."

"Do you think a sword did that, or another demon?" Madira asked.

"I cannot say," Azreth replied. "We should find the lord and ask him."

"A summoning gone wrong?" Adamus suggested. "It's hardly rare for a demon to kill its own summoner." He glanced up at Azreth. "No offense."

Azreth looked at Raiya instead of at him. "The truth does not offend me."

"Or Lord Han-gal killed her after she helped him," Jai suggested. "He seems like the type to get rid of someone after they've outlived their usefulness."

Raiya stepped around the corpse and kept moving. Whoever had killed Gereg was probably still somewhere in the castle. "The summoning circle the last cultist made was in the tunnels below the castle. We should start there."

Wind whistled through the corridors as Raiya led them toward the staircase to the dungeon. They passed more dead creatures on their way, none of them human. Raiya stared at their twisted, bloodied forms. They looked terrifying, but when they were lying dead and motionless on the cold floor, she couldn't help but pity them.

"The inhabitants of the hells are so strange," Jai murmured.

"Especially when you consider the fact that these must have been killed by something even bigger and stranger," Adamus said, his expression dark. "They have the same puncture wounds the priestess had."

They entered the great hall. Snow and moonlight were drifting through windows that had been broken recently, their glass littering the floor. Raiya stopped when she heard a soft fluttering. Something was moving near the ceiling. Azreth raised his ball of mage light higher until the rafters were illuminated. Raiya's jaw dropped and she took an automatic step back.

The rafters were lined with roosting demon-birds, their heads tucked into their feathers in sleep. Raiya could see the beginnings of several nests in the corners. They'd made themselves right at home. Something small skittered along the railing of the balcony that overlooked the space from the second floor, and more crept around in the shadows on the floor. More unwanted visitors from the hells.

Azreth put a hand on her shoulder. "Just birds. They're small."

"They're quite large by our plane's standards."

"But not bigger than I am."

Her home had become a graveyard and a demon nest. It looked like it had been abandoned.

They watched the creatures for a few moments longer, and then the birds shifted, lifting their heads in unison. As if one of them had spread a telepathic command, all of them spread their wings and flew, fleeing through the narrow windows or down the corridors, not seeming to care which way they went as long as they got away.

"Something frightened them," Azreth said. Raiya felt him grow tense. A shadow shifted in the corner of her vision, and then a bright projectile flew toward them.

Azreth spun, putting himself between her and the projectile and raising a shield of magenta magic. The projectile exploded against the shield with such force that Azreth stumbled and Raiya was shoved off her feet.

Disoriented, Raiya looked up. Beyond Azreth's shield, a figure approached from the shadows of an adjacent corridor. It was tall, humanoid, and horned. He had violent red skin, almost like he was covered in blood, and his eyes were like embers.

Unlike Azreth, each of his fingers tapered into enormous claws. Raiya's throat went dry. She had thought Azreth was enormous, but this other demon made him look scrawny by comparison.

The demon swung an arm, releasing another projectile. It was a solid beam of light not unlike Azreth's own light weapons, but these ones seemed somehow more aggressive, more wild and powerful, sparking and crackling like lightning. Azreth rushed forward, deflecting the projectile and then tackling the demon. To her surprise, he swept the other demon off his feet with a dive into his legs.

Someone grabbed her arm. "Get up!"

She obeyed, letting herself be dragged backward as she stared at Azreth wrestling the other demon. Every other time she'd seen him fight had been like a child play-wrestling compared to this. Their bodies contorted and struck out with ferocity and speed unlike anything she'd ever seen.

He was going to be hurt, or killed. He couldn't beat someone so much bigger than he was. She aimed her baton, waiting for an opening. Beside her, Adamus had drawn a bow and an iron-tipped arrow.

A screech pulled her gaze upward. One of the birds was swooping down on her. She jerked her baton up, and a blast of magic *boomed* out of it, sending the bird spinning. More of the birds were coming now, as if spurred by the commotion, perhaps an instinct to protect their new nests. Raiya shot another one as it tried to dive for Jai. The sharp smell of raw, crackling magic filled the air.

As Raiya's eyes followed the circling birds through the air, her gaze caught on a pair of eyes peering down at them from the shadows in the corner of the balcony.

Nirlan. He was... *hiding.*

Instead of fear, her heart filled with fury at the sight of him. "Nirlan!" she snarled.

His eyes widened. He spun and disappeared down the hallway. The coward. The *worm.*

"*Go,*" Azreth shouted to her. "*Go after him.*" He and the other demon had separated for a moment, but he hardly had time to take a breath before the other one struck out with those terrible claws, catching Azreth across the chest. Four deep lines appeared on his pectorals, dripping black. Raiya's breath caught, but then Azreth conjured a sparkling beam of light that struck the other demon, knocking him back. Azreth was holding his own. For now.

Adamus nodded to her, drawing the iron sword from the sheath at his waist. "Go with the elves. I'll stay with him."

Jai took Raiya's hand, pulling her toward the stairs. Raiya's chest felt like it was tearing in half, but she forced herself to turn away from Azreth and run toward the curving stairs that led to the balcony.

Jai's magic flowed through her as they took the stairs two steps at a time, and when she looked down, her body had faded to shadow. Madira's feet were silent behind them, but she knew he was following a step behind. As a bird flew down at them, talons extended, Raiya fired another shot and kept running.

At the top of the stairs, she slowed, following the elves' lead in staying low and quiet. They came to the intersection of corridors leading to the bedrooms and the servants' chambers. Raiya turned down the hall to the bedroom. Nirlan would have wanted to run to a place that felt safe, where he probably had weapons hidden away.

She slipped through the door to the bedroom in time to see him squeezing into the gap between the wardrobe and the wall. Raising the baton, she shot at him, but he disappeared behind the wardrobe at the last moment, and the blast hit the wall. Blackened stone rained down on the floor. Another wasted shot.

Raiya circled closer to the wardrobe, her baton raised, and then she saw the opening. There was a hidden door behind the wardrobe, half obscured by the rubble. A dark tunnel lay beyond.

Cursing, she ran to the wardrobe and shoved at it ineffectually until Madira came to help her. With their combined efforts, they shifted it a few inches, then climbed over the rubble and into the tunnel. Far down the passageway, she could see a faint light disappearing around the corner.

"Nirlan!" she shouted again, breaking into a run. They rounded the curve of the tunnel, and then came to a fork. She stopped, listening, but she heard nothing. Tiny mage lights lined the walls in both directions. He could have gone either way.

Without having to discuss it, Madira went one direction, and Raiya and Jai went the other, running hand in hand. The tunnel turned into rough stairs cut from the rock, and Raiya sensed they were below ground. The tunnel had exited into the dungeon beneath the castle.

Ahead, a light flashed briefly. She sprinted toward it, her lungs burning. This time, when they rounded the corner, she was fast enough to see Nirlan still running down the corridor ahead of them. She lifted her baton and fired again. In her rush, her aim was off, hitting the wall ahead of him. Nirlan ducked, flinching as rock shattered around him, but he kept running. Raiya nearly screamed with frustration.

But just as he started to round another corner, he stopped short, grunting as his head abruptly jerked back. Madira flickered into view in front of him, wincing and shaking out his fist. Before Nirlan could recover, Madira had grabbed him by the hair and raised his sword to his throat. Nirlan's eyes widened.

"You bastard," Raiya hissed, stalking toward him. He was responsible for this. He had killed all those people in town. He had summoned that demon who was trying to kill Azreth as they spoke. "What were you thinking? How could you do this?"

Nirlan held up his hands, grimacing as Madira gripped his hair tighter. "Wait! We're on the same side."

"Like hells," Raiya scoffed.

"That red beast downstairs—he's wild. He needs to be put down. That's what you want, right?"

Raiya was dumbfounded. "Are you telling me you've lost control of your demon? Again?"

Nirlan sneered. "No great works ever came to fruition without risk, Raiya. Ambition has its costs. Next time, I will succeed, and when I do, everyone will say I was lucky. But it's not luck. Success takes work and time and sacrifice, and yes, sometimes failure."

She rolled her eyes, wanting to strangle him. How had she ever tolerated him? "For the gods' sake, be quiet."

Madira's blade nicked Nirlan's throat. He seemed eager to bleed him out.

Nirlan glanced nervously between Jai and Raiya. "So... Is this it? Are you going to kill me, wife? After two years?"

Raiya clenched her teeth. "How do we get rid of the binding you put on Azreth?"

"Azreth?"

"The demon."

"Which one?"

"The blue one," she said through her teeth. They were losing time. Every second they spent with him was one that they could have been spending helping Azreth. If she hadn't still been hearing distant thuds and crashes vibrating through the walls, she might have thought the fight was over already.

Nirlan smiled smugly. He was pleased to have something he could withhold from her. "And why would I tell you that?"

"So we don't kill you, idiot," said Madira.

"If you kill me, you'll never have your answer."

"The answer is in the runes," Raiya said. "I will figure it out eventually, with or without your help. But if you tell me now, you might live longer."

Nirlan chewed his lip for a moment, glaring at her. "Tell your servant to release me, and I'll show you."

"I'm not a servant," Madira growled.

"Let him go, Madira."

Nirlan shot a pointed look over his shoulder at Madira, waiting. Madira snarled and lowered the sword.

Nirlan straightened, smoothing his hands over his coat. "That zealot mucked up the binding. You can't depend on these people for anything, even the one thing they're supposed to be good for."

"The priestess?"

"Yes."

"Did you kill her?"

"The demon killed her. Don't get me wrong, I don't mourn her, but I didn't want her dead. Now I have no one to fix this mess she created. But you can help me send him back to the hells. I can't have a wild, unrestrained demon running loose in my home."

Raiya hesitated. She wouldn't put it past him to stab her in the back the moment he had what he wanted. But what other choice did she have? "Fine. Show me the summoning circle."

Nirlan gave a sarcastic bow, gesturing down the corridor. "Follow me."

Madira leaned in to whisper in Raiya's ear. "This is a mistake. We should kill him now."

"I agree, actually," Jai whispered.

"Not yet." If he knew how to send his demon back to the hells, and how to remove that lingering half-binding from Azreth, they needed him. And she didn't want to admit it, but she still hadn't found the courage to end his life. Some kind of internal block kept her from just raising her baton and blasting him in the face.

Nirlan glanced over his shoulder as they walked, peering apprehensively at her baton. "What have you done with that thing?"

"It's a demonic weapon," she replied, her lips curling up. "Does it frighten you?"

"You've certainly changed in the past few weeks. Being a demon's whore has made you think rather highly of yourself, haon't it?"

"We don't need your help for this," she said. "The sound of your voice grates on me. Insult me again and I'll silence it."

Predictably, he looked like he wanted to say something else, but he sealed his lips. There was outrage on his face, but there was also apprehension that she'd never seen there before. The fact that she had put that fear there filled her with satisfaction. She didn't think she'd ever made Nirlan afraid before. Their power dynamic had never, not once, swung in this direction, and the thrill it gave her was intoxicating.

"Tell me what happened when you performed the summoning," she said. "How did all the other monsters get here?"

"That's none of your concern."

"Of course it's my concern. They're terrorizing the entire countryside."

"I mean that you don't need to worry about it."

"What is that supposed to mean?"

She stopped short as they passed beneath an iron gate and reached the central chamber where he had summoned Azreth.

The room was teeming with magic. Glowing runes radiated from the middle of the chamber, even more of them than the last time she'd been here. At the center of them all was a strange object that she had trouble making sense of.

It was a shining irregularity in the air, an ovalish shape a little larger than a human, floating a step above the floor. Vague images flashed in the shadows within the shape, never quite becoming anything recognizable. She could not decide if it reminded her more of a mirror, a window, or a rune shimmering with magic energy.

As she looked at it, a shape appeared inside, like a creature from the ocean depths coming to the surface. It was another bird, like the ones upstairs.

There was a flash and a snap, and to Raiya's shock, the bird burst forth and soared over their heads. It circled the room once before choosing a tunnel seemingly at random and disappearing down it.

Nirlan had opened a gate to the hells.

The planes of hell were not her area of expertise, but even a layperson knew that you couldn't just open a gate. This wasn't how you were supposed to go about summoning demons.

The gate itself was jagged and messy, like a rip in the air. It shouldn't have been there. It felt wrong. A mistake born of desperation and hubris.

"What have you done?" she asked, dazed.

"Don't be so dramatic," Nirlan said. He had crossed the room and picked up something from a table. He turned around to face them, raising a small metal disk. Runes on the disk glowed to life, flashing as its enchantment activated.

Raiya didn't have time to figure out what the thing was before a wave of something hit her. She felt herself falling, and then there was nothing.

THIRTY

Raiya felt that something was wrong even before she awoke, before she remembered what had happened.

The first thing she became aware of was the cold, hard stone at her back. It felt cruel and unwelcoming, bruising her where it dug into her shoulder blades. Somewhere nearby, she could hear something large breathing.

Fear spun through her. She was in danger.

She tried to lift her limbs, to open her eyes, but her body was heavy. She was unnaturally tired, like she'd been drugged. Eventually, she pried open her eyelids, turning dry eyes on a scene that slowly came into focus.

Nirlan was standing over a table near the gate, his back to her. Raiya blinked, shifting her gaze across the room, and her heart stuttered. The red-skinned demon lounged in a too-small chair nearby. He'd propped the side of his head on his hand as he watched Nirlan doing whatever he was doing at the table, wearing no expression whatsoever. His red eyes flicked over to hers briefly.

He looked bored.

Raiya drew a shuddering breath. It felt like she'd been in

hibernation for months. Trembling, she pushed herself up onto her elbow. Her baton was gone, as were her bow and arrows. Her satchel had been emptied onto the floor beside her, presumably when Nirlan had checked it for more weapons. Her book of notes had been carelessly tossed upside down beside her stylus, its delicate pages crumpled.

Deep, ragged breathing drew her attention again. She followed the sound until she spotted the large figure lying on the floor in front of the red demon's chair.

Azreth.

He was alive, but vicious claw marks covered his body. Worst of all were the deep punctures in his belly. The demon's claws had cut into him so far that she could see the glistening, black viscera inside him. She didn't know how he was still alive. The wounds were catastrophic.

"Azreth," she said, without really meaning to. Her voice was choked and hoarse. Azreth's breathing hitched. He slowly tilted his head to look over at her, the muscles in his neck straining with the effort.

Nirlan turned as she spoke. "I can't lie—it stings that the first thing out of your mouth when you awaken is another man's name."

Raiya pushed herself up to a sitting position. "You said he wasn't bound to you," she said.

"And you believed me."

She was a fool. He had lied to her about everything. The demon had never been out of his control. Nirlan had no intention of sending him back to the hells.

Beside Azreth, there was another bloodied body. Adamus. He was very still, and Raiya couldn't tell whether he was still alive.

She looked around until she located Madira and Jai just behind her. They were both still unconscious from whatever magic Nirlan had used on them, but she could see them breathing. She was relieved they were alive, but a part of her was also relieved they were still unconscious—she didn't want to see the judgment in their eyes.

She'd led them all here. It was her fault. She had wanted to trust Nirlan so badly that she'd put them all at risk, and she didn't even know why. She'd spent so long wanting him to love her and wanting so badly for him to change that she'd taken the hand he offered her like a fish taking bait from a hook.

She wondered why the demon hadn't just killed Azreth and the rest of them, and then she realized the obvious answer. He couldn't feed off of them if he killed them. Even now, he was probably soaking in Azreth's pain, letting it bolster his own power.

"You're not so mouthy without your weapon," Nirlan observed, cocking a dark eyebrow. He picked up the metal plate from the table. "Thank you for this, by the way. I never thought any of your trinkets would come in handy, but with a little help from that priestess, this one proved useful at least once." He tossed it onto the table with a clatter.

She recognized the object now. It was a sleep aid she'd created over a year ago, which had been sitting on a shelf in the parlor gathering dust for most of that time. It was supposed to be placed on a nightstand to help gently lull you to sleep. Someone, apparently Gereg, had clumsily modified the enchantment, turning it into a blunt weapon.

"You opened a gate to the hells," Raiya said, still disbelieving. "Why?"

"That part was incidental. The priestess looked at Eunaios's work from the last summoning, but she didn't fully understand it. She said this was the best way for her to adapt his spellwork to connect to the hells and find another demon to bind."

Raiya wondered if that was true, or if it had just been

Gereg's way of sowing the chaos and death she craved. "This is madness. Anything could come through it."

Nirlan shrugged. "I can find a way to close it later. The important thing was finding the demon."

"But why? Why is it so important to you?"

Rage flashed across his face. "Because you *disrespected* me, you unfaithful—!" He regained control of himself, swallowing the outburst. He lowered his voice again. "Because you deserve this. You were a fool if you thought you could cheat me out of my wife and my demon."

This was all because of her leaving. He probably didn't even care about Azreth escaping—he was just angry she'd gone with him.

She glanced up at the red-skinned demon, who just blinked slowly at her. Something shifted behind her. She looked over her shoulder. Jai was moving a little, close to waking.

Raiya looked up at Nirlan. "Let them go. Please."

"Why?"

"They're just children."

"If they're old enough to fight, they're old enough to die."

"Bastard."

"Ah, there's that mouth." He walked over to her, and she flinched when he took her jaw in his hand. She tried to push him away, her arms weak. The lingering magic was making her body sluggish.

"Don't condescend to me," she hissed.

He looked her up and down with disdain. "You think you don't deserve it? What have you ever achieved in life, other than spreading your legs in exchange for status and power, first with me and then with this creature? You're weak without that weapon, without your demon, and without me. You have nothing left but yourself, and you alone are nothing."

He leaned in, hovering his mouth near hers. "But that's all

right," he murmured. "You'll come crawling back to me now. Kiss me. Be a good girl." He paused there, waiting for her to come to him. It was worse than if he had just forced himself on her. He wanted to watch her realize she was powerless and then capitulate.

She swallowed a hard lump in her throat. "Fine," she said quietly.

Nirlan's eyebrows went up slightly. He looked pleased.

He glanced behind him to see if Azreth was watching, and he was. His eyes, glowing very faintly, followed every movement without blinking. The muscles in his jaw stood out as he clenched his teeth.

"No man will take what's mine," Nirlan said. "And no demon, for that matter. Not without suffering dearly." He turned to Raiya, his mouth twisting into something that was too hateful to really be a smile, and leaned in. "You're worthless without me," he whispered. "Never forget that. Never forget this moment."

She surreptitiously reached into the pile of items that had been dumped out of her bag until she felt the smooth, cold metal of her enchanting stylus. She wrapped her fingers around it. "I won't," she said. Then she stabbed the pointed end into his throat.

Warm blood burst across her cheek. She gasped involuntarily at the same time as Nirlan. His eyes were wide with shock. She'd hit him in the artery just beneath his ear. When she jerked the stylus free, another gush of blood flowed forth. It streamed down his throat and over his collar as if from a spout.

He clapped a hand over his neck. Panic and confusion flashed across his face. For a moment, he began to scramble backwards, but then he changed his mind and reached for her, fury in his face. With a shout, Raiya stabbed the stylus into his chest. He lurched, grabbing her arm to try to disarm her. She stabbed again, and he crumpled, grimacing in pain. Shoving him away, she clambered out from under him.

Azreth looked down at his palm. As Nirlan bled out, the runes changed, going flat and dull. They no longer shone with lingering magic. The enchantment was broken.

A shadow fell over Raiya. Nirlan's demon had risen from his seat, giving her a curious frown as he towered over her. For a moment, she was relieved. Nirlan was dead, and so the demon could not be compelled to protect him.

But then the demon started toward her.

Nirlan's death presented a new problem. The demon was unbound. He could do as he pleased. Kill who he pleased. Azreth tried to reach for him, just missing his ankle as he walked by. Gathering all the strength left in his dying limbs, Azreth turned over and climbed to his hands and knees, but he trembled and fell when he tried to get up.

Raiya turned and ran, but her legs were slow from the sleeping spell. The demon caught her before she'd taken five steps. He wrapped a massive hand around her forearm and turned her around to face him. He looked at her for a moment, taking stock of his next victim.

She almost sympathized with him. He was like Azreth. He'd been imprisoned here against his will, and he couldn't change the fact that he needed to feed to survive. That didn't mean he needed to look so pleased about it, though.

Whatever emotions she felt, he would take them and use them to make himself more powerful. She steeled herself, determined to feel nothing. "I saved you from a life of servitude to a cruel master. You should thank me and go."

The demon laughed softly. Rather than answering, he moved a clawed hand to the soft, vulnerable flesh of her stomach, and pushed. Raiya froze, her heart pounding in her ears as the claws slowly began to cut, first through her clothes and then deeper, pricking her skin, drawing blood. She stopped breathing.

Feel nothing. Feel nothing.

The panic came anyway, drowning her. She opened her mouth to scream or cry, but no sound came out. The demon held her wrist in a steel grip, keeping her from pulling away. Sharp pain burst through her as the claws pierced through her flesh.

And then, a sword sprouted from the demon's chest.

Everything stopped. The demon jerked, and he released her. Raiya backed away, her legs shaking so hard they barely held her up.

Azreth was standing behind the demon, holding Adamus's iron sword in his fist. Madira's black cloak was wrapped around the hilt in a thick bundle to make a barrier between his hand and the iron. Azreth let go of the sword with a shudder. His palm was dark where it had burned him even through the cloth.

The sword remained stuck in the demon's body, and he clawed at it, his limbs already trembling from the effect of the iron. Raiya ran to the table, where she found the sleeping device, her baton, and her bow and quiver. The enchantments had both gone dull, their power depleted. Before the demon could dislodge the sword, she picked up the bow and drew an iron-tipped arrow, aiming it at him.

"Get back!" she shouted. She circled around so that he was between her and the gate to the hells. The demon glowered at her, but she held his gaze, trembling. "Go!"

He gave a furious, defeated exhale, and took a step backward into the gate. He took another step, and then he was gone, lost among the swirling images beyond.

Raiya dropped the bow. A sigh rushed out of her. She put a hand to the wounds beneath her ribs, and her hand came away bloody. Beside her, Madira was watching the gate with a look of shock. Jai was just waking up.

"Azreth," Raiya said, spinning to face him. He'd dropped to his knees. She rushed to his side, started to put her arms around him, then stopped, afraid of hurting him. He seemed not to care about his grievous injuries, though, as he lifted his lacerated arms to touch her.

"You're injured," he said.

"Gods, I'm fine, Azreth. Look at you—" She sobbed. "I'm so sorry."

His hands came to her face, his eyes on hers.

"Your rage is beautiful," he said reverently.

"Take it," she said. "Take all of it."

Magic gathered around him as he fed from her. White light sank into his wounds, slowly sewing them shut.

"Kiss me," he said.

Raiya held his cheeks tightly as she pressed her mouth to his, her eyes still overflowing with tears.

She wanted to stay there, in that very spot, embracing him for the rest of her life.

THIRTY-ONE

As much as Raiya wanted to just lie down with Azreth and sleep for the next day or week or several months, she had other things to consider now. Nirlan was dead, and there was no one else left to clean up the mess he'd left behind.

She and Azreth spent the morning sealing off the room with the gate so that no other creatures could come through. Once they'd closed the area, Azreth approached the gate, hands raised and glowing with powerful magic. Raiya's hopes climbed when the gate shrank smaller and smaller until it was just a narrow, glowing line in the air. Azreth's arms shook with the effort of goading magic into the gate, but it had stopped shrinking.

Finally he lowered his arms, glaring at the gate in defeat. "This is as much as I can do. Opening and closing gates between planes is not simple magic."

"I imagine there would be a lot more demons visiting our plane if it were simple."

"Yes."

She could no longer see through the gate like a window,

but she wondered whether someone could still pass through the crack if they had a mind to. "Perhaps this will be enough. It looks like it will be more difficult to move through, at least."

"More difficult, but not impossible. Someone who knows where to find it could still use it."

"Does that worry you?" she asked, wondering if he was concerned about the safety of the people in town.

"I like your plane the way it is, without demons. There is a peace here that I never knew in the hells." He looked down at her, putting his hands on hers. "Will you come with me?" he asked, gesturing for her to follow him upstairs.

Casting another glance back at the ominous split in the air, she followed him out of the dungeon and up to the more pleasant parts of the castle. They came out on the balcony overlooking the gentle hills below. Soft snow covered the land and coated the roofs in Frosthaven. Smoke was rising from a few chimneys in the town.

Raiya moved closer to Azreth, and he obligingly wrapped an arm around her, pulling her against the furnace of his body. For a long while, they looked out at the landscape in silence.

"I wish I had been born here instead of the hells," he said. "I wish this was my home."

"It can be."

He gave her a sideways glance. "No one will welcome my presence here. Except for you."

"And Jai and Madira. And the Roamers."

"I will be hunted. As you will, if you harbor me."

"Let them hunt, then." She turned around to face him. "Nothing has changed between us."

His hand went to her face, touching her hair and her cheek, and he focused intently on placing a lock of hair behind her ear. He was delaying saying what he wanted to say, but as

Raiya leaned into his touch and brushed her fingers along his back, he worked up the courage he needed.

"I want to stay here," he said. "I want to be with you."

"I want that, too."

"But I am putting you in danger by remaining near you."

"No. I have never felt safer than I have when I'm with you."

"I doubt that."

"You shouldn't." She felt foolish now for ever having stayed with Nirlan. But before she'd met Azreth, she hadn't known it could be like this. She hadn't known this sort of love was possible. "Even before you knew me, when you could have hurt me—even when you needed to consume me in order to keep yourself from starving—you resisted. Even then, you protected me."

"You seem to forget sometimes, but I am a demon, Raiya. My world is one of destruction and danger. I was designed to deal death and take violence. You weren't."

"You are more than the circumstances of your birth. You are not wrong just for being what you are."

"What about the other mortals who will want to come for me? If you do not fear me, you should at least fear them."

"If you're being hunted, then I must stay with you to protect you."

His eyebrows went up a little.

"I've made my decision," she said. "I want you here beside me for whatever comes next, and for whatever comes after that." She motioned to the sturdy, ancient stone walls around them. They'd stood for hundreds of years, and they'd stand for hundreds more. "We have a whole castle to ourselves. A fortress to protect you."

"You want to take over the castle? Someone will stop you."

"No one will stop me, because it's my inheritance. It was

Nirlan's land. I am his closest remaining relative. That makes it my land."

Suddenly, she could see a future for herself. It had been a long time since she had envisioned anything other than boredom and misery ahead of her.

She was going to make this place hers. Hers and Azreth's.

"We can watch over the gate to the hells from here, in case anything else comes through," she went on. "We can fix up the castle and make it a real home. I could have a study to work on enchanting, and you could put some behelgi in the stable if you like. And we can leave whenever you want, of course," she added quickly, not wanting him to feel trapped. He'd been caged enough. The last thing she wanted was for the castle to become yet another prison for him.

He studied her for a long time, and she could see him breaking. He leaned down, touching warm lips lightly against hers.

"For a violent creature designed for dealing death, you kiss very sweetly," she said wryly.

He seemed not to know what to say. "Am I doing it incorrectly?"

"No. You do it very well."

"Oh. Thank you."

"I hate to interrupt," came a voice.

Madira had appeared in the doorway behind them. He handed her a burlap sack that was nearly empty. There were a few shriveled apples inside.

"Breakfast," he said. "There was also a bag of flour, a sack of sprouting potatoes, and some kind of pickled vegetables in jars."

"Asparagus and carrots," she supplied.

"Ugh."

"The cook and the rest of the staff must have left after

Azreth and I first escaped. I can't blame them. I suppose the kitchen has been unattended for a while."

"Well, it's tended right now. Jai is cooking."

"Really? She doesn't have to do that."

"She was excited to get to use a real kitchen for once. Don't ruin her fun."

"Staff?" Azreth repeated, frowning. Raiya could read his mind. He didn't like the idea of living with strangers.

"Just a few. There was the groundskeeper and the cook, who was also a housekeeper. I think we can do without the guards."

He made a face.

"Surely you didn't think Nirlan was cooking and cleaning for himself," she said, amused by the thought. "We'll need to try to get them to come back. This place won't take care of itself." She frowned, thinking of the bookkeeping Nirlan used to do. He didn't do actual work often, but she recalled him spending long hours muttering irritably to himself over stacks of papers on his desk whenever the time for tax collection came. There were things lords needed to do that he'd never bothered to explain to her. If she was going to inherit his title and his possessions, she would have to learn what those things were. The thought made her grimace. She had always been better with words than numbers.

She looked over the edge of the balcony into the bailey. Adamus was below, carrying the corpse of a guard out of the castle. Azreth had healed his injuries, and he was looking nearly recovered from the previous night. The Paladin had lined up the dead neatly along the outer castle wall. Raiya would need to make arrangements to notify their relatives of their deaths.

"Adamus," she called. "I wonder if I could ask another favor of you."

He rested his hands on his hips and stretched his back. "I'm at your service, as always, lady."

Azreth made a soft, almost imperceptible sound of annoyance deep in his chest, which Raiya ignored.

"I remember you saying that you know about law and accounting."

"A little, yes."

"With my husband gone, I will need some help learning my duties and getting our books straight. Would you be willing to stay and help me?"

Adamus looked surprised. He tilted his head at her and Azreth as he thought about it. "What are you paying?"

She blushed a little. "I'm not sure what amount would be appropriate for such work. You'd have to educate me about that, too."

"I'd be happy to stay a while and help you set things in order. You can count on me."

Azreth made another, slightly louder, sound of annoyance. "The castle is going to become a zoo at this rate."

Raiya looked up at him. "How do you know what a zoo is? Do they have them in the hells?"

"No. Jai told me it's a place in the capital of Ardani where they keep all kinds of animals."

"Ah. I imagine you'd like to see a place like that."

He gave her a tentative glance. "Perhaps."

"We'll go there someday," she said, then returned to the topic at hand. "But Adamus isn't an animal, and we aren't a zoo. You'll be fine sharing a castle with him for a little while."

He made a sound of vague disagreement.

ADAMUS and the elves had stayed with them for several weeks before moving on. They'd stayed longer than they needed to—

long enough to make sure she and Azreth had settled in safely and that the gate was no longer posing an immediate threat to the town. Raiya sent them back south with enough coins from the castle's vault to feed and house them for several weeks.

She stood on the balcony over the bailey, bundled up in many layers, because she'd wanted to watch the sunset while she worked. She looked up from her notebook, her breath puffing in front her face as if to remind her that it was far too cold to be outside.

As vibrant reds and oranges in the sky gave way to gray-blue and lavender, she felt a hand on her shoulder. She turned, expecting to find Azreth behind her. Instead, there was only a disembodied magenta hand. Amused, she took the hand. Its fingers folded around hers.

"Azreth?" she said, looking around. No one answered.

She looked down toward the castle gate, and there were two figures standing beneath it—one outrageously tall one, and one mortal-sized man. Azreth was wearing his human glamour.

The visitor was a stranger, probably from Frosthaven. He was standing back from the gate a fair distance, and Azreth wouldn't get too close to the iron portcullis, which left an uncomfortably large gap between them. But they were talking, which pleased her.

Azreth had become somewhat infamous. Everyone knew, or at least suspected, what he really was, but the people in town also knew he was the man hunting down all the beasts that had escaped from the gate. It wasn't unusual for people to cautiously come asking for him when they needed a demon hunter.

She raised the hand to her lips and kissed its palm as Azreth spoke to the human. The hand calmly accepted the kiss until she began to move away, and then it grasped her face, brushing its thumb over her lower lip. She kissed the pad of the finger. The only acknowledgment Azreth gave her was a single sly glance before he went back to speaking with the man in front of him.

Raiya pushed the obliging palm against her mouth again. "I'm going to make you scream later," she murmured into it. Azreth glanced up at her again, curious. She knew he could feel her speaking against the hand, but couldn't hear what was being said. She just smiled at him.

Azreth came to her after he'd finished talking to the human, who had hurried away from the castle gate as if he might be set upon by hellspawn if he lingered too long.

She turned to him as he joined her on the balcony. "What was it this time?"

"Just rumors," he said. "They're saying that the Temple of Moratha in Ontag-ul is attempting to open another gate. They say that the Paladins are refusing to interfere in cult business, so they want me to investigate it."

"Are you going to do it?"

"Perhaps. What do you think I should do?"

She hesitated. "I think you should do what you want. You're not obligated to guard the entire country from the hells, you know."

"That is true." He was waiting for her to say more.

"On the other hand, you are uniquely equipped to deal with other demons."

He nodded, having received the approval he'd been looking for. "I will go if you will come with me."

She smiled. "To be honest, I'd started to feel cooped up here. Now that I've had a taste of the rest of the world, it doesn't feel right staying in one place for so long."

"Then you should not be kept in one place."

"But you like it here."

"I like to be where you are. And I have also started to feel...

cooped up," he said slowly, as if he wasn't completely sure what the phrase meant.

She'd watched him settle in to quiet life at the castle and its surroundings. When he wasn't with her, he spent his days exploring the land nearby or lying curled up in front of the fireplace in her study. She'd learned that he liked the heat, despite his invulnerability to the cold, and he gravitated to the warmest nooks in the castle like a house cat.

They had obtained two behelgi from the Roamers' herd. Fu-lon had selected a strong, white doe for Raiya, and a smaller male for Azreth. The choice of the male had surprised her. It was fully grown, but too small and weak for anyone larger than a child to ride, and its coat was gray and patchy. At first, she had suspected Fu-lon had chosen to give them this one because it wouldn't fetch a good price anywhere else.

But then she realized that the male had another critical flaw: it was painfully unintelligent. It wandered aimlessly instead of following the herd, it had to be led by hand to its food and water, and it stared dumbly at predators the other behelgi ran from. It seemed to have no sense of self-preservation.

So when Azreth had reached out to touch the creature, it hadn't moved. It had stood still, eyeing him calmly while he stroked its fur. Azreth had glanced up at Raiya in surprise, his eyes bright. She would never forget the look on his face.

She could tell he enjoyed the calm of their new life. And she took joy in watching him experience luxuries he'd been denied before now, like warmth, love, good food made by the cook she'd rehired the previous month, friendship with the elves—who had already planned a return visit—and peaceful coexistence with the people and wildlife who lived nearby.

And yet, she had suspected there was a part of him that missed conflict. It was the part of him that claimed to crave blood. She saw it in him whenever he lost himself in the pleasures of her body and sank his teeth into her. She felt it in herself, too. There was a hunger in both of them.

Now, untethered by curses or cults or bad husbands, they were free to go where they wished when they wished. They could choose peace and quiet or adventure and battle as it suited them. That in itself was a luxury.

There was just one last thing to be addressed.

"Are you ready?" she asked.

He nodded.

"Come on," she said, picking up her notebook and pulling him inside. They wound slowly through the castle and down many stairs, deep into the heart of the dungeon below, until they came to the central chamber where Azreth had first been summoned. The gate still shimmered in the center of the room.

Azreth stood patient and still as Raiya painstakingly painted runes all over his body in dark ink. She had already spent long weeks on the runes in the rest of the room, painting over ones that needed to be modified and scrubbing away the ones she didn't need.

"It will work this time," Raiya said, more to herself than to him.

"I know." He went to stand beside the gate in the center of the room, then waited. Runes striped his body and radiated out from him in all directions. They were flat black, waiting to be charged with magic.

"Are you ready?" she asked.

"I am."

Her heart was in her throat as she recalled what had happened the last time she'd tried this. What if she'd gotten it wrong again?

"Be calm, Raiya," Azreth said. "The runes are all in place? Everything is correct? You have nothing to worry about."

She looked around one last time. The runes were right.

She'd researched and experimented for weeks. She'd done everything as well as she possibly could. They were ready.

She nodded. "Do it."

Azreth didn't move, but she knew the exact moment that he charged the runes, because they began to shimmer, filling the room with rainbows of light.

He didn't contort with pain as the runes on his own body lit up. Instead, he held up his hand, watching the inert binding mark on his palm. Raiya leaned closer to watch with him.

The mark faded, and then it was gone.

Azreth looked up at her, sucking in a breath. He bent over her, taking her face in both hands as he kissed her hard.

"Thank you, Raiya," he said emphatically.

She was surprised by his delight. "It was nothing. I doubt it would have done any harm to you, now that Nirlan is gone. It was just an unwanted tattoo at this point."

"It means a great deal to me," he said. "My body is my own again."

That, she could understand. She nodded. "I'm glad."

The runes around them began to fade again. Raiya shook her head a little. "Gods. I've been working on that for so long. I don't quite know what I'll do now that it's finished."

"Now we will begin the rest of our lives. I will supply some ideas, if you wish."

"I have some ideas of my own."

Whatever came next in life, they would do it side by side.

HELL SENT
DEMONS OF ARDANI BOOK 1.5

Azreth has always faced life alone. Trust is dangerous.

Like all demons, he is a monster, forced to kill and abuse to survive.

When he's imprisoned on the mortal plane and bound to a cruel human lord, his only hope for escape is the lord's mistreated wife, who offers herself to him in exchange for his protection.

She may be small, but her mind is as sharp as any sword. Trusting her to help him navigate this strange new world is probably a mistake.

Her kindness is a trap, and he won't fall for it.

No mortal could love a demon, and a demon shouldn't love anyone at all.

Hell Sent is a novella-length spicy fantasy monster romance featuring a prickly cinnamon roll hero and a gentle heroine on a journey of mutual healing and self-acceptance. Hell Sent is a retelling of Demon Bound through Azreth's eyes.

Free Bonus Epilogue

Newsletter subscribers can download a free short story/epilogue about Raiya and Azreth, *Sanctuary*. This content isn't available anywhere else, so sign up for the newsletter via my website to read it!

Thank You

Thank you for reading Demon Bound! If you enjoyed this book, please consider supporting my work by leaving a rating or review. It doesn't have to be long—just a few words is fine —and it really does help!

The next Demons of Ardani book, Hell Sent, is an alternate POV version of Demon Bound from Azreth's perspective! There is so much of Azreth's history and thoughts that I didn't get to include in this book, but now you'll be able to read everything he was thinking and feeling, too.

If you're new to my books, I hope you loved this introduction to the Ardani universe. If you're eager for more, try Elves of Ardani: a series of fantasy romance standalones with plenty more spice, angst, and adventure for you to binge on.

As always, I owe a big thank-you to all my readers. Your support means so much. I feel privileged to be able to share my world and characters with you all, and knowing that other people are enjoying my books along with me is a big part of what keeps me writing.

Special thanks to my beta readers for this book (Jenna, Rachel, Shanon, and Tiff) for all your thoughtful comments, gushes, and many exclamation points. Extra special thanks to my parents for accepting and nurturing my obsession with fiction, and to my wonderful partner for being endlessly supportive of me and my writing career.

— Nina

About the Author

Nina K. Westra is an elf enthusiast and fantasy romance author with a love of antiheroes, outsiders, and feminist men. Her books feature sweetness and spice, action and adventure, and heart-wrenching (usually forbidden, always angsty) romance with non-human men.

She lives in the ridiculously beautiful Pacific Northwest, and when she's not writing, she can usually be found petting someone's cat.

For news, ARCs, and free stories, sign up for her newsletter at ninakwestra.com

instagram.com/ninakwestra

facebook.com/NinaKWestra

bookbub.com/profile/nina-k-westra